As she searched the wall for the light switch, her fingers caught a cobweb. A metallic click caught her attention and her heart stalled while she tried to localize the sound. She shook the web off her hands and shivered as a chill raced down her spine. Kelly closed her eyes and breathed out slowly. She opened her eyes and scanned the hallway. A fluorescent green exit sign shone at the far end of the hall and she could make out two glowing stickers on the restroom doors.

Shaking her head, Kelly abandoned the search for the light switch and headed toward the glowing sticker on the nearest door. Just as she pushed on the door, a hand brushed over her shoulder and clamped over her mouth.

Visit

Bella Books

at

BellaBooks.com

or call our toll-free number

1-800-729-4992

The Unknown Mile

JAIME CLEVENGER

Bella BOOKS

2004

Bella Books, Inc.
P.O. Box 10543
Tallahassee, FL 32302

Printed in the United States of America on acid-free paper
First Edition

Editor: Christi Cassidy
Cover designer: Sandy Knowles

ISBN 1-931513-57-0

For everyone who's given me good advice and bear hugs, especially Corina, Jackie and Linda.

Chapter 1

050001

Truck headlights glared in the Volkswagen's rearview mirror. The Ford was gaining ground fast and Kelly Haldon had to floor the gas pedal to keep the lead. Buildings bordering the unmarked avenue passed in a gray blur. She had lost track of the block numbers and cussed the punk who'd ripped off the street signs. Apparently no one replaced stolen signs in this part of Oakland. At the next intersection, the traffic light switched from yellow to red, taunting. She slammed on the brakes as the truck swerved around her and raced through the intersection.

The Ford's rear lights quickly blended with the streetlights until neither was distinct. Kelly sighed, relieved to finally lose the unwelcome escort that had been pacing her since she'd turned off the freeway. She flipped on the radio and static buzzed through the speakers.

As she tuned in a rock music station, her hand brushed the edge of a slip of paper poking out of the cup holder. It was the hardware store receipt with Shannon's name and phone number neatly printed in blue ink. Avoiding the slip of paper and thoughts of Shannon, Kelly eyed the other objects in her car. A flashlight with no batteries, a knife that wasn't hers and a box wrapped in brown paper littered the passenger seat. Her karate uniform and sparring gear were strewn across the back seat. She hadn't cleaned her car in weeks and the smell of dried sweat was as ripe as a locker room.

Kelly glanced back at the box. She'd been trying to guess the contents for the past three days. A handgun would fit, but this package was too light. The contents rustled when she shook the box. Maybe it was only the shuffle of papers. But why wrap the box so carefully if there were only paper documents inside? A yellow Post-it note listing an address and delivery time was attached to the box. No name. She'd probably never know what she was delivering.

Rick had given her the package on Friday without any hint to the contents. He didn't ask if she wanted to make another delivery. They both realized that she would not quit now. As Kelly was locking the door to the Ashton karate dojo, Rick had tapped her shoulder.

"Last one to leave?" he asked.

She nodded.

Rick handed her the package, about the size of a shirt box and wrapped up in brown paper like a present. She knew Rick wouldn't tell her what was inside.

"Deliver it Monday night at ten. Hide it until then." He glanced down the sidewalk anxiously, as if sensing that someone was watching. The karate dojo was on a quiet street that had little pedestrian traffic in Ashton, a suburb just east of Oakland. Unlike its two big-city neighbors, Oakland and San Francisco, downtown Ashton had no nightlife and no crime. In fact, most of the other businesses on Main Street had already turned off their lights and the sidewalk was clear on both sides of the road. He continued, "The address is on the label and the house should be vacant then. Just leave it on the doorstep."

Rick continued to scan the sidewalk and she wondered why he acted so tense. Rick usually handed off the deliveries like they were laundry he was too lazy to fold himself. *What was different about this package?*

"Questions?" Rick cleared his throat and eyed Kelly. With a nod, he turned and strode away quickly.

Kelly focused on the odometer as she waited at the intersection. Her Volkswagen had just cleared its fifty-thousandth mile. A movement at the side of her car caught her eye and she spotted a man walking down the sidewalk. He paused at the bus stop and lit a cigarette. The man took a drag and the orange ember burned bright red. She realized he was watching her and quickly pressed the lock button for the passenger door, wondering when the traffic light would finally turn green. There was no reason to be afraid, but her nerves were on edge. She stared directly at the man to memorize his face. He turned away from the streetlight and took another drag. Kelly's thoughts shifted to Gina's ruby as the cigarette's ember burned a deeper red.

Last night she'd awakened to the sensation of Gina's fingertips tracing a line across her forehead. Alex had left the front door unlocked and Gina had slipped inside undetected. Kelly's brother lived in the suburbs and often left the house unlocked.

"Hey, sleepy," Gina said quietly.

Dazed, Kelly squinted in the darkness and rubbed her face. She realized who was standing next to the bed as a shiver raced up her spine. "What happened? Why are you here?"

Gina held her finger up to Kelly's lips and shook her head. "I had to see you. Don't tell me to leave."

Kelly had been resisting the urge to call Gina but had desperately wanted to see her. Gina slipped off her shirt. A small ruby hung from her neck on a thin silver chain. As she undressed, the red stone glided over her skin. She had slipped under the covers and curled up next to Kelly.

Shaking her head, the image of Gina's ruby disappeared. At the flash of green on the traffic signal, Kelly squeezed the gas pedal. The muscles in her neck and back refused to relax. She hunched forward and hugged the steering wheel to concentrate on the road.

The Volkswagen passed under a highway bridge and veered to the west, following the road that climbed the steep hills of the city. Street signs dotted each intersection. Nearing the top of the first hill, Kelly watched San Francisco's skyline fill the horizon. Across the dark bay, the city lights sparkled. The rich claimed the hills of Oakland and held dominion on the best views of the famous city across the bay.

Continuing on the road lining the ridge, she focused on the street names as she drove slowly through each intersection. Mansions were cradled behind tall gates on well-manicured yards. Porch lights shone brightly. She spotted the road sign that matched the address on the package and made a quick right turn. Scanning the house numbers, Kelly rambled through a list of excuses to explain why the delivery was late. Maybe no one would notice. It was only five minutes after ten and this was just one more delivery.

As soon as she found the right address Kelly tapped the brakes, drove slowly past the mailbox and squinted at the front porch. The package would soon belong to the doormat of a Mission-style stucco home. A wrought iron fence lined the front yard. No porch lights were lit to identify the color of the stucco or welcome visitors. Kelly drove past the house and parked a few blocks down the road. Grabbing the knife and the box from the passenger seat, she slipped out of the car. The night sky was a somber dark gray with no stars in sight. Kelly skirted along the bushes lining the pristine front lawns of the row of expensive houses. Carefully checking each parked car before passing, she hedged up to the wrought iron fence of the stucco home.

At the front gate, Kelly paused to feel for the latch. Her fingers curled around a padlock. The hinges of the gate were rusty and would scream with movement. A red tile walkway led from the gate to the front door. At six feet, the fence would be easy to clear with one quick jump. Rick had given her two rules when she started delivering packages: "Never ask questions and don't let anyone see you make the delivery." The deliveries were an easy side job and the pay was good. Kelly didn't ask questions.

A soft rush of wind rustled the leaves of a bush near the fence. Her skin prickled with uneasiness. She turned to steal a quick glance down the sidewalk. The neighborhood was eerily quiet, even for a Monday night. Ignoring the sensation that someone was watching her, she slid the box under the gate. The cold rail of the fence held solid as she jumped. Kelly landed on the red tile, grabbed the box and raced up the stairs. She dropped the package on the mat and pulled off the yellow Post-it note.

The sound of each heartbeat pounded in her ears as she turned to run toward the fence. With four steps remaining before the gate, Kelly froze. A low growl, steadily gaining in volume, shook the stillness of the night. Flipping out the knife blade, she felt her chest tighten as her breathing stalled. A Rottweiler stood to the side of the path, waiting. The seething look in his eyes broadcast his intentions. If she took one more step, his fangs would sink into her throat. Kelly rubbed the knife's handle, planning her only defense against the guard dog. She'd have to stab his body as soon as he lunged. *Would this blade stop him?* His lips curled back in a snarl as he placed one paw on the red tile.

A gun fired suddenly. The bullet exploded in the bushes near the gate. Narrowly missing the dog's backside, the gunshot sent the Rottweiler running toward the side yard. The dog howled and a sharp whistle pierced the air. Kelly recognized the whistle and ran toward the gate. Just then, lights in a second-floor room of the stucco house switched on. Someone was home and probably already dialing the police. She caught the flash of Gina's ruby as she grabbed

5

the top rail and sailed over the fence. Her feet slipped on the landing and her knees pounded into the cement. Gina reached down to grab Kelly's arm as she helped her stand. The pistol vanished into the lining of her leather jacket. Kelly hadn't told Gina about her work with Rick or any of the deliveries. *How did she know about this?*

Suddenly the porch lights flashed on and Gina pulled on Kelly's arm. "We need to run," she ordered. "Now."

Chapter 2

0 4 9 0 0 1

A white picket fence lined the front lawn of a yellow paneled tract home. The fence paint had been chipped off on several boards to expose an underside of weathered gray pine. Kelly parked in the driveway and stared at the Volkswagen's odometer that had just rolled over to forty-nine thousand miles. Forty-nine had been her lucky number since the day she won a carrot cake by standing on the chalk-marked number forty-nine in her grammar school cakewalk. She hadn't liked carrots, but the thick layer of cream cheese frosting and the fact that she was the only cake winner in the third-grade class made up for the vegetables hidden inside the dessert.

Final exams at Bridges University had ended that afternoon and summer break officially began four hours ago. After helping her sublet tenant settle into her apartment, she'd squeezed the contents of her bedroom closet into the Volkswagen's back seat. She left San Francisco and headed east toward Ashton. For the next three months she would be stuck in suburbia.

Although there were no historical points of interest and no theater or arts programs, Ashton did boast hundreds of acres of over-priced housing tracts and a prime commute location. Until some yuppies discovered the short commute to San Francisco, most people had never heard of the town. Then the city workers came in a slow but persistent dribble, paving over the farming community and planting strip malls in place of peach orchards. The town was soon crawling with conservative upper-middle-class families. Kelly hated the place and referred to it as the town that made homogenized vitamin D milk seem exciting. Eighteen years after her first birthday, she finally moved out of Ashton. If anyone asked, she always claimed she grew up on a ranch, not the suburbs. This wasn't exactly a lie, but it wasn't quite true either.

While she was still running around in Wonder Woman Underoos, Kelly's parents built a single-story ranch house with a red barn on some acreage just outside the Ashton town border. Kelly spent half her youth chasing chickens, scaring cows and mucking out horse stalls and the other half attending Ashton public schools, kicking goals in the youth soccer league and cruising the cinema and mall scenes. Between the tract-home suburbanites and the aloof ranchers was a sign that read, "You Are Now Leaving Ashton," one speed bump and two stop signs.

Kelly and her brother, Alex, both left the ranch three years ago. They swore they'd never settle in the suburbs. She rented a dive apartment in San Francisco and started classes at Bridges University. Denim cut-offs were traded for tight-ass leather pants, and she started to dread mornings without caffeine. Alex rented a beach house and took a union construction job. His commitment to avoid the suburbs didn't last long. A year after he left the ranch, he got sucked into a marriage proposal and home ownership in downtown Ashton. He became hell-bent on remodeling a Fifties' version of a middle-class

American dream. Now the wedding plans were canceled, the bride had been kicked out, and he was stuck with a mortgage in suburbia.

Kelly usually spent university breaks at the ranch with her parents, but they had finally sold the place in May. They sunk a small fortune into a Winnebago and were traveling across the country as they settled into retirement. In their last phone call, they informed Kelly that gas prices were cheaper in the Midwest and that their arthritis was worse in the mornings. They gave her weekly updates on their travels and were currently somewhere between Denver and Detroit.

This year, Alex had convinced Kelly to spend her summer break helping him remodel his house. In exchange for free rent, Kelly had agreed to paint Alex's house Daisy Yellow. Her other commitment in Ashton was a job teaching karate at the local dojo, where she had taught the children's classes for the past three summers. Teaching karate was a good change from life at the university, and she'd often daydream during lectures of canceling her grad school plans to become a full-time karate teacher. Her karate Sensei, Sam, had offered a teaching position after graduation—no benefits and a salary just above minimum wage. She knew she shouldn't even consider the job offer. There was no way she could afford to pay off her school loans working at a minimum-wage job, and her parents urged her to decide on a *real* profession. Her dad had sent weekly e-mails about M.B.A. programs while her mom was pushing her toward pharmacy school. Grad school applications were due in the fall, but she wasn't ready to make a decision.

Kelly shifted in her seat and stared at her reflection in the rearview mirror. Her blue eyes were bloodshot and her skin looked even more pale than usual. She smoothed her mousy brown hair into place, tucking the loose strands behind her ears, and sighed. The final exams, house painting and future careers could wait. Tonight she just needed to relax. She grabbed her backpack and suitcase and traipsed across Alex's freshly watered front lawn.

Alex opened the front door and crossed his arms. "Where have you been? You told me you'd be here hours ago."

"Stuck in traffic," Kelly replied.

"You look sick." He shook his head. "When was the last time you slept?"

"Well, you're the picture of good health, nice tan by the way," she said. "Did you shower for me? You smell almost civilized."

At six-feet, Alex was four inches taller than Kelly and had the ability to look domineering even while wearing only a pair of boxers. She squeezed past him, dragging her suitcase through the doorway. His dark brown hair was still wet and his tan skin lacked the usual sweaty odor of a day spent pulling cables at a construction site. Her hair was usually a shade lighter than her brother's but it was damp now from a sweaty drive in a car without air conditioning and nearly the same color. Her eyes were burning from the past three sleepless nights and too many hours of studying. She envied Alex's tan. Even if she'd had the time to go outside, there was too much fog in San Francisco to get any color.

"Why didn't you call to tell me you were running late?" he asked. "It's almost seven."

Wondering why he would care what time she arrived, she glanced at her wristwatch and slipped off her backpack. "I can't call when I'm stuck in traffic. Remember, I don't have a cell phone."

"You just don't care about my feelings," he pouted.

"Your feelings? You know Monica used that line the first time I tried to break up with her. Have you been taking lessons from my ex-girlfriend?" She laughed.

Alex didn't smile. His arms were still crossed against his chest.

"Look, Alex, I'm sorry. I didn't think you'd care when I got here."

"Whatever. I know you don't think I'm important." His face twitched and the corner of his lip pulled up in a sly grin.

She shook her head as she realized his joke. He started to laugh and she swung at his arm in a half-hearted punch. He leaned to the side to avoid the slow strike. "You almost had me. I swear you sounded just like my ex."

"Yeah, mine too." He grinned. "It's good to be single again."

Kelly nodded. In the past month, she had broken up with Monica and Alex had called off his engagement with Laura. For the first time in five years they were both single. "It's good to see you."

"You too, punk." Alex ruffled her hair. "Feeling smarter?"

"No," she admitted.

He sighed. "Well, maybe living in the city has hardened you. You've lost that innocent look. I keep expecting a call from the county hospital. They're going to notify me that you've been shot in some drug heist in that ghetto apartment."

"It isn't that bad, really. No one's been shot in months. We had a stabbing a few weeks ago, but it's been quiet ever since."

"Your eyes are bloodshot," he noted.

Kelly shrugged. "I've been pulling all-nighters. I hate finals."

"Well, welcome to your vacation in sunny Ashton." He spread his arms in a sweeping gesture. "There's no place with an ocean view, but I can promise restful nights and absolutely no exams. There's nothing to do in Ashton and no reason to stay up late."

"I know. This town is boring as hell," she said. "Which is why you fit in perfectly here."

"Shut up, brat," Alex replied. He playfully pushed her shoulder. "Hey, speaking of fitting in, the neighbors can't wait till you start painting my house. I think they're about ready to turn me in for community review."

"Community review?"

"The Ashton housing tracts each have annual reviews of the properties to ensure they abide by the community standards." Alex thumbed his nose in mock disgust. "Yeah, and I've been advised by a few *friendly* neighbors that my exterior house paint is peeling. They also told me that Mustard Yellow is outdated." He laughed. "I figure there's no point in fighting them. The house does need a fresh coat of paint. I'd pay money to see their expressions when they find out that the new paint is an even brighter yellow."

"You really decided on sticking with Daisy Yellow?" Kelly asked. She hoped he had changed his mind since their last conversation when he suggested staying with the obnoxious yellow theme. She had voted for some shade of blue.

"What's wrong with Daisy Yellow?" he asked with a sarcastic grin. "Hey, do you want to see my other remodeling project? Come check out the back porch. I finished installing the deck last week."

Kelly followed her brother through the house. The end tables, entertainment unit and stereo were missing as well as the kitchen table and chairs. Laura had left Alex with only a sofa, a coffee table and a TV that sat on the floor. Kelly knew he had been miserable living with Laura and was glad he finally called off their engagement.

When they reached the back porch, Alex proudly pointed to each of the improvements he had made to the yard.

"The deck tiles were a big pain. I screwed up and bought two different types of tile and then had to exchange everything. My trips to Home Depot are becoming so frequent that most of the employees know me by my first name. I think I may be addicted to that store. Speaking of which, we have to pick up lights for the deck—wanna go for a drive?"

"No. I've been sitting in traffic for the past two hours. Let's walk."

"All the way to the store?" he asked in disbelief.

She smiled. "You've been living in the suburbs for too long. It's less than a mile to Home Depot. We can walk."

Alex started to argue, but Kelly stubbornly refused to drive anymore that night. While she waited for Alex to change his clothes, she hunted through the kitchen for a snack. There were no fruit or vegetables in the refrigerator, or anywhere else for that matter. The milk was two weeks past due and mold had claimed a slice of pizza and a pint of chow mein. Kelly investigated the pantry and found a box of graham crackers and the peanut butter jar. Jabbing the cracker into the peanut butter, she flipped through the newspaper on the kitchen table. The news headlines hadn't changed over the past month—they were still fighting in Iraq and the economic experts on Wall Street forecasted a sluggish market. Kelly flipped to the comics and read the first few strips.

Alex reappeared in a pair of jeans and a clean blue shirt. He glanced at the items on the counter and then raised his eyebrows at Kelly. "What the hell you eating?"

"Graham cracker peanut butter sandwich. You're out of bread and I couldn't find any jelly. Did you know your milk is expired by two weeks? And you have no produce in this house anywhere. Maybe we should go to the grocery store instead of Home Depot." Kelly licked the peanut butter off her fingers and swallowed the last graham cracker. Judging from the state of Alex's cupboards, she guessed that Laura had been in charge of grocery shopping.

"No, I hate grocery stores. Let's go pick out the deck lights," Alex insisted. "Come on, it'll be a quick trip."

Kelly didn't want to go to the hardware store. She wanted instead to collapse on the couch and take a nap. But Alex had an uncanny ability of convincing her to go along with almost any plan. She blamed it on his smile. For as long as Kelly could remember, Alex had got away with things just by flashing his perfect grin. Nearly all of her friends from grammar school through high school managed to have a crush on him and mostly it was because of the smile. Her friends would develop a sudden inability to speak and used to giggle whenever he was around. They called him a hottie behind his back. At age eleven, her friends' behavior made her nauseous. By age fifteen, it was just annoying. He was two years older and had mastered the art of charming chivalry at a young age. Although his smile won him many dates and even got him out of detention on a few occasions, his most distinctive feature was the jagged scar that ran across his chin. He joked that the scar was a battle wound. Really, it was because of the rat wars.

On the ranch, much of their childhood was spent riding horses, building tree swings and waging battles against the rodents around the barn. Rats routinely killed chickens and baby kittens, stole eggs and ravaged the grain bins. To defend the farm animals from the vermin, their father taught Alex and Kelly how to shoot BB guns and construct pop-bombs. They usually missed the rats with the gunshot, but the pop-bombs almost never failed. Pop-bombs were made out of an empty soda can stuffed with firecrackers, rocks and a kerosene-drenched rag. The two of them would search for rodent holes, light the rag, drop the can and wait for the explosion.

After finding a rat den behind the barn one morning, they made one of their trademark pop-bombs. Alex lit the kerosene rag and dropped it in the hole. He ran for cover behind the hay bales where Kelly was waiting with fingers stuck in both ears. Thirty seconds passed with no explosion. You could never tell if the rats had blown out the flame or if the pop-bomb was a dud. A full minute passed in silence. Frustrated, Alex ran to check the fuse. As soon as he leaned over the hole, the chain of firecrackers exploded in the can. A rock propelled out of the hole and struck his chin. The skin split and blood gushed out. Fourteen stitches later, Alex declared that on that day, the rats had won the battle.

After leaving Alex's house, they walked a few blocks through the tract home park and turned onto Main Street. They reached downtown Ashton within a few minutes. The hardware store was on Main Street, sandwiched between the bank and a fast-food Mexican restaurant. Alex selected two lightbulbs and a home improvement magazine. An overly friendly cashier recognized Alex in the checkout line and asked how his remodeling projects were coming. As she waited for Alex to finish his conversation with the talkative employee, Kelly picked out a flashlight from the bin of clearance items. She'd been meaning to buy a flashlight to keep in her car since she'd had to change a flat tire on her way home from a late-night study session. Alex and the cashier finally finished their conversation. After purchasing the flashlight, Kelly pulled Alex away from the talkative cashier's hold to finally leave the store.

"Let's take the bike path through the park," Alex suggested as they stepped out of the store.

"Why don't we just go back the way we came?" Kelly asked. It was still light out, but she was starting to feel tired and the bike path was a longer route home than the main road. She'd overdosed on caffeine to make it through her statistics final that morning and the buzz from her three cups of coffee had finally worn off.

"It's a nicer walk this way. And it's eight o'clock on a Friday night. I want to show you something," Alex finished cryptically.

Kelly shook her head but followed his lead anyway. The path led through the community park bordering Alex's neighborhood. A woman's softball game was in full swing in the corner field.

Alex pointed to the softball field and smiled. "Thought you'd like to see where all the lesbians hang out, in case you want to flirt. This is the only place I've seen dykes congregate in Ashton—every Friday night they have their games here. I bet we could hook you up with someone."

Kelly laughed. "Thanks, but I don't think I'm up for checking out girls tonight."

Alex stepped off the path and headed toward the field despite Kelly's protests. "Why not?" he asked. "You finally got rid of the last girlfriend and it's the beginning of June. You need to start thinking about a summer fling, right? What's holding you back?" Alex didn't wait for a response. "Want me to introduce you to someone? I don't know anyone here, but I don't mind making a fool of myself for you."

"Alex, don't even think about it!" Kelly said as she turned down the bike path leading away from the softball diamond.

"Hold up, Kelly," Alex called. He jogged over to her. "Come on, we'll just watch for a minute so we can pick out the cute girls. You know you want to. I'm not ready to go home yet."

A ball game was a good excuse to enjoy the warm summer evening, but she wasn't interested in checking out women tonight. She was too tired to argue with Alex though. Once he had made up his mind, he was unbelievably stubborn. "Okay, fine. But I swear I'll leave if you try setting me up with someone."

Alex agreed and they headed back to the field. After choosing a spot on a grassy mound behind the chain-link fence surrounding the dugout, they settled in to watch the game. Kelly figured out the score, nine to six, in favor of the team in blue jerseys. One of the women in the dugout caught her attention. She was about Kelly's height, with a lanky build, tan skin and spiky bleached blonde hair. A player in a blue baseball cap called over to her, "Hey, Shannon, you're up."

The spiky-haired woman picked up a bat and jogged out to the plate. She joked with the catcher and then swung the bat a few times to practice. The pitcher threw the ball toward her and the muscles in her forearms flexed as the bat struck the ball with a resounding crack. She sprinted to first base as the ball sailed out to left field. A woman in a green jersey ran to catch the ball. Fortunately, it hit the ground and bounced out of her reach.

The woman in the blue cap yelled, "Keep going, Shannon! Take the next base."

She sprinted past second base and slid onto third just as the ball was thrown toward the plate. Kelly stopped staring at Shannon only when the next player stepped up to bat. She reminded herself that she wasn't looking for any dating drama right now, but it was hard to ignore Shannon.

For the next ten minutes, Alex kept up a running commentary on the game with his input on each player's merit. This critique of the game and each player was annoying and she hoped no one could hear.

"Hey, Kelly, what about this batter? She had a good hit during the last inning and she's pretty cute." He motioned to the spiky-haired woman who was stepping up to the plate to bat again. "Except for her haircut. I don't know why lesbians like short spiky hair. But I'd bet she's your type, right?" he asked.

Kelly shrugged. She wouldn't admit to Alex that she was already forming a crush on this player. The woman swung her bat in the air a few times and then nodded at the pitcher. She bunted the ball and dashed to first base.

"Well?" Alex pestered.

Knowing Alex, he'd jump up and introduce himself to the woman just to be helpful. "I don't have a type," she replied.

He shook his head in frustration. "Everyone has a type."

"Well, from ten yards away I have no idea what her personality is like," she countered.

He sighed. "We're not interested in personality right now. Come on, I can tell you were watching her earlier. Why not talk to her? Flirt a little."

"No way. I'm not going to flirt with some stranger just because we're both lesbians stuck in Ashton. Anyway, she probably already has a girlfriend," she argued.

"You don't know that. Anyway, what are you scared of?" he taunted.

"I'm not scared." After a long week of exams and a recent sour breakup, she didn't want to think about dating tonight.

"You just don't have the balls." He grinned.

"Thank God—that's the last thing I need."

He laughed. "No one enjoys being single for long."

"I don't know. We're both happier being single than when we had dates last month. Who knows how long our bliss could last?"

Although she told herself she was happy being single, she watched the woman with spiky hair intently. Kelly remembered the phone conversation she'd had with Alex a month ago. They complained about their girlfriends and dating in general often, but on this occasion Alex had more to tell. He'd suddenly realized, in an epiphany over a cup of coffee, that he was not in love with his fiancée, Laura. And it occurred to him that he didn't have to settle into a marriage simply because that was the natural course of a relationship that had lasted five years. He had nothing in common with Laura and didn't want to grow old with her. That same day he broke off the engagement. Laura moved out of his house two days later.

"Alex, I think you need a rebound girlfriend more than I do," Kelly said. "Five years is a long time to only sleep with only one person."

"It's called commitment, but I wouldn't expect you to understand that concept." He shook his head. "No, it's too soon for me to date anyone."

"Maybe you have a point. Five years is commitment." Unlike Alex, she had been in and out of relationships with several women over the past few years. Nothing lasted long and she'd never found a reason to make a commitment to anyone. But she wasn't satisfied with any of the relationships. Maybe Alex could give her some advice.

She had dated her last girlfriend, Monica, for only two months, thanks to Alex. Monica was a freshman at her university, and a few weeks after they stated dating Kelly realized she'd lost her attraction to the younger woman. But since it was Monica's first lesbian relationship, Kelly decided to stick it out for a while. She didn't want to hurt her feelings or turn her off other lesbians. Alex, however, encouraged Kelly to cut ties before Monica got attached. She'd broken up with Monica just before final exams.

The softball game finally ended. The spiky-haired woman had made the winning run for her team in the last inning. She was gathering her sports bag and glove from the bench in the dugout as the other players congratulated her.

"Now's your chance." Alex elbowed Kelly. "Just say hi to her."

Kelly shook her head, concentrating on the scene at the dugout. A small group of fans, probably mostly made up of the players' girlfriends, waited to congratulate the teams.

"I dare you to go ask her out on a date," Alex prodded.

She shook her head. "No way."

"You know, there's only one way to face your fears."

"I'm not scared. It's just stupid," she said defensively.

"I double-dog dare you."

She grinned and shoved his shoulder. "I'm not ten years old anymore. You can't get me to do something stupid just by daring me."

"Why not? It used to work all the time." Alex smiled. "You know, it never hurts to flirt with someone and you could use something to spice up your life."

"I just broke up with Monica—there has to be some kind of waiting period."

"Excuses," he replied.

"Maybe." She shrugged. Her relationship with Monica didn't really count as one that needed recovery time.

The spiky-haired woman hugged a few of the other players and then downed a bottle of Gatorade. She caught Kelly's gaze just as she dropped the bottle into her sports bag.

Kelly considered asking her out on a date. *I'll need some distraction from the dojo this summer anyway.* "Okay, I'm going to go talk to her. What do I have to lose?"

"Nothing. I'll see you at home," Alex said, grinning. He picked up his bag of lightbulbs and swatted her with the home improvement magazine. "You make me so proud."

"Shut up." Kelly resolutely grabbed her bag with the flashlight and approached the dugout. She couldn't believe his double-dog dares still worked.

Kelly paused a few feet from the chain-link fence. The woman was watching her expectantly, but she hadn't thought of anything to say before waltzing over.

She fumbled through a fog of ideas then began, "Umm, I had a question about softball. I was wondering if you could give me some advice on joining a team. By the way, good hit tonight."

With the back of her hand, the woman wiped sweat off her forehead. "Thanks. The team played a good game." She smiled. "Unfortunately, I'm not the best person to help you with advice on joining a team."

"Oh." Kelly couldn't think of anything else to say. She glanced at a group of players just leaving the dugout, wishing she could think of some other excuse to detain her while she got up the nerve to ask her out. "I'm Kelly, by the way."

"Shannon." They shook hands. "You know, if you're really interested in joining a softball team, I can introduce you to someone who knows more about the league. Our captain will know which teams are looking for players. We might even have space on our roster."

Kelly remembered that Shannon's team had had a few less players than the other team. "Yeah, I thought it looked like your team could use some extra help tonight."

Shannon's eyes flashed at Kelly. "Some help?" she shot back skeptically.

"No, wait, I didn't mean help, I meant—"

Shannon laughed. "Relax, I'm joking. You just looked too serious and I had to lighten your mood. But you're right, we were short a few players. Maybe we could use you."

Kelly bit her lip. Why had she brought up softball at all? She couldn't hit a ball to save her life.

"It's kind of late in the season to start a new player, but let's go talk to Beth." Shannon gestured toward the end of the dugout.

Beth was the team captain. Shannon introduced them and explained that Kelly was interested in playing on their league. Beth said she thought there might be room on their team since a few players hadn't attended the recent games. She then launched into a discussion of rules and team practice times.

Kelly tried to pay attention but found herself focused on Shannon. Below the spiky hair, each ear was pierced with five or six rings, and a small Chinese character was tattooed on the back of her tan neck. She could have been a poster girl for the sporty butch club. Kelly had a weakness for a girl who could pull off that look. After a few minutes, another player called over to Shannon. A group had gathered around an ice cooler in the parking lot and Shannon quickly excused herself to join them.

As soon as Shannon left, Kelly admitted to Beth that she didn't think she'd be good enough to join their team. She promised to come to their next game with a glove to practice catching.

Kelly walked past the parking lot, hoping for a second chance to talk with Shannon. But Shannon was engrossed in a conversation with her teammates about where to go for dinner that evening. Kelly decided not to interrupt and turned to head home to Alex's place.

Just as Kelly passed the group, Shannon jogged over to her. "Hey, Kelly, wait up. Did Beth get you signed up for our team?"

"Honestly, I don't think I'm good enough to join. But I'll come back to watch the next game."

"Oh," Shannon responded. "Well, did you have any other questions?"

Can I ask you out? Kelly stared at Shannon without responding. Her skin was growing warm with a blush. *Damn, say something.* "No. I don't think so." Kelly cringed at her own shyness.

"Okay. Well, have a good night," Shannon said.

Kelly nodded and turned away.

"Hey, wait." Shannon caught her arm. She grinned sheepishly as Kelly turned to face her. "What happened to that guy you were with? Are you two together? I mean, is he your boyfriend?"

"Boyfriend? No, he's my brother." Kelly laughed. Don't say anything stupid, she told herself. "We were on our way back to his house from the hardware store." She held up the Home Depot bag. "That's when we stopped to watch the game."

"Do you live with him?" Shannon asked.

"Only for the summer—I'm helping him remodel his place."

"That's good. I mean, it's good that you're on vacation. And that you're here." Shannon paused. A hint of apprehension was apparent in her voice. "I was wondering if, maybe, you'd be interested in going out . . . You know, for coffee or something. We could talk about softball if you still had questions."

Kelly hoped she wouldn't have to talk about softball again. "Yeah, I'd definitely be interested." She smiled.

"I don't usually ask out strangers. I mean, I try to keep a low profile around here." Shannon shook her head and then added, "But I got the impression that you might not be back here for our next game and I didn't want you to disappear without knowing if you were flirting or just being nice."

"I'd bet you get a lot of practice flirting in this park," Kelly teased, feeling more bold. "Why else would you play softball?"

Shannon grinned and swung her sports bag off her shoulder. She searched through the bag and pulled out a pen. "Do you have any paper?"

Kelly found the Home Depot receipt under the flashlight in the plastic bag and handed it to Shannon. Shannon printed her name and number on the back.

"Here, call me if you want to go out sometime, okay? I gotta go— the team is going out for pizza to celebrate." Shannon shouldered her sports bag and turned toward the parking lot without waiting for an answer. She glanced back at Kelly just as she passed the softball field and hollered, "You'll call me?"

When Kelly got home she found Alex perched on the steps of his front porch. He looked up from the home improvement magazine and smiled at her. "Well, you're glowing. Must be good news. What happened with our softball lesbian? Did you talk to her?"

"Yes." She unlocked her car door and tossed the flashlight into the glove box. She realized that she'd forgot to buy batteries and left the Home Depot receipt in the car's cup holder as a reminder to go back to the store. "And thanks for abandoning me," she added, slamming the car door. "I almost got roped in to playing softball."

"What?"

"I don't know, I wasn't thinking very clearly. You know that feeling when there's a cute girl staring at you, just waiting for you to say something, and you forget how to say, 'Hi, how are you?' For some reason, I asked her about joining their softball league. You know I can't play softball. I hate team sports. I don't know what I was thinking."

Alex's hand landed on her shoulder as he laughed. "Don't worry about it. Everyone says stupid things when they flirt. I bet she liked you. What's her name?"

"Shannon. That's about all I know about her," she admitted, leaning against the door of her car.

"Well, at least you talked to her. I'm impressed. So, did you set up a date?"

"Got her number." Kelly grinned. "God, look at me. One day in Ashton and I'm already flirting with the softball players."

"You can thank me later."

Kelly shook her head. "Yeah, I guess I needed to flirt. Who knew it'd be this easy to find a date in suburbia?"

Chapter 3

049051

In her first week back at the karate dojo, Kelly remembered why she had hated Tuesday afternoons—Colin McNally. She'd last taught at the dojo eight months ago and since then Colin's karate skills hadn't improved at all. He still wore the same purple belt that she'd given him two summers ago and was the worst student in the intermediate children's class, by a long shot. About the only thing that seemed to have changed for the better was his height, if being above four and a half feet by age ten was a good thing. Colin had little control when he sparred, sloppy karate techniques and an expanding vocabulary of annoying cartoon sounds. He practiced the cartoon sounds whenever he was bored.

Colin and his brother, Isaac, had a private class every Tuesday at four o'clock. At twenty-five minutes after the hour, Kelly told the boys to meditate. Isaac kneeled immediately, closed his eyes and sat perfectly still with his hands clasped in his lap. Colin slowly dropped to one knee, glanced out the door, then tightened his belt and grinned at his reflection in the mirror before finally sinking all the way to the ground and closing his eyes. After ten seconds of silence, Colin started practicing his cartoon exclamation sounds and boxing the air.

Kelly was glad that no one else was in the dojo to hear the noise. She waited for the minute hand to finally signal the end of their lesson, the longest half-hour of her week, and then clapped her hands. "Rise up. Front position," she called.

Isaac jumped up quickly. Standing with his back straight and chin tipped up, the eight-year-old immediately clasped his right fist in front of his chest and covered the fist with his left palm. Isaac's hair was wet with the sweat of a long sparring match. Kelly glanced down at Colin, waiting for him to stand. He sighed and climbed to his feet slowly. Shifting his weight from his left to right foot, he fidgeted with his purple belt and impatiently gazed out the front window of the dojo.

With a glance at his older brother, Isaac waited for the boy to assume the traditional front position. "Stand still, Colin," Isaac whispered.

"I thought class was over. When are we gonna be done?" Colin whined, ignoring his brother. He lost interest in the scene outside the dojo, glanced briefly at Kelly and then stared at the mirror. He stuck his tongue out at this reflection and then laughed.

Isaac scowled at him. "Cut it out. Stand in front position." Concentrating on Kelly, the boy added, "I'm sorry. He never listens." Isaac's hazel eyes silently asked for help. Colin had turned his attention back to the view out the front window.

"Colin. Focus here. Now," Kelly ordered. She could grab his attention with harsh words and didn't need to yell. His eyes focused quickly and his hands clasped together in front position.

"What? I just want to go."

"No talking, Colin. Feet together, back straight, chin up and eyes forward. Do not move your hands. Concentrate on standing in a perfect front position. Look at me and pay attention." She knew he was laced with Ritalin. Isaac had confided that their father made Colin take his "behavior drugs" each morning.

Colin glared at Kelly. She hated to see the anger in his eyes, but he was finally concentrating. He could focus if he was forced to do so. "Fine. I'm looking at you. Happy?"

"No, I'm not happy," Kelly replied, refusing to match the anger in his voice. He was testing her. Colin was accustomed to pushing people and he'd learned that eventually everyone reached a point where they just stopped arguing with him. His teachers decided he was a lost cause. His parents agreed. "Colin, you won't train at this dojo with that attitude."

"Good."

"Think about what you just said. Do you mean that? Because I can make that happen."

Colin didn't reply. His body swayed back and forth as he turned to look at the door. Kelly guessed the drug levels were shifting in his blood again. Some days were better than others.

"Why do you bow when you enter the dojo?" she asked.

"Because I have to," Colin responded indignantly.

"No." Avoiding the urge to raise her voice, Kelly kept her tone even as she continued, "We all bow as a sign of respect when we enter the dojo and we agree to respect everyone here. You need to work harder at showing that respect."

"Yeah. I know, I know, okay! Everyone tells me to work harder. I don't have to hear it again," he snapped. The anger rippled under his skin, distorting the little boy features into a seething gremlin. "I know what respect means. It means I don't talk. Everyone says, 'Do this, don't do that! Look at me! Pay attention!' 'Listen to me and do what I say!' They all say the same thing, 'You need to work harder and you need to pay attention!' Well, I don't care."

Kelly wondered what he'd be like in ten years if this anger continued. "Colin—"

"Did you hear me? I don't care," he interrupted. "I already know what you want. *Pay attention! Do as you're told!* See, I don't need to hear it again," he yelled.

Kelly's tone was steady and quiet. "Colin, no one raises their voice at anyone in this dojo. If you show anger again, you won't be allowed to train here."

"My parents pay for this. You have to let me—"

"Don't finish," Kelly interrupted. Silently she added, *I could drop you with one strike*. She'd never hit him, but her expression portrayed enough venom to silence him. "Take off your belt."

Colin stared at the ground, avoiding her gaze. His anger had been quickly replaced by fear and his lower lip trembled as he opened his mouth to protest. Kelly shook her head once. He clearly understood the threat and bowed his head. "You know I didn't mean what I said."

"Colin, I gave you that belt because you earned that rank. Now you have lost it." Kelly held out her hand and waited.

"I'm sorry."

She shook her head. "Too late."

Dropping to one knee, Colin untied the purple belt. He folded the belt neatly before giving it to Kelly. His belt signified an intermediate level in the children's class. Colin had trained for nearly three years before passing his test for the rank of purple belt. It took most children his age one year to reach the same level. Moisture wicked at the corner of his eyes. "Does this mean I'm not a purple belt anymore?"

"You earned this belt by training hard for months and committing to improving yourself. You told me that you wanted to be a black belt someday. I don't think you care about your karate training anymore. Do you want to prove me wrong?"

Colin nodded. He rubbed the tears out of his eyes quickly and stared down at his plain white karate uniform with a crease in the fabric from where his belt had been.

"You need to respect people," Kelly said.

"I'm sorry I yelled."

"Show me that you mean that apology." She was struggling to make her tone of voice sound as strict as her Sensei's did when he corrected a student's behavior. Surprisingly, it appeared to be working. Colin was finally standing still and focused on her. "Your attitude needs to improve in the dojo, at home and at school. You need to show that you can be a black belt someday or I won't waste my time training you anymore."

Colin pleaded for a second chance, but Kelly's sharp look silenced him. Maybe taking his belt was a bad decision, but she didn't know another way of getting his attention. His father had mentioned that Colin's last report card had failing marks in several courses and the child's therapist didn't think his medications were at the proper levels. If his grades weren't improved this quarter, he'd have to take summer school in order to pass the fourth grade. Kelly wondered if the boy would work harder to get the belt back or just lose confidence. Unfortunately, psychology was not a requirement for her bachelor's degree in biology. Probably some therapist would tell her she had made the wrong decision. "Okay, boys, front position and bow. Class dismissed."

"Thank you, ma'am," Isaac called out as he ran to the front door. He stopped at the edge of the mat and bowed perfectly.

Colin trudged behind his brother, dragging his feet slower as soon as he saw his father waiting by the door. He bowed at the edge of the mat and looked up at Kelly. "I really am sorry."

"Me too, Colin. By the way, your punches and side kicks are looking great," she lied. "I know you could be a great martial artist someday. Don't give up."

With a serious nod, Colin grabbed his shoes. He left the dojo barefoot, waving meekly at Kelly as he stepped outside. Isaac and the boys' father were waiting by the minivan.

Kelly entered the waiting room and found a paper Dixie cup. She leaned against the wall and closed her eyes as the water filled her cup. She had three more hours of teaching before her own sparring class.

Through the front window, Kelly watched the scene in the parking lot. Isaac ran up to greet him and the father hugged the younger boy quickly before opening the back door of the minivan and helping him inside. Colin was trudging toward the minivan with downcast eyes. His father yelled for the older boy to hurry and shook his head with disapproval as Colin dropped one of his shoes. Colin climbed into the back seat and his father slammed the door shut. He didn't seem to notice that Colin had lost his belt. Kelly hoped that next week would be better. Colin didn't have anyone else on his side.

After teaching the last children's class, Kelly took her position on the mat in the adult sparring class. Nine other students were lined up in order of rank, facing Sam. As the chief instructor of the karate school, or Sensei, Sam held every student's respect. It was well earned. Sam was committed to the martial arts and to every student who demonstrated that they wanted to learn. His first lesson in the martial arts came the day after his eighth birthday. He was the target of the school bully one morning. Right before class, the bully had punched Sam in the belly and stole his book bag. During recess, Sam found his bag in the boy's bathroom with the word *Foriner* scrawled on the canvas. That evening he asked his dad what the word on his book bag meant. His dad immediately gave Sam a lesson in self-defense as an explanation. After a few classes, Sam had decided to spend his life training in the martial arts. Now in his early thirties, he had his own karate school and hundreds of students.

Sam was Kelly's first, and only, Sensei. He'd tied her first belt, clean and white around her waist, showing her how to make the knot and adjust the length so that the ends fell evenly. Then, many years later, Sam tied the knot on her black belt. To her the different ranks really had little to do with karate, and Kelly forgot all the colors that passed between the white and black belt tests. But she remembered the countless bruises Sam had delivered during her training. He had repeatedly crushed her ego, criticized every aspect of her life, and twice recommended that she seriously consider quitting karate. Last summer, he fired her for slouching after an eight-hour day of teaching. The next day he called to find out why she was late for work. She would do anything he asked.

Kelly and another black belt, Kevin, were scheduled for the first sparring match in the adult class that evening. The other students in the class kneeled on the mat to watch the fight. Bowing, first to Sam and then to Kevin, Kelly stepped back into a fighting stance and waited for Sam's call to start the match. Kevin faced her in a fighting stance. His lips were pulled back in a grin. The plastic mouthpiece distorted every fighter's face into one of two expressions, a grin or a grimace. Sam's hand sliced the air between Kelly and Kevin. "Spar!"

Instantly, Kelly threw two punches, high then low. She chased the strikes with a roundhouse kick to Kevin's right ear. Her strikes were fast and she dodged out of Kevin's target zone quickly. Kevin was stronger than she was. He had tagged her helmet with a deafening hook punch more than once and she knew she couldn't afford to get close. They sparred frequently and knew each other's secrets. A light smack sounded as her foot hit Kevin's helmet. He grabbed at the foot, but she pulled her leg back forcefully. As he stepped forward, she pushed the same foot out in a side kick to his ribs.

A cell phone rang in the front waiting room. Kelly threw an uppercut toward Kevin's head just as he turned to look into the front waiting room. At the same moment Sam called, "Break!"

It was too late to pull back the strike. Her glove glanced off of Kevin's jaw and struck his nose. Sam had already stopped the match.

"Break!" The second time everyone in the room heard Sam's voice. The cell phone rang again. No one turned to look into the waiting room this time.

Kevin and Kelly stood at attention facing Sam. A bead of blood formed under Kevin's nose and Kelly bowed her head. She knew her last strike had hit Kevin after Sam had stopped the match. The bead of blood skirted around the edge of Kevin's lip, then turned into a red ribbon, dripping fast down his chin and cutting a wide swath of red across his pale skin. Tugging his glove off, Kevin's hand leapt up to form a cup at the base of his chin. The blood pooled in his palm.

"I'm sorry—" she started. There were a lot of rules in karate sparring. One, never apologize to an equal opponent. Two, never hit the face or below the belt. Three, pay attention. She thought of Colin and remembered the words everyone told him. *Pay attention.* The apology raged in her head. If you made a mistake that injured another student, it was customary to kneel on the mat facing the door. The judge would help the injured student. Kelly immediately turned to face the door. She fell to her knees and waited for Sam's punishment.

A gray-haired man in a black business suit stared at her. A silver cell phone was clipped to his belt. The front door to the karate studio was open and Kelly guessed he had wandered inside to watch the fights. It must have been his cell phone that had interrupted the match. After a moment, she recognized the man. He was the investor who owned part of the karate dojo. Sam had only mentioned a few details about the investor. She knew his first name was Rick and that he had worked for the FBI for several years. Apparently, Rick had invested in a few local businesses. Over the years, the investments had provided handsome returns and Rick had recently settled into a wealthy retirement. Kelly rarely saw Rick at the dojo and had never had a conversation with him. She figured he had better things to do in his retirement than micromanage a karate school.

Now Rick was watching her intently. She felt him measuring her up against the other students in the class. But the only judgment she cared about was Sam's. She had thrown a punch with poor control after the match had been called. Her opponent was still bleeding. Kelly closed her eyes to block out the investor's face. After a few minutes of meditation, she forgot about Rick and concentrated on her breathing. The touch of Sam's hand on her shoulder made her shiver. It was the signal to rise. Sam offered no punishment. Kevin pressed a bloody tissue under his nose. Kelly's next opponent was called on the mat and the next match began.

At the end of the last match of the evening, the sweaty men crowded into the waiting room to take off their sparring gear. Sam and Rick disappeared into the office at the back of the dojo. Kelly stayed on the mat to stretch her muscles. She pulled off her helmet and listened to the noisy banter in the waiting room. The guys were comparing their bruises from the last week.

Kevin looked over at Kelly and smiled. "You don't look like you are ready to leave. Are you hoping to find another guy to beat the crap out of tonight?"

"I feel terrible about throwing that punch. Sam had already called break and I should have—"

He held up his hand to stop her. "It was a sweet strike. Relax, I'm just teasing you. I was surprised that Sam didn't yell at me for bleeding so much."

"Kevin, you know the way karma works around here . . . I'll wear a red shirt the next time we spar so the blood won't show."

The other students began discussing the other notable strikes from the evening matches. Most students denied their own talent and attempted to laugh about the mistakes. It was better not to dwell on success. The next sparring match could change everything.

"So, who was that guy with the cell phone that disappeared into Sam's office?" Joe asked. He was one of the brown belts in training for the upcoming sparring tournament. His clothing stank of sweat even before their sparring class began.

"Rick Lehrman," Kevin replied. He gave a quick description of his position as an investor in the karate dojo and ex-FBI agent. Kelly eavesdropped on their conversation, curious to learn any more gossip about him.

"What do you think the cut is on the investment in the karate school?" Joe asked. "Sam does all the work around here."

"I don't think his cut is very big." Kevin shoved his sweaty spar-ing gear in his black canvas bag. The gear barely fit and he had to yank at the zipper to close the bag. "Lehrman has other business investments besides the karate school. And after he retired from the FBI a few years ago, he started a private investigation service here in Ashton. You know, some guys go crazy if they stop working."

"Who does he investigate in Ashton?" Joe asked incredulously.

"Jealous housewives hire him to follow their husbands when they're having affairs," one of the other students quipped.

Kevin laughed. "No. He works for lawyers on high-profile cases. My neighbor is a D.A. in San Francisco. He knows Rick Lehrman well. Apparently, Lehrman has had his hand in quite a few cases recently. He investigates leads on witnesses and does background checks. It sounds like he makes a killing at the business. Lawyers pay better than the FBI." Kevin stood up and slung the gym bag over his shoulder. "Well, have a good night everyone. I'm going home to ice all my wounds." He laughed easily and nodded at Kelly.

After Kevin left, the other students began discussing baseball players and the current stats on the Giants. Kelly kneeled on the mat and closed her eyes to meditate. She concentrated on her breathing to block out the chatter from the waiting room.

Distracted from her meditation, Kelly remembered the softball game and the receipt with Shannon's phone number that was still in her car. The receipt was supposed to remind her to buy flashlight batteries. Instead, it just made her think of Shannon every time she got in the car. Over the past few days, Kelly had considered calling her several times. But excitement at the prospect of another relationship mixed with uneasiness from her last few failed attempts at dating. She didn't want to start something that would only last a few months.

Footsteps padded past her place on the mat, bringing Kelly's attention back to the karate dojo. She was not sure how many minutes had passed since she closed her eyes. Time was fluid during meditation. She guessed that the footsteps belonged to Rick. They sounded like expensive dress shoes. The front door closed and the dojo was finally quiet. Kelly opened her eyes. The waiting room was empty. The other students had left for the night. Sam was slowly henpecking on the computer keyboard in the office. Kelly walked over to the bags hanging against the back wall. She swung a few strikes at the bag to loosen her muscles. The bag swung back at her body, eager for a fight. She bounced on her feet and started to pound her fists against the black canvas, finding her rhythm with the bag's movement.

Sam cleared his throat. She stepped back from the bag and glanced at Sam. He leaned back in his chair and stared at the account register book. His feet were balanced on the desk and he spun a pencil around his fingers. Kelly knew that business was booming. Rick was probably happy with Sam's numbers this month. She turned back to hit the bag and noticed a wet stripe smeared against the canvas. Kelly stopped to check her knuckles for blood.

"Impressive strike tonight. You nearly gave Kevin a cheap nose job." He laughed. Sam gave only a hint of censure. He penciled something into the account register and then closed the book.

"The strike wasn't impressive. I hit Kevin after you called break. The match was over. I completely screwed up." Kelly slugged the bag again. She loved the smell of sawdust that puffed out of the canvas with the hard punch. She pounded the bag repeatedly. The pain raced from her knuckles through her wrists. Her shoulders burned. Somehow seeing the red liquid seep out of the cracked skin on her knuckles was a relief. She wanted to drain emotion out with the blood and paint the bag red.

Sam shook his head. "Kevin stepped into your strike because he was aiming a spinning back fist at your head. You clocked him before he could land his strike. Your mistake was that you didn't anticipate your opponent's next move. Pay attention."

Kelly nodded. She had given Colin the same reprimand.

"You need to focus. Don't get distracted. Keep the outside world off the mat."

❧

Kelly left the dojo immediately after the scolding. The last thing she wanted was for Sam to see her emotions, and tears were pushing at her eyes. She drove home, memorizing the phone number on the Home Depot receipt and debating whether she had the energy to start dating again. When she entered the house Alex's cat ran up to greet her. He meowed loudly and brushed between her legs. "Hey, Elvis," Kelly replied.

Alex had left a note taped on the refrigerator: "We're out of milk, beer and cat food. All the essentials."

Kelly opened the refrigerator and stared at the leftovers. The cat butted his head against her leg, begging for food. She handed Elvis a slice of chicken and the mewing stopped immediately. Kelly fished out the jar of jelly and the peanut butter. She reluctantly spread jelly over a slice of bread. She'd gone to the grocery store that weekend but had only had enough cash to afford the jelly and bread. Unfortunately, payday wasn't until next Friday and this was already her third peanut butter and jelly dinner.

She sat down at the kitchen table. Her mail had been forwarded to Alex's address and a letter from Bridges University was at the top of the mail pile. She opened the envelope and stared at the last line on the page. Payment for next year's tuition was due in July. The university fees had increased. Kelly sighed, knowing she wouldn't have the money to cover the bill by the due date. If she kept working full-time at the karate school, she'd have enough money saved to pay tuition by the end of August. She didn't want to take out another loan. Her options were to find a second job or ask the university for an extension on the payment.

Kelly folded the tuition bill and shoved it back in the envelope. Another issue preoccupied her thoughts. She wanted to talk to Shannon and had stared at the hardware store receipt in her car for enough miles to have finally memorized Shannon's phone number. Still, she wanted someone's encouragement before picking up the phone. Unfortunately, her best friend was on vacation in Spain and she had no way of contacting her. And Alex was already asleep. For the past few days, he had worked overtime at the construction site and was asleep by eight every night.

She picked up the receiver and dialed the phone number.

"Hello?" Shannon's voice was sweet and instantly recognizable.

"Hi . . . umm." Swallowing resolutely, she started again, "Hi. Is this Shannon?"

"Yes."

"I'm Kelly. We met at the softball field last week and talked about going out for coffee sometime."

"Right. Hey, I'm glad you called. I wasn't sure if you would."

"So, do you still want to go out for coffee?"

"Definitely," Shannon replied. "My schedule at work is crazy. I get off early Thursday—would that work for you?"

Kelly paused, wondering where Shannon worked and trying to recall her plans for Thursday. Sam had scheduled her to teach the afternoon classes. The adult sparring class ended at eight. "Is nine o'clock too late?"

"Sounds perfect."

Chapter 4

049101

Sam announced the last sparring match of the night at five minutes to eight. Kelly didn't want to go another round. She was anxiously eyeing the clock and hoped she could dodge out of the dojo early to get ready for her date. Sam called her on the mat to spar with Joe and she guessed that he'd read her thoughts. Joe and Kelly faced each other after bowing to Sam.

"Spar," Sam called out, slicing his hand through the air between the two opponents.

Joe immediately threw a roundhouse kick at Kelly's face. As she shielded her head with a forearm block, Joe's foot collided into her elbow and a sharp pain shot up from the joint. Following the block, she threw two punches at his helmet, missing on both attempts, and a hook punch that barely scraped the foam padding over his ear. Joe shoved a front kick at the middle of Kelly's chest. She stumbled backward and lost her balance. The moment after she hit the ground, his body was on hers. She struggled to keep him from pinning her and quickly trapped his neck between her arms. Squeezing her forearms, she tightened the headlock as Joe aimed a knee strike at her side. The knee struck her lower back, right at the kidney. Joe was gasping for air as she tightened her choke hold. He kneed harder the second time aiming at the same kidney. The second strike was too painful to ignore and she felt her forearms loosen on his neck. Joe slipped out of her hold and they tumbled on the mat, each fighting to gain control.

"Break!" Sam called.

Instantly, they released each other and scrambled to their places on the mat. Sam pointed at Joe. "Point for the front kick to the solar plexus. Good power, Joe, and nice follow-through." Sam didn't look at Kelly.

Alex was yelling at the TV when Kelly opened the front door, "That's crap! He was safe!"

"Hey, Alex. Let me guess, the Giants are losing to Red Sox?" Kelly asked. She always enjoyed watching Alex's reactions to baseball games, especially interleague. He'd throw potato chips at the players he didn't like and cheer as if his favorite pitcher could actually hear him when he struck out an infamous batter. And he uniformly hated the team coaches. His reactions were more entertaining than the actual game.

"The ref made a bad call. We're down by two runs." Alex sighed and shook his head. He glanced at her face and then surveyed her disheveled uniform. "Are you okay?"

She nodded. The black fibers of her karate uniform had faded to a muted gray after years of sweat and laundry detergent. The loose cotton pants and jacket were damp with moisture. Tonight's fight was a hard loss. Kelly removed her belt. The jacket hung open and the sweaty undershirt clung to her. A drop of blood had stained the shirt. Kelly gazed at the blood smear. One of her sparring partners had probably scraped their knuckles raw during the warmup exercises on the punching bags. Her own hands were clean for once. "I guess I look like hell."

"Maybe worse," he replied. "I hate to ask, but did you win?"

"Does it look like it?" she asked with a smile. Elvis pawed at the screen as the pitcher threw the ball. The cat loved watching the game as much as Alex and often attacked the ball as well as the players.

Alex watched the batter swing and sighed as the ball sank into the catcher's mitt.

He shook his head. "Do you always lose?"

"Winning's overrated. I always have a good time." She went to the kitchen to get a glass of water.

"I think that's only what the losers say."

Kelly laughed. "Probably."

He came into the kitchen for another beer. His eyes were still focused on the screen. Alex moaned as the batter missed the third pitch. "Damn, they're going to lose again."

"Winning's overrated," Kelly repeated. "How's work been? We never see each other anymore. Now I know why Laura was feeling neglected."

Alex nodded. "It's crazy right now. I have a big inspection with the contractor at the building site next week so I'll be working more overtime. But I don't mind. Overtime pays the mortgage and it beats getting a second job."

"Hey, speaking of which, I've been looking for a second job. Do you know of anyone who's hiring around town?"

Alex shook his head. "I saw your tuition bill from Bridges on the table. Is that why you're looking for another paycheck?"

"Yeah. And don't tell me to borrow money from Mom and Dad."

"No, you're too stubborn to ask anyone for anything." Alex smiled knowingly. "Want to go out for dinner with me after the game? My treat."

"Thanks, but not tonight." Tasting salt from the dried sweat on her lips, Kelly glanced at the clock on the microwave. She had to meet Shannon in a half an hour and still needed to shower and make dinner. Staring at the jar of peanut butter, Kelly contemplated another sandwich. "Alex, we need to go grocery shopping again, although I see you got more beer."

Alex nodded. "Add it to my list of things to do. It's right after laundry, mowing the lawn and cleaning out my car. There's sand on all the seats from the last surfing trip. Are you coming with me next time? I've got an extra surfboard now that Laura won't be tagging along."

"You know I hate sharks," Kelly replied, shaking her head.

"Come on, you aren't really scared, are you?"

"No," she lied. "Not really."

Alex took a sip of the beer. There was a commercial break before the last inning of the game. "When we were kids you'd surf anything."

Kelly sighed. Alex had been the risk-taker throughout their childhood. He had pressured Kelly into breaking their parents' rules countless times. She'd do anything he put her up to and had surfed with him on every family trip to the beach. But she'd always dreaded sharks.

"I'm sure you'll change your mind and come on a surfing trip with me before the end of summer." He stared at the peanut butter and jelly sandwich in Kelly's hands. "How many times can you eat that for dinner?"

"I don't know. I'm trying to set a record." Kelly smiled sarcastically.

"Why don't you want to go out to dinner?" Alex asked.

"Hot date." Kelly grinned. She didn't like first dates, but she was excited to see Shannon.

"Date? With who?"

"Shannon—the woman from the softball game."

"Why didn't you tell me? Where are you going?" he asked.

"The café down the street next to Sweet Stream bar." Kelly finished her sandwich and tossed the bread crusts in the trash.

"Congratulations on actually calling her back. I'm impressed." He smiled. "And glad I'm not you. First dates suck."

"You actually remember your last first date?" Kelly asked sarcastically. Alex sighed and shook his head. He entered the family room and sank down on the couch with his beer. Wishing she could take back the last comment, Kelly guiltily headed for the shower. She would have to remember to apologize later.

The coffee shop was a few blocks past the hardware store, just off Main Street. Kelly arrived five minutes late and found Shannon at a table in the far corner of the room. She stood up as Kelly approached. The smell of softball sweat was missing but Shannon still modeled the sporty butch look well. Her handshake was firm and warm and Kelly felt her skin blush with the touch. She knew Shannon was attractive, but her responsive blush surprised her. *Relax. You've been on a dozen first dates,* she thought.

They ordered drinks at the front counter and then returned to the table Shannon had claimed. The cafe was mostly empty and the waitress was singing along with the Sixties rock music playing on a little radio behind the counter as she prepared their coffee.

"So how long have you been in Ashton?" Kelly asked. She knew the usual first date questions well. First dates were like job interviews without the typed résumé. Maybe that was why she hated them.

Shannon responded, "Three months. I'm in the Army Reserves and just finished my training. They stationed me at the San Francisco base, but I decided to live in Ashton rather than the *big city* after I looked into rent prices. And I had a few friends here. My friend Gina hooked me up with a job at sports store in town—she's friends with the manager. And I moved in with Vicky, a friend from the army. In less than a week, Ashton felt like home. I can't believe I've only lived here three months."

"So you like Ashton?" Kelly asked, careful not to reveal her own distaste for the town. She was surprised at how positive Shannon sounded.

"Well, I grew up in Southern California. In my hometown, no one talks to their neighbors unless they're bragging about their new car. And for the past six months I've been training in North Carolina. The army sent me to this town that I swear is literally in the middle of nowhere. The hottest spot on a Friday night was Wal-Mart. So, compared to the other places I've lived, the Bay Area feels like a big gay party." Shannon laughed. "Yeah, I love it here."

The waitress appeared with the drinks and a plate of biscotti. "Free samples for you two. It's my own recipe so you'll have to tell me what you think." She winked at Kelly as she handed her an iced coffee. "Enjoy."

Kelly didn't know what her wink meant but thanked her anyway. Maybe she could tell that they were on a date. As the waitress left their table, Kelly eyed Shannon. She didn't want to start off a date with an argument but couldn't let Shannon's comments go. "You know, Ashton isn't San Francisco. I think every dyke in town has joined your softball league. Everyone else in this town is straight, white, middle-class and conservative."

"You sound like Gina. She calls herself a Latina lesbian and always complains that Ashton is too white and too straight." Shannon smiled. "I've been friends with Gina since grade school and we bicker like sisters. She moved to Ashton a year ago and hates it. Her family is still in Southern California and I think she'd like to go back. She can't understand why I love it here. Go figure."

Kelly remembered seeing one attractive Hispanic woman on Shannon's softball team. She hoped she'd get a chance to meet this woman again and hear her impression of the town.

Shannon continued, "So what about you? You mentioned you were just in Ashton for the summer, right?"

"Yeah, I'm on summer break. I'll be starting my senior year at Bridges University in the fall."

"You're going to be a senior? Do you mind if I ask how old you are?"

"Not at all. Twenty-one." Kelly took a sip of her iced coffee.

"Ah, so young and innocent," Shannon replied. "I'm twenty-two, by the way. So what's the rest of your story?"

"I'm too young to have a story," Kelly returned with a smile. There was no reason to give too much information at this point.

"Come on, give me a few details. Otherwise I'll think you have a secret identity."

"Sometimes I wish I did." Kelly smiled. "Well, as far as current details go, I subleased my place in the city this summer so I could vacation in sunny Ashton. I'm working full-time and staying at my brother's so I can afford next year's tuition."

"What do you do for work?"

"I teach at a karate school." Kelly looked away from Shannon. She didn't want to talk about karate tonight. Two customers were waiting for their drinks at the front counter and chatting about the Giants game. The team had gained three runs for a win in the last inning. Alex would be happy with the score.

"Really? See, you do have a secret identity. How'd you get started teaching?"

"Money," Kelly replied honestly. "Wish I could say it was because I was good at it. But I love the job most of the time."

Shannon picked up a piece of biscotti. After dipping the cookie into her mocha, she bit the corner. "This is good. You should try it." She extended the plate to Kelly and then continued, "Don't be offended, but you don't look very tough. I wouldn't guess that you're a karate kid."

"Yeah, the element of surprise always helps." Kelly smiled as she took the other piece of biscotti.

Shannon laughed. "Do you fight in competitions?"

"Sometimes. I like to fight, but I lose all the time," Kelly answered as she tasted the cookie. "There's nothing like the feeling of landing a perfect kick on some guy's helmet. And it's empowering when you realize you can actually defend yourself with your bare hands. I mean, I'm no match for some crazy man with a gun and I'd probably freeze up in a real fight . . . But the adrenaline rush of sparring is addictive."

Shannon didn't respond after this comment. She took another bite of the biscotti and glanced away from Kelly.

Kelly wasn't ready to admit that she lived to fight, even to someone who was in the military. She decided to change the subject. "So, why did you join the army?"

"I ask myself that a lot," Shannon said. "You know, they promise you a lot of benefits—job training, travel opportunities, money for college . . . At the time, I didn't have any real goals in life and I wasn't ready to go into debt for college. I wanted some direction."

"And I bet the army is great at giving recruits direction." Kelly smiled. She wondered if Shannon was out when she first joined the military. She pictured the media clips of gays who'd been abused or kicked out of the army and couldn't understand why anyone would willingly join.

"Direction? You have no idea. They tell you exactly where and when to go to the bathroom, to eat, to sleep, to think . . . I wanted to quit after the first week, but I stuck it out. They make you feel like crap and I think they really want you to quit. The accomplishment at the end makes the rest of it worthwhile. Now it's only one weekend a month."

Kelly thought about the Iraqi war in the news headlines from the morning paper. She'd started reading the paper every morning now that she lived with Alex. He left the paper on the kitchen counter with his half-full cup of cold coffee every morning after he left for work. "I thought they were sending more reservists to Iraq. Couldn't you be called up for that?" Kelly asked.

Shannon nodded. "A lot of my friends in the reserves have been called into active duty. They're sending new troops to Iraq every day." She took a sip of her mocha.

"You don't sound worried." Kelly shook her head. She didn't understand Shannon's nonchalant attitude. The thought of being sent to fight in a war made her nauseous. "What if they send you?"

Shannon shrugged. "I knew that it was a possibility when I signed on, but we've been told that our unit is scheduled to stay in California." The tough army girl attitude was in full swing. "They have control of your life once you sign up. And if they want to, they can destroy your future if you don't play by the rules."

"Like rules for gays in the military?" Kelly asked. She wasn't sure if this was a subject Shannon would want to discuss but decided to ask anyway.

"There are no gays in the military," Shannon corrected in an official tone. She nodded when Kelly arched her eyebrows. "Yeah, I know, it's bullshit. The military has the same mentality as a bunch of boys in a treehouse—they've posted a sign about who can join their club and made rules for everything from how to walk to how to think. But so many gays are in the military that it's a running joke now—they say it's easier to find a dyke in uniform than at the local gay bar." Shannon laughed.

"Doesn't sound too bad." Kelly grinned. "So is that the real reason that you joined?"

"No, I wasn't looking for a date. But I did find a few." She smiled. "I don't have any regrets. Let's just say I made a lot of friends during my training."

Shannon seemed to gloss over the restrictions on gays and made it sound like no one was really discriminated against because of the *Don't ask, Don't tell* policy. Kelly still had more questions she wanted to ask about the military, but Shannon switched from the military topic to softball.

Shannon relayed that Beth, the team captain, was hoping Kelly would make it to their next practice. She gave a description of the players on their softball team and said that her friend Gina was their star pitcher. When Shannon mentioned they needed a shortstop

Kelly ignored the hint and simply nodded. She knew she had to tell Shannon that she wasn't interested in joining their league but wasn't ready to admit she'd lied.

As Shannon continued on about softball, Kelly's attention drifted to the scene at the front of the café. The waitress who had provided their biscotti was serving an older man with a ring on his left hand. Kelly guessed the waitress was about her age. She had a low voice, long brown hair and an hourglass figure. As the waitress leaned over the counter to hand him a coffee cup, the married man stared at the young woman's chest. The waitress's low-cut blouse accentuated her full breasts and she didn't seem to mind the man's stare. She flirted with him, in spite of his obvious ring, and the man nearly spilled his coffee while stirring in the milk and sugar. Kelly wondered how much of a tip he'd leave. He was the last customer in the café, aside from Shannon and Kelly. The other café employee, a scrawny teenage boy, had begun noisily stacking chairs and cleaning the empty tables.

Shannon shot an accusatory look at the boy's backside when one of the chairs banged against their table. "I think the staff may want us to leave," she said.

Kelly nodded. She didn't mind the interruption from the softball stories but wasn't quite ready to end the evening with Shannon. As they stood to leave, the married man ended his conversation with the waitress. They followed him out of the café. He also seemed reluctant to be leaving.

The air was cool outside and stars dotted the sky. Music drifted into the parking lot through the open doors of the bar next door. They walked toward Kelly's car silently. Shannon turned to face Kelly and stretched out her hand. The handshake felt awkward, but in the middle of a parking lot in downtown Ashton, there were few options for intimacy. And it was only their first date.

"There's something I have to tell you," Kelly started. She paused, procrastinating. Shannon looked at her expectantly. "I can't play softball and I don't really want to join the league."

Shannon shook her head. "Why didn't you tell me earlier?"

"Softball was the only excuse I could think of for a reason to talk to you at the park," she admitted.

"So now that I know you lie, I better tell you I never date liars. I guess this is good-bye." Shannon waved and turned to walk away.

"Can I call you again anyway?" Kelly asked.

Shannon laughed. "I hope you will. Assuming that's your last lie." She paused and stared at Kelly. "There's one other thing that I better ask. You're not dating anyone else, are you? Cause I don't date players either."

"No, I'm single." Kelly reached out to grab Shannon's hand. "Can I ask you something too?"

Shannon nodded.

"I've been trying to pay attention to our conversation all night, but I keep getting distracted. You're really cute." She stepped forward, closing the distance between them. "Would you mind if we drop the handshake and kiss instead?"

Glancing back at the café, Shannon shifted uneasily on her feet. Kelly's hands slipped down to hold Shannon's hips. When Shannon looked back at her, Kelly leaned closer and kissed her. Shannon pulled back and blushed.

"I'm sorry," Kelly said quickly. They stared at each other awkwardly. She hadn't expected that Shannon would be so shy.

"Don't apologize. You just caught me by surprise." Shannon laughed with obvious uneasiness.

Kelly touched Shannon's arm. "I'll give you more warning next time. I mean, if you want to go out again and we get another chance to kiss."

"I'll think about it," Shannon replied. She turned toward a red Jeep parked a few spaces away from Kelly's Volkswagen.

Kelly watched Shannon climb into the front seat of the Jeep, half expecting her to simply drive away without looking back. She wasn't sure why Shannon had responded so strongly to the kiss and hoped she wasn't offended.

After a moment Shannon said, "Okay. What's your phone number?"

Chapter 5

049151

Kelly had Sundays off at the karate dojo. She spent the morning scouring the classified ads for a second job. The only job that would fit with her teaching schedule was a part-time position at a bakery. She circled the ad and called the number. They needed help every morning starting at four a.m. and the pay was minimum wage. She thanked the baker who had answered her questions, hung up the phone and then crossed off the ad. Cinnamon rolls might smell appetizing before dawn but there was no way she could make it out of bed that early. Kelly headed into town to check the other local businesses. There was an opening at the hardware store for a cashier position that she didn't want. She took an application anyway and headed home.

The front door was locked and Kelly walked around to the back-

48

yard. She spotted Alex leaning against the handle of his shovel in the middle of the garden. He lit a cigarette and stared at the rows of dirt mounds. Pushing open the back gate, she called out to Alex, "Hey, I'm not interrupting anything, am I?"

Alex looked over at her and smiled. He took another drag on his cigarette. "I'm in the middle of a stress-reduction program."

"Let me know when it starts working and I'll order your casket." She swiped the cigarette out of his hand and he looked at her with surprise. "When did you start smoking anyway?"

"When I kicked Laura out. So do they teach you how to steal cigarettes in karate? You're pretty quick." He grabbed the lit cigarette back and jabbed it in his mouth.

"We practice with knives instead of cigarettes."

"That's comforting," he said sarcastically. Pointing to a row of newly planted tomato plants, Alex smiled and asked, "What do you think about my garden? I'm picking out recipes for homemade salsa, tomato and mozzarella salad, pasta with roasted tomatoes and garlic, grilled shish kabobs . . . I can't wait until these tomatoes start ripening. I have a whole menu lined up. This garden was Laura's best idea. Of course, she didn't do anything to help. You know, her acrylic nails wouldn't look good with mud caked underneath. Finished planting the rosemary, thyme and chives against the fence. Snap peas and corn are set in the big plot over on the right. Hungry?"

Kelly held up a paper bag from the Mexican fast-food restaurant and nodded. "Yeah, but until I can see something green sprouting around here, we may have to settle for cheap tacos."

"Sounds perfect. Let me wash up." Alex pushed the blade of the shovel deep into the soil.

"You know, I wouldn't mention your little herb garden to the guys at the construction site. You'll lose that tough-guy image." Kelly sat down on the newly remodeled back porch.

Alex ignored the comment and turned on the garden hose to wash off the dirt. After drying his hands on his jeans, he joined Kelly on the porch. "How do you like the bench?"

She brushed her hand across the wood surface. He must have spent hours sanding the redwood. It was as smooth as glass. She shifted her weight on the bench, testing the joints. "Well, there's no splinters and the legs don't wobble. It's an improvement over that other bench you made for Dad. Maybe this one will last through the summer."

"The last bench I made in tenth grade wood shop. Give me a break."

She smiled and handed him the bag of tacos. "It looks good."

"Thanks for dinner." He fished through the bag, searching for the hot sauce and his taco. "I was supposed to meet Laura tonight, but I called to cancel our plans."

Kelly remembered that the front door had been locked when she came home. Alex never locked his door when he was home. Maybe he was trying to keep Laura out of the house, but she probably still had a key. "Why did you have plans with her?"

"She wants us to talk about getting back together." Alex ripped open the packet of hot sauce and tasted the sauce before squeezing it on his taco.

"You're joking, right? Please tell me you're not going to get back into a relationship with her. That engagement was almost as healthy as your smoking habit." Kelly took the bag from Alex and grabbed her taco. She set a napkin on his knee.

"I know . . ." He stared at the mounds of dirt in his new garden as if he could see the green that would cover the area. Everything grew fast under the warm California sun. "I told her I didn't feel like talking tonight. She may drop by the house later though. She never really listens to me and I don't think she cared when I told her that I was tired. She kept saying that she had left a few things in the garage and wanted to get them tonight." As he took a bite of the taco, hot sauce dripped out of the shell and splattered on the deck tiles.

"She probably left the things in the garage on purpose. It's an excuse to get back into your life," Kelly said.

"That would be something Laura would definitely plan. I know

it's crazy to even talk about dating again, but I did love her, once."
Alex stared at the spots of red sauce on the blue deck tiles. The useless napkin was still balanced on his knee.

"Well, whatever makes you happy, right? You're the one who's always telling me to not listen to what anyone else says. If you both want to get back together, maybe you can make it work this time. Who knows?"

"I don't want to try to make it work. The fights aren't worth it. Maybe I need a rebound girl to get Laura off my mind."

"That's the first thing you've said tonight that I believe." Kelly smiled. "Hey, if you're serious, there was a cute girl working at the café where I met Shannon."

"Shannon? Oh yeah, your softball player. How'd it go?"

"Not bad. Until I tried to kiss her—she blushed and acted like I was pushing too fast. It was just a kiss. I don't know what went wrong."

"Maybe it was a bad kiss. Try less tongue next time," Alex teased.

"Shut up. I've never had any problems kissing before," she said defensively.

"Maybe she isn't as butch as she acted on the softball field. You don't know her that well."

"Hell, you never know about women. Some act butch in public, but they want to cuddle all the time and bake cookies. Some femmes hide a whip under their bed. I've given up on the labels."

Alex laughed at her description. "So where do you fall? I've never seen you bake cookies or carry a whip."

Kelly shook her head. "I hate labels." She finally bit into her taco, carefully preventing any hot sauce from dripping on the new deck. "But, you'd think that someone who plays softball, works at a sports store and is in the army wouldn't act shy. She said she wasn't ready for a kiss. Who knows, maybe I was reading her wrong. I have this weird feeling that she doesn't always tell the whole story."

"She's in the army? Maybe she's worried about starting a relationship right now. They are sending more troops to Iraq every day."

"Her unit is supposed to stay in California. She's in the reserves and stationed at the San Francisco base."

"Well, did you set a second date?"

Kelly shook her head. "Not exactly. She asked for my phone number. I don't know. Anyway, let's change the subject. Can I tell you about the girl who works at the café?"

Alex finished his taco and crumpled the wrapper. "Why not? I don't want to think about Laura tonight and I'm done planting my garden. I have some time on my hands for someone new. How old is she?"

"I'm guessing in her early twenties. She has long brown hair and the hippie-kid look. You know the type—earthy colors, handmade bracelets and wrinkled hemp clothes. She looked a little rough around the edges. I'd bet she'd be a complete change of pace from Laura."

Laura worked at a bank. She insisted on a weekly manicure and had her hair colored regularly. She sharply criticized any woman who was not well groomed or stylishly clothed. Laura only went surfing with Alex so that she could get a tan while floating around on her board.

Alex nodded. "She probably has a boyfriend. Or a girlfriend."

"Well, I don't know if she's single, but I'm pretty sure she's into men. She was flirting with some guy at the café last night. He had a ring on his finger though and was too old for her." Kelly finished her taco and leaned back on the bench. The sun was setting and the horizon was streaked with shades of purple. She wanted to leave before Laura arrived. Their mutual dislike always made meetings tense. "So are we going out for drinks or are you chickening out?"

Alex stretched his arms and yawned. "Let's hang out and watch a movie instead."

"Come on, Alex, you dragged me to a softball game to meet a girl. If we go, I'll buy dessert. If you aren't interested, we can turn around and come home without even saying hello to her." Kelly waited for his response.

He shook his head and closed his eyes. "There's probably some-thing good on TV tonight."

"There's never anything that good on TV. They bake great cook-ies at this café. Since when do you turn down free dessert?"

"I'm too old to go out cruising for dates."

"Since when? Okay, fine. Stay here and wait for Laura to come over and make you miserable." After a moment of silence, she added, "I know you like the guilt trips."

He smiled. "All right, you've convinced me. I really don't want to see her tonight. She still has a key and can pick up the stuff without my help. And I don't need an hour-long psychoanalysis of our failed relationship."

They arrived at the café and claimed a table near the front. In case they needed a reason to linger with their drinks, Kelly had grabbed a few paperbacks from Alex's bookshelf. The café was crowded with customers tonight. At the back of the room, a group of teenagers were boisterously recapping their theater performance that evening. Bits of *West Side Story* song lyrics punctuated their conversation.

To keep up with the increased business, the busboy had been reassigned from cleaning tables to managing the coffee machines. The same waitress was serving at the front counter. Tonight her hair was pulled back in a braid and rings flashed on every finger. Kelly waited at the cash register while Alex scanned the dessert display.

"Uh-oh. Did the last date not work out?" the waitress whispered. "You brought a new one already? This one's cute, by the way." She added the last sentence in a louder voice and winked as Alex looked up at her.

Kelly laughed. "No, I brought my brother this time. How'd you know I was here on a date last night?"

"No one looks that uncomfortable unless they're here on a first date. How'd it go?"

"You're right. First date . . . I think it went okay." She still couldn't decide if it had been a good first date. The kiss was awkward and Shannon never really seemed that comfortable.

"Personally, I think your date needed to loosen up a little." She looked over at the group of teenagers. Their noise level was building. Three singers were belting out "Officer Krupke," each in a different key. The coffee machines were running at full steam and the busboy was racing to clean a stack of mugs. He tossed the mugs in a sink full of rinse water and then spun back to his position by the espresso machine. "But, I guess that's not for me to say. She's in the military, right?"

Kelly nodded. She wondered how much of their conversation had been overheard. Between the busboy and the waitress, she probably had few secrets about her last date.

"Well, good luck. I've dated a few military guys and it's never lasted longer than a few weeks. They're either shipped out or I wish they were. Anyway, what can I get you tonight?"

"Iced coffee. Hey, Alex, what's for dessert?"

Alex pointed at the plate of biscotti and approached the cash register.

"Good choice, Alex," the waitress remarked. She extended her hand. "I'm Starr. I was just giving your sister some dating advice."

Kelly sat down at the table with her coffee. Alex was still at the front counter flirting with Starr. It was a relief to be out of the hot seat for one night. She had no impressions to make tonight. As she pretended to read one of the paperbacks, she focused on the front counter. Starr was an easy flirt and obviously attracted to Alex. Kelly knew Alex well enough to guess that he was thoroughly enjoying their conversation.

After picking up the biscotti and his cappuccino, Alex returned to the table. His face was beaming. "Okay, I think we're even. Thanks for the introduction."

The high school group had finished their drinks and left en masse. The noise level immediately dropped as the last teenager slammed the front door.

Alex breathed a sigh of relief. "Were we ever that obnoxious?"

"Probably." It was strange to think that she was only a few years older than the high school students. A few years at Bridges had changed her perspective on a lot of things. Or maybe it was living in San Francisco. The last time she had a crush on a guy was in her 11th grade history class. Fortunately, only a few notebook sketches of his handsome profile ever came out of that crush.

Starr served the last customers in line and then looked over at Alex. She slipped around the counter and approached their table. Starr pointed at Alex's plate. Only a few crumbs remained. "Can I bring you another?"

He smiled. "No. But, you were right—you make awesome biscotti. It could be addicting."

Kelly cringed. Listening to Alex flirt was almost as painful as if she were saying the same cheesy lines. She focused on her book and tried to ignore the rest of their conversation.

Chapter 6

049201

According to the clock at the karate dojo, it was 7:10 p.m. Kelly had been given the task of setting the clock and had decided to set it back five minutes from the actual time. If the clock was slow, she reasoned, she could show up for work five minutes late and Sam would think she was on time. Unfortunately, that also meant she had to stay five minutes later. This only bothered her on Friday nights. At the end of a full week, the last thing she wanted to do was spend five more minutes in the dojo. And she had a date with Shannon tonight. Over a week had passed since their first date and now she couldn't wait to see her. "I don't think my next student is coming."

"Whose lesson was at seven?" Sam asked from his seat in front of the office computer.

"Maria was supposed to be here. She's not usually late." There was no sparring class tonight and Kelly hoped that she could leave early.

"You act like you have something better to be doing tonight. Hot date?" Sam pushed his chair away from the desk and looked through the office doorway into the studio.

Kelly glanced again at the clock and shook her head. "Well, maybe," she admitted.

"Really? Now this is the first time I think I have heard you mention anything outside of schoolwork."

"I'm not mentioning anything," she replied defensively. As Kelly's boss, Sam was easy-going and personable. He gave Kelly extra credit for her patience with the toddlers in the beginner class who drove most instructors crazy and appreciated that she worked hard to earn her minimum wage paycheck. As her Sensei, he was harsh and forceful. He expected things that Kelly often felt she could not achieve. And his influence was not restricted to the dojo. Sam seemed to expect success in every aspect of her life and routinely grilled her about school and career goals. Kelly wouldn't talk about other aspects of her life because she was afraid of disappointing him. Mainly, she wouldn't admit she was queer. Sam's opinion of her wasn't the only thing that mattered. As an instructor, she wanted her private life to be separated from the dojo. Even in the suburbs of San Francisco, some students or parents might be uncomfortable with a lesbian instructor.

Glancing at the clock again, Kelly watched the second hand tick slowly over the black marks. "She isn't coming."

"So, are you going to tell me about him?"

She looked at Sam quizzically. "Him? What?"

"Your date."

"Oh." Kelly stalled for a moment. The switched pronouns caught her off-guard. "Yeah, my date. I don't really want to talk about it."

"Big secret, huh."

"No. I just don't want to talk about it."

"Kelly, do you know how boring my social life is? I met my wife in ninth grade. We started dating. She was a year older than me. We got married two years after I graduated from high school. I have a baby girl and my wife is pregnant again. I am thirty-one years old. Do you think I am going to have any more hot dates?"

"Hey, some people would argue that there's nothing wrong with a kid's burger meal and a bargain matinee."

"Okay, don't hit too close to home," Sam replied with a grin. His dark eyes were happily taunting Kelly. "So, what about your hot date? You never talk about any dates."

"I don't want to talk about it, sir." Kelly added the last word to make Sam understand that despite his casual approach, he was her Sensei and boss. This was too personal.

"Fine. I understand if you don't want to tell me." Sam entered the front waiting room. Avoiding Kelly's gaze, he filled a blue paper Dixie cup at the water cooler. "You know, I have a brother who is gay." The cup was emptied in one swallow and he crushed the paper before tossing it in the trash. "My parents disowned him from the family as soon as he came out to them. He moved to New York and settled in with this guy who runs a theater company. They have lived together for the past six years. My brother sends me a Christmas card every year. I send him pictures of my daughter. He would make a great uncle . . . We used to be very close. Unfortunately, my wife sides with my parents on the gay issue. I wish I could include him in our family again."

Kelly felt her cheeks burn. "How'd you know?"

He shrugged. "You've been my student for years. How could I not know? I guessed it the first day you asked to start training here."

"I didn't even know I was a lesbian at thirteen."

"You walked into the waiting room and sat down to watch a room full of men beating each other up in the adult sparring class. Do you remember that?"

Kelly nodded.

"I thought you were one of the guys' daughter. But after class ended no one claimed you. The men all left and you came up to me and asked if I would teach a girl to fight like the rest of the students in that class."

"Yeah, and as I remember, you told me no."

Sam paused and looked out the door. "Yep. And you didn't walk away. I knew by the sound of your voice that you weren't interested in fending off boyfriends. You wanted to take classes because you wanted to learn how to fight."

"That doesn't mean I was going to grow up to be a lesbian," Kelly countered. She'd known plenty of other tomboys who'd eventually dated men.

"Well, maybe it was intuition. Anyway, I wasn't wrong, was I?" Sam asked confidently.

"No. But you could have told me that you knew sooner. Like when I started high school." Kelly hadn't realized she was a lesbian until her first year of college. She couldn't believe that Sam had known all along. "So, why did you tell me you wouldn't teach me when I asked that first night?" Although she didn't know it then, plenty of other women were enrolled in the martial arts school. But most women avoided the adult sparring class.

"I wanted to see how stubborn you'd be. You came back every night that week to ask if I would reconsider. I knew you weren't the typical teenage girl. You asked me to train you to fight like the other students in that class—all men. I wouldn't do that. Women are different, even here. Now, you don't fight like the rest of the guys. You're half the size of some of the guys in the adult class and they laugh at some of your weak punches. But you can drop them to the ground in a good match." Sam glanced at the clock. "I guess Maria isn't coming for her lesson. You might as well leave early."

Kelly nodded.

"But you owe me some details about the hot date," Sam finished with a grin.

She headed to the back room to change out of her karate uniform. After untying her belt, she hung it around her neck and stared in the mirror. The air in her lungs felt lighter as she exhaled. The pressure of the secret had finally been lifted. She had wanted to tell Sam for a long time. And all this time he had already known. She wondered why he hadn't mentioned it sooner. High school would have been so much less painful if she had realized she was queer. Kelly sighed. She didn't have time to bemoan the past.

That morning, Kelly had found a message on her answering machine. In one quick sentence Shannon left her address and invited Kelly to stop by that evening. Kelly was not the only one who had a date tonight—Alex was heading back to the café to meet with Starr for another piece of biscotti. Kelly was happy to see his excitement.

After a few circles through the tract home neighborhood, she found Shannon's place. Climbing out of the car, Kelly gazed up at the night sky. The moon had not yet risen and only tiny stars cluttered the blackness. She walked up the driveway and paused to smile at the orderly rows of flowers. A knock on the door brought a round of barking from inside. Shannon opened the door, one hand wrapped through the collar of a Dalmatian whose front paws were waving in the air as he dangled in her grip, caught in mid-lunge. She let go of the door to adjust the phone cupped against her ear.

"Hi. Come in. This is Paco, the crazy beast. I'll just be a minute." She held a finger up to the phone to signal she was waiting for a break in the conversation.

Squeezing past the dog, Kelly entered the house and quickly closed the front door. The Dalmatian slipped free from Shannon's grasp and lunged again at Kelly. This time, Kelly caught the dog and wrestled with his paws in the air. Holding the dog's collar, Kelly sat down on the only couch in the front room and rubbed the Dalmatian's head. When the initial excitement of meeting someone new had passed, Paco sat down next to Kelly and patiently stared up at Shannon.

After a moment, Shannon's voice interrupted the caller. "Let me ask what she wants to do." She dropped the phone from her ear and sank down on the couch next to Kelly. "Do you want to go to the bar for a drink with some friends of mine?"

"Honestly?"

"No, a lie would be fine." The response surprised Kelly. Before she could answer Shannon started to laugh and casually rested a hand on Kelly's thigh. Kelly felt a rush of excitement at Shannon's touch. She looked away quickly as she felt her skin warm with a blush. Shannon was distracted by Paco's attempt to jump into her lap and didn't notice. After pushing the dog down, she returned to the phone conversation. Kelly inspected the ID tags on the dog's collar. The address on the tag didn't match Shannon's house and the phone number was different. Shannon continued the phone conversation. "No, we won't be able to make it tonight. Have a drink for me, okay, Beth? And tell Tasha I said hello." She hung up the phone and laid back against the couch cushions.

Although Kelly wanted to spend time alone with Shannon, she did not want to seem antisocial. "You know, I think it would be great to go to the bar with your friends. I don't want to keep you from spending time with them."

"I think you want to keep me here," Shannon teased.

"No, not at all." Kelly shook her head. "Wait, I mean, I do want to keep you here, but . . . I think we should go to the bar and meet your friends."

"Why?"

"Because I want to meet your friends." Paco pushed his nose at Kelly's hand. She had stopped rubbing the dog's head for a moment. She resumed petting Paco. It was a good distraction from Shannon's steady gaze.

"You're a bad liar."

Kelly nodded. "I know."

"Fine. At least you agree with me. So, how are you?" Shannon began, as if just starting the evening's conversation.

"Fine. How are you?"

"I had a busy day at work. Too many people are trying to get new shoes for summer sports. I'm ready to relax and not think about anything to do with other people's feet." The Dalmatian was again attempting to jump up on the couch and she pushed his paws off the cushions. "Paco has no manners."

"He's just friendly and a little hyper. If he was a kid, someone would give him behavior drugs." Kelly patted the dog's head and tried to avoid the slobbery tongue that lolled out of his mouth. He paced between Shannon and Kelly with his tail wagging furiously.

"You're defending him, but he doesn't deserve it. Paco is crazy—you can't teach him anything . . ."

The dog suddenly spun in a circle chasing the flash of white fur from his waving tail. Shannon caught his collar as the dog was in mid spin. He looked up with a bewildered expression. She pulled the dog out of the front room and down the hallway. Kelly followed, surveying each room that they passed. With one quick push, Shannon sent Paco out the back door.

"Paco is my parents' dog. They're having some work done on their house and I'm stuck with the beast for a few weeks." Shannon glanced at the door leading to the backyard. Paco was whining to be let inside. "He's sweet, but if you turn your back he'll destroy everything in sight."

"How long have your parents lived in Santa Barbara? Is that where you grew up?" Kelly asked. They moved back toward the family room and passed three closed doors. She wondered which one led to Shannon's bedroom.

Shannon nodded, then stopped in the middle of the hallway and turned to face Kelly. "Wait, how'd you know my parents live in Santa Barbara?"

"Paco's ID tags."

"Oh. Yeah, I lived there for almost twenty years. My parents have the same house that they bought when they got married. Gina's family lives next door to my parents. I never thought I'd forgive her for moving away. She started college in Oakland but dropped out after two years. My other friend, Vicky, left Santa Barbara when she signed up with the army. She got stationed in San Francisco and moved in here. Vicky was so excited when I told her I was being stationed at the San Francisco base. She had an extra room here and the rent was cheap so I moved in. Then Vicky ditched me."

"What?"

Shannon smiled. "She's on a six-month mission in Iraq."

"Wow . . . Is she doing okay?"

"Yeah, but she's ready to come home. She's been there for two months now. I'm happy our unit is staying in California. Six months in the desert is a long time to spend with army boys for company."

"A lot of women wouldn't mind that company," Kelly taunted.

"Lucky for you, I'm not one of those women." She shook her head and then lightly pushed her fingertip against Kelly's chest. "Just to set the record, I am not planning on letting you off on anything easy. I didn't really want to go to the bar tonight, but I don't like the fact that you tried to lie to me. *Twice.* So, tell me the truth—why did you want to stay here tonight?"

"The truth?" Kelly smiled, hesitating. She realized that Shannon would not accept another lie but was reluctant to be honest. "I wanted to have you alone, without any distractions. We don't really know each other yet."

"Hmm." Her eyebrows arched, playfully tempting Kelly. Shannon took one step closer and grabbed Kelly's hands. "And what were you planning to do once you got me alone?"

What happened to the demure woman who'd blushed after a goodnight kiss last week? Why is she so forward now? Kelly wondered. Her gaze dropped from their clasped hands to the leather belt lacing through the loops of Shannon's jeans. Kelly brushed her cheek softly against Shannon's hand. Shannon let go of her hands and stepped back. Instinctively Kelly stepped forward again. She grasped Shannon's hips and kissed the smooth space of exposed skin on her neck, just above the shirt collar, then kissed her lips before slowly pulling back. Tracing the line of buttons down Shannon's shirt, Kelly imagined unclasping each one, until she reached the leather belt.

"Mmm. Not bad." Shannon smiled. "And it's good to know that you aren't too shy to answer," she added, clearly unable to hide the excitement that Kelly's touch had brought on.

"No, I'm not usually shy. But I don't want to make you blush yet."

"All right, enough teasing. Let's go—" Shannon paused as Kelly leaned forward to kiss her again. She blushed, despite the warning, and turned away from Kelly. "Let's go rent a movie."

"A movie?"

"Yeah, a movie. We need a distraction," Shannon replied, opening her bedroom door. "I just have to find my keys."

A queen-sized mattress took up most of the room, leaving only a narrow pathway between a faded brown couch, an old wooden dresser and a shiny black entertainment unit. On the shelf above the stereo, a framed photograph leaned against a potted plant. In the picture, snow was flying off of a board several feet above the ground. Secured to the board, a figure in a blue ski jacket and puffy black pants grinned happily. Kelly guessed the figure was Shannon but couldn't make out her face past the goggles in the picture. With her keys and wallet in hand, Shannon motioned for Kelly to follow.

They headed toward the garage. Shannon's loose-fitting Levi's moved easily on her body. "Hmm, cute butt," Kelly said softly.

"What?" Shannon asked.

"Umm . . ." Kelly struggled for a quick response. "I can drive."

"No, I love my Jeep."

"Why do we need a movie to distract us?" Kelly considered what Shannon's reaction might be if she grabbed the leather belt on Shannon's jeans to pull her close. She wanted to feel their bodies touch again.

"We might need something to keep us from getting too entertained with each other. And you don't want to meet my friends, so we need another distraction."

"It's not that I don't want to meet your friends," Kelly repeated, returning the sarcastic tone, and then continued, "There are just other things I'd like to know about you." Maybe Shannon wasn't ready for more intimacy, Kelly thought.

Shannon held the handle of the garage door as she looked over her shoulder at Kelly. "Let's rent a movie and stay in for the night. You can meet my friends later."

"Maybe we can ask your friends to join us for breakfast when we wake up tomorrow morning." The sound of the garage door opening muffled Kelly's words.

"Wait, did I really just hear that?"

Kelly shook her head. She wasn't ready to act as aggressively as her body desired. She glanced back at Shannon's bedroom door. "I'm kidding, relax."

"Oh," Shannon responded, deliberately letting her voice drop. "Damn."

They spent an hour wandering through the aisles of movies, discussing the actors and the plots, or lack thereof, and flirting. The cashier announced that he wanted to close the store and they decided to rent the movie that Shannon had just picked off the shelf. By the time they left the store, the parking lot was nearly empty. A black sedan and a blue Honda were parked under the row of alder trees near Shannon's Jeep. Kelly squinted at the black sedan's front window. The rear windows were tinted. She could barely discern the features of an older man waiting in the driver's seat. She guessed he was waiting for someone inside the rental store. None of the other shops in the strip mall were still open. She couldn't remember seeing anyone else in the store when they left, but they had been distracted.

Shannon handed her the movie as she unlocked the passenger side door. Kelly couldn't remember the title they had finally selected and glanced at the cover. "I may be more interested in watching you than this movie."

"Wow, I didn't count on your being so forward."

Kelly shrugged and smiled at her. Shannon pushed Kelly playfully toward the Jeep. Their bodies pressed close as Shannon pinned Kelly against the door. "You know, I've never dated someone who could beat me up," she teased.

"Don't worry. I won't beat you up."

"But you could. You have a black belt," Shannon stated evenly.

"That doesn't mean I like beating people up."

"I know, but if we get caught in a dark alley sometime, it'll be nice to have you around."

"Gee, thanks." Kelly smiled. "As fair warning, the color of the belt doesn't mean much. We should probably avoid dark alleys. I'm really not very good at fighting, despite the black thing that holds up my karate pants."

"Hmm, I doubt that. And I'm still going to make sure I don't do anything to piss you off."

"Don't worry—I won't touch you."

"What if I want you to touch me?" Shannon let go of Kelly's shoulders. She turned quickly and headed to the other side of the Jeep.

As she opened her door, Kelly grabbed her from behind. Shannon shivered at her touch. "You know, it's not fair to walk away after saying something like that," Kelly said.

Shannon turned to face her. Their bodies brushed against each other and Shannon's jeans rubbed between Kelly's legs. Kelly wanted to kiss her but waited for Shannon to make the first move. Finally their lips pressed together. Shannon's tongue lightly flicked between her lips. They kissed for a moment longer and Kelly closed her eyes, enjoying the sensation of lost equilibrium.

Finally, she leaned back and caught Shannon's wrists in her hands. "I think we have the kissing thing down now."

"Was that okay then?" Shannon asked.

Kelly nodded. "Better. But I may go crazy if we never get past the one-good-night-kiss phase."

Shannon grinned mischievously. "Who said good night?"

As they climbed into the Jeep, Kelly glanced from the dark sky littered with a few stars and gray clouds to Shannon. "Can we skip the movie?"

"Not yet," Shannon answered.

Chapter 7

049251

Kelly was late to work the next morning. She had left Shannon's house at four a.m. and slept through her alarm three hours later. Alex finally banged on the wall between their bedrooms after the alarm had beeped for a half an hour. He was pissed.

Technically, the dojo opened at eight. Fortunately, no classes were scheduled until nine on Saturdays and Sam left the place in her hands. She unlocked the door five minutes before the crowd of toddlers arrived for the first class. Three and a half hours of sleep was not enough to handle teaching a group of 20 energetic four- and five-year-olds. Instead of working on karate forms, the toddlers ran through endurance courses that morning. After the first kids kicked the bags and shouted in high-pitched voices as they'd been taught to do, Kelly announced that they were going to learn the secret art of

Samurai silence. The drill lasted about ten minutes before the toddlers realized it was a ploy to keep them quiet.

Kelly closed the dojo at three p.m. and went home to sleep away the rest of the afternoon. She awoke two hours later to Elvis's persistent cries for dinner. The cat was overweight but sounded half starved when he cried for more kibble. Kelly filled Elvis's bowl and headed for the shower just as the phone rang. She picked up on the second ring.

"Hey, Kelly." Alex's voice echoed on the line. His cell phone crackled with static. "Guess where I'm driving to right now?"

"Well, it's Saturday night. Are you going to miss the Giants game for more biscotti?"

"No, she likes baseball. I'm picking her up from work and we're going to the ballpark. But she may bring some biscotti." Alex laughed.

"So your last date went well?"

"Kelly, Starr is great. We spent the evening discussing philosophers and politics. Pretty good for a waitress and a working guy like me, huh?" He laughed. "She's smarter than she acts. She's a history major at Cal State. And she surfs."

"Not just to get a tan?" Kelly thought of Laura paddling around on her surfboard in a string bikini.

"No. She grew up in some little town on the coast down south."

"Alex, she sounds perfect. When are you two going surfing?" Alex usually spent his days off driving down Highway 1. He'd rather spend a day chasing waves than do anything else.

"Tomorrow. Want to join us?"

"Tomorrow? Wow, aren't you moving kind of fast?" Kelly teased.

"No, I think I'll skip this time."

"Okay. Leave a message on my cell phone if you change your mind." Alex wasn't going to push her this time. "Are you staying home tonight?"

"No. I'm going to the bar downtown with Shannon's friends," she answered. Shannon was bent on going to meet her friends. Kelly had agreed to go but was regretting the decision. She wasn't interested in meeting Shannon's friends yet. Although she had stayed at Shannon's house late last night, they had only kissed and there was still a palpable distance between them. She wanted more time alone with Shannon.

"You don't sound too excited about that. Don't tell me you're already bored with this girl. Has it even been one week?" Alex insisted that her relationships didn't last because she had a short attention span.

"The softball game you dragged me to was two weeks ago . . . And I'm not bored yet, so I guess that's a good sign." She had dated a few women who never made it to the two-week mark. She always knew it was a bad omen when she was bored after the first week. "Though we've only gone out a few times. Who knows what could happen? I still don't really know her and all I can think about is making out. Why do people always want to introduce you to their friends."

"You have a one-track mind. Once you have sex, you'll be ready to move on to the next challenge," Alex predicted.

"You have so little faith in me," Kelly joked. She knew that Alex's predictions were often true.

"So, go meet her friends—find out what she is really like when she hangs out with them. That may be an important part of her."

"Well, thanks for my free relationship consultation. I don't know about your credentials, but . . ."

Alex laughed. "I just know how you think—everything is a sparring match. You play with the girl, win her over and move on to the next match. How many women have you dated in the past year?"

"Okay, I get the idea. I'll go meet her friends. Have a good time with Starr."

Kelly hung up the phone. She wished Shannon would call to change their plans and stared at the phone hoping it would ring again. Finally she gave up waiting for the ring and headed to Shannon's house.

Alex's comments about her past relationships weighed on her mind. She had dated four women in the past year. From Alex's perspective, given a five-year relationship with Laura, four women a year was excessive. And it wasn't that she liked the short flings. She was looking for something that would last and was tired of losing interest after a few months. Kelly thought of the cool distance she felt with Shannon. There was no doubt that Shannon was attractive, but was Alex right? After she slept with her, would she get bored with the relationship? Maybe she needed to open up more. It was easy to break up with someone if you never let yourself get close.

Shannon had tried to prepare Kelly for the bar meeting by running through the list of twelve names and hinting at the myriad of relationships. Everyone had dated at least one person in the group. Some of them had dated three or more. Kelly had no intention of remembering everyone's name or the incestuous connections on the first night. A few of the friends were from the army. The rest of the group had met through work or college.

After attempting to jump into a few conversations, Kelly lost interest in their chitchat. She didn't understand any of the inside jokes. Every time she opened her mouth to add a comment, it seemed that someone was judging whether or not she would fit in with the group. She abandoned chatting and moved over to the jukebox. From her corner of the room, she watched a few couples dance and scanned the music titles so she could avoid eye contact with anyone from Shannon's group. They were on their third round of shots. Kelly watched Shannon slug down the tequila and slam her glass on the bar seconds after the group called out the toast.

A few minutes later, Beth, the softball captain, and her date, Tasha, approached Kelly. Shannon had mentioned that Tasha was also in the reserves and that they had met at the army base in San Francisco. Kelly couldn't remember where Beth worked, but she knew she wasn't in the military. Tasha and Beth were both in their early twenties and dressed alike in designer T-shirts, jeans and baseball caps pulled low on their heads. Tasha's hair was streaked with red highlights while Beth's was streaked with blonde highlights. Tasha was a few inches taller than Beth, but otherwise the women were nearly identical.

"Are you sure you don't want a drink?" Beth asked, placing her shot glass on the table next to the jukebox. Tasha sat down on a barstool by Beth and smiled at Kelly.

"Yep."

Beth winked at Tasha. "Shannon's got a cheap date. Where'd I go wrong?"

Tasha swatted at Beth. "Don't even try and tell me that."

Beth laughed. "So, Shannon told me that you don't want to play softball. Can I change your mind?"

Kelly shook her head.

"Okay. We need to talk about something else then." Beth grabbed Kelly's arm and leaned close as she whispered, "I know what Shannon would like tonight." Her breath reeked of alcohol. Kelly looked at her credulously, inviting her to continue. "Why haven't you kids slept together yet? It's been a while now since you met her."

"One week." She wanted more contact but Shannon didn't seem ready. She wondered how well Beth really knew Shannon.

"Well, she's waiting for you to make the first move. She thinks you're the type who likes to take it slow. If you want anything to happen, I think you're going to have to just take her on—you know? I know it would make her happy." Beth grinned. Kelly hoped she wouldn't remember any of this conversation. "She'd be pissed if she knew I was talking to you about sex." Beth laughed. "Shannon and I dated for a few months. Did she tell you that?"

"No." Kelly glanced over to the bar. Shannon was laughing at someone's joke.

"Yeah, I'm not surprised. Anyway, she likes you."

"Well, she isn't giving me very good signs. Actually, she's kind of pulled away." Kelly looked over at Tasha. She smiled back. Kelly guessed that she was one of the sober drivers of the group. Tasha was too quiet.

"Because she doesn't think you are interested in sex." Beth smiled knowingly.

Kelly sighed. It was strange to have this conversation with Shannon's ex-girlfriend. She doubted that Beth would have mentioned sex if she'd been sober. "When did you guys break up?"

"Years ago. We met in Santa Barbara. By weird coincidence we both ended up here in Ashton, but we were both dating other people."

Kelly tried to remember when Shannon had moved to Ashton. "Did she just break up with that other person?"

"It's been a while. The last woman she dated was some officer in the army, but I don't think they've talked for months. Just have sex and get it over with. You will both be happier if you can relax."

"Yeah, I agree. But you can't just jump on somebody and—"

"You could," she interrupted, leaning close to Tasha and batting her eyes suggestively.

"Ignore her, Kelly," Tasha advised. "She was trying to get me in her bed on our first date." Turning toward Beth, Tasha continued, "Some people want to get to know the women they date before having sex—that way the sex means something."

"Really? Who would want that?" Beth asked with sarcasm.

"You're hopeless," Tasha replied. "It's a good thing I already love you. Ordinarily, I'd never sleep with someone who had that attitude."

"You know I'm joking."

"Who knows? Maybe you're serious—you did try and get me to spend the night at your place the first time we went out." Tasha pointed a finger at Beth's chest. "Get this, Kelly, I met Beth at this bar four months ago. I had just relocated to the San Francisco base from Los Angeles. Shannon invited me here after our drill one night. So, I was already a little nervous about going to the suburbs and hanging out with some dyke—don't want to blow my image, you know. Beth walks up to me, ten minutes after we're introduced, and offers to buy me a drink if I'll marry her. I thought she was joking so

I said sure—why not? The next thing I know, we are both plastered and she's trying to convince me to spend the night in her bed. Fortunately, Shannon was the only person from the army at the bar that night. No one else saw Beth seduce me." Tasha laughed. She winked at Kelly. "Then I found out that Beth was actually Shannon's ex-girlfriend. As a warning, this group is a little too close, if you know what I mean."

Beth grabbed Tasha's hand. "See, you knew what you were getting into on the first night."

Tasha shook her head. "Anyway, can you believe I actually decided to go on a second date with her?"

Kelly laughed. "Well, you look like you were made for each other. And four months is longer than a lot of lesbian relationships last."

"I told you I was a good decision." Beth smiled and leaned forward to kiss Tasha again.

Tasha turned to avoid Beth's advance. "What are you thinking? People from my unit will see us. We can't kiss here."

Kelly moved away from the jukebox corner as the couple fell into a more intimate conversation. She scanned the room to find Shannon. She was leaning against a pool table on the other side of the room with her back to Kelly. Shannon's arm was ensnared by one of the guys in the group. He was telling some story in a loud drunken voice and had wrapped his audience in the saga. As Kelly watched Shannon interact with her friends she realized that this world was foreign to her. For the past few years, she'd spent all her time studying or working. When she had a free moment to go out with friends, they always went to gay clubs in the city. She'd never considered hanging out at a straight bar in Ashton and felt out of place. She searched for a dark corner where she could disappear.

The clientele in the bar were a strange mix. Straight older men sat hunched over beer bottles and argued about the baseball game playing on the large-screen television. A few straight couples and some single women danced on the small wooden dance floor. Shannon's military friends and buddies from high school crowded around the pool tables. They shouted noisily over the din of dance music and the baseball game.

Kelly caught the gaze of a woman who was sitting at a back table. Shannon had introduced the woman, her best friend, Gina, earlier that evening. Kelly gave a nod of recognition and Gina looked away quickly. Gina hadn't smiled once that night. Kelly sighed, fighting the urge to leave. She could walk back to Alex's place from here. It was only a few miles and she'd be happy to be away from the crowd of strangers. Unfortunately, she had to give Shannon a ride home.

She looked back at Shannon and then over to Gina's corner. Gina was staring at her and this time didn't look away. Her hands clutched a beer bottle and the remnants of the bottle's label were scattered on her table. The sharp angles of her face were set off by brown hair pulled back in a low ponytail and she might be described as striking if she'd smile. Her light brown skin was flawlessly smooth and the dance lights flashed in her dark eyes. Kelly shook her head. Gina was very attractive, but she was Shannon's best friend. She resisted the urge to continue appraising her and turned away.

Tasha and Beth had left the jukebox to join the group at the pool tables. They were recruiting dance partners. Gina watched Tasha and Beth intently. She only shifted her eyes away when the women stepped out on the dance floor. Tasha had coaxed two men from the group by the pool tables out to the dance floor. It was strange to watch the lesbian couple dance with the men. Kelly wasn't accustomed to a bar where it was necessary to maintain a straight appearance. Kelly ordered a bottle of mineral water and approached Gina's back corner.

"Hey, Gina," Kelly started. Gina remained silent, staring blankly at the bottle in her hand. "I don't think we were properly introduced. I'm Kelly."

"Yeah, I know. You're Shannon's date."

"I like to think I have an identity beyond that, but maybe not tonight." She pulled a barstool over to join Gina. From this seat, she could watch Shannon across the room.

"Not tonight, not in this bar. With this group, you're just the girl Shannon brought for the night."

"Yeah, it's a little uncomfortable," Kelly responded. There was a long pause and Kelly tried to think of something to make conversation. "So is *Gina* a nickname, or is that your full name?"

"Are you asking because *Gina* doesn't sound Latina enough?" Gina snapped.

Kelly immediately regretted her question. Stumbling through an apology, she continued, "I just thought there might be a story. Most people have a story that goes along with their name. But I'm sorry if I offended you."

Finally Gina responded, "Gina's short for Angelina. But my father used to call me by my full name when I was in trouble, so I hate that name now."

Kelly waited for Gina to continue the conversation, but Gina acted like that was the end of their interaction. After a few awkward minutes, Kelly considered moving back to her post by the jukebox. Beth and Tasha were still on the dance floor and Shannon was caught up in a drinking game. Kelly didn't know anyone else in the bar and didn't want to be Shannon's token girlfriend for the night. The bar's exit signs glowed green as traffic lights and she stared at them longingly. Gina's sullen face was unsettling. Resolved to stay at the bar, Kelly decided to find out more about her. "So, Gina, what's wrong? You look like you've lost your best friend."

Gina made no response.

"Feel free to chat openly with a stranger who you will probably never see again," Kelly added.

"You mean you aren't going to stick around as Shannon's little buddy?" Gina asked sarcastically.

"You're crushed, I can tell," Kelly replied. "To tell you the truth, I doubt it."

Gina nodded. "Well, I like people who are honest. By the way, nothing's wrong. I don't need to talk about anything. I'm just fine."

"So much for honesty," Kelly said. She knew Gina was upset. Her bitter attitude and the shredded beer bottle label littering the bar were telling signs of a tortured soul.

"I like people who are honest—that doesn't mean that I am. But don't worry your pretty head, I'm just a little drunk . . ."

"Are you always annoying and standoffish?"

"Yes. And the alcohol helps. But I'm glad I'm drunk. I felt like shit four beers ago and now I don't remember why. So, I hear you aren't drinking tonight."

"News travels fast," Kelly said bitterly.

"Oh, you have no idea."

"I don't want to know what else this group is gossiping about me," she responded.

"You would blush. There are more than a few people watching you tonight." Gina took a sip of her beer.

"I don't care." Kelly was embarrassed and didn't really know how to respond. Gina seemed to be flirting with her.

"So, why aren't you drinking? Are you Shannon's sober driver?"

"I don't like alcohol."

"Meaning, you never drink?" Gina's voice was incredulous. "Why not?"

"I've been using the excuse that I'm a strict Mormon." Kelly smiled.

"Are you?"

"No. And I don't think that religion allows lesbians anyway. No caffeine, no booze, no lesbians. I'm sure that's on their list."

Gina smiled. "Why don't you drink, really?"

"It makes me moody. I want to hit things when I'm drunk," Kelly admitted.

"You? I don't believe that. I think you should stick with the Mormon excuse, even if it isn't true. At least people might believe it."

"I don't care what people believe."

"Yeah, I don't care either," Gina agreed. She took another swallow of the beer. They stopped talking, suddenly at ease with each other, and listened to the music. Gina quietly pushed the strips of the beer label into a circle. Without looking up at Kelly she asked, "So are you happy with Shannon?"

"I think so. We don't know each other that well." Kelly paused. Shannon was caught up in the drunken banter of her friends. She wondered if Shannon wanted to get to know her at all. She had thought that Shannon was someone she could really have a relationship with, rather than the usual fling, but she was beginning to doubt that after seeing her at the bar with her friends. She couldn't think of anything they had in common and her only reason to get to know Shannon now would be to sleep with her. This realization made her stomach queasy. Maybe after they had slept together neither would want to continue dating, but Shannon was too sexy for Kelly to ignore. She turned back to Gina. "I don't know."

"I'm only asking because I have to watch out for my friends."

"I think she can take care of herself." Kelly grabbed her bottle of mineral water and tapped it against Gina's bottle. "And you're not the only one watching out for Shannon's interests." She nodded at the dance floor where Beth and Tasha were dancing, then continued, "Beth was drilling me for reasons why I haven't had sex with Shannon yet."

"Yeah, that sounds like Beth. Don't worry, she's only like that when she's had too many." Gina signaled the bartender and ordered another beer. "And we could be having more fun if we were both drunk. Why don't you turn your back on that Mormon religion and join me?" Gina joked.

"No, thanks. I'm not in the mood."

"By the way, I really don't buy your line about wanting to punch things. You wouldn't hit a fly." Gina paid the bartender as he set a fresh beer on a napkin.

"You don't know me," Kelly replied.

Gina arched her eyebrows. "Now that sounds tempting. If I didn't know better, I'd think you were flirting with me. You're not flirting, are you?"

"No," Kelly said quickly. She was surprised that Gina would think that.

Catching Kelly's wrist in her hand, Gina stared directly at her. "You know, I'm good at catching a liar . . . I'm a cop."

Kelly averted her eyes. "You're too young to be a cop."

"Nope. I just graduated from the academy." She let go of Kelly's wrist.

Kelly took a sip of her water. "Where do you work?"

"San Francisco P.D.," Gina stated. "I love the city, but it's nice to come home to Ashton. This town is so calm."

"I think you mean boring," Kelly corrected.

Gina smiled. "Maybe."

"I know I shouldn't say this, but you have a beautiful smile."

"Careful, Kelly. You're flirting with your date's best friend."

Kelly shook her head. "I'm not flirting."

"I'm going to give you some advice. You can ignore it if you want . . ." Gina pointed over at Shannon and her group of friends arguing about the contents of some mystery mixed drink. "This is Shannon's scene. She loves to come to this hole in the wall, shoot pool and get drunk. If you want to fit in her world you have to join the party."

"Thanks for the advice. I'm not trying to fit in. I just came to have a good time."

"So, grab a beer. Otherwise, you won't ever feel like you belong."

Kelly shook her head. "I feel like I belong here with you."

"Wow, we're having a little moment," Gina said in a sarcastic tone. "You aren't supposed to be here with me. You are supposed to be hanging on to Shannon and laughing at her jokes."

"I don't follow the rules." Kelly realized that she was more comfortable with Gina, whom she had known for less than an hour, than with Shannon. She suddenly wanted to go home with Gina tonight. "So, do you dance?"

"Not without a partner."

"Hmm, want to dance with me?" Kelly knew what Gina's answer would be.

"No, but thanks for the offer," Gina quipped. "You're off limits, remember? How old are you?"

"Twenty-one. You?"

"Twenty-two, almost. My birthday is this month," Gina ended abruptly. She seemed to be distracted by Beth and Tasha's exit off the dance floor.

The two men who had served as Beth and Tasha's dance partners were called back to the pool game. It was obvious that these women were together and Kelly doubted that anyone was fooled when they invited the men to dance with them. But this bar was in Ashton, not San Francisco. Around here, being straight was the norm.

"I like being drunk," Gina said, staring at the corner where Tasha and Beth were. "Give me a few beers and I'll forget all my problems. I'm happier then."

"You don't look happy."

Gina sighed. "Beth is one of my ex-girlfriends. I don't really like to watch her dance with Tasha, even if they drag a couple of boys out on the floor to pretend they're not lesbians. Tasha is worried about the military. She thinks that someone is watching her and detailing all of her lesbian secrets. Shannon used to worry about it also. Now she thinks that she'll never get caught. Did Shannon tell you that she dated Beth also?" Gina asked.

"I heard it through Beth. Sounds like Beth has dated just about everyone."

"Yeah, watch out. You never know about this group." Gina shook her head. "We play softball together, drink together and sleep together."

Kelly wished she could ignore the impulse to kiss Gina. She knew her cheeks were turning red just thinking about a kiss. Scanning the bar, Kelly spotted Shannon still standing by one of the guys from the army unit. In a few hours Gina would probably forget that Kelly existed. She couldn't let herself fall any deeper into the sordid love entanglement of this group.

Shannon's laughter broke Kelly's train of thought. Beth and Tasha had wandered across the dance floor to join Shannon and the guys by the pool tables. Kelly could hear Beth recounting a scene from a party the group of friends had thrown a few years ago. She wondered what details Shannon would later add about her friends. After meeting Gina, Kelly had renewed interest in hearing the gossip. "So, how'd you get to know this group? Are you also in the Reserves?"

"No," Gina replied adamantly. "Thank God I never joined. My ex-girlfriend Vicky, Shannon's old roommate, is in the army. Vicky is in Iraq now. She sends me letters all the time. The stories sound like nightmares. I thought about joining the Air Force but applied for the police academy instead. Best decision I ever made."

"Do you miss your girlfriend?"

"Well, she's my ex-girlfriend." Gina stopped for a moment. She seemed lost in thought. With a quick turn of the bottle, she downed the last swallow of beer. "Yeah, I miss her. And I'm pissed that I broke up with her when I did—it was bad timing. We weren't getting along and then I found out she was leaving. I wanted to be single. But as soon as she left, I realized I had made a mistake. I look around me and know that I miss her. I don't want to be here with any of these people." She shook her head and then glanced at Kelly. Her expression was contrite. She seemed to realize that until an hour ago, Kelly had been a complete stranger. Gina added, "No offense, you actually seem like a great person . . . I just miss her. She's out there doing these crazy missions and risking her life every minute. I can't convince her that I made a mistake. I'm desperate for her to come home. She doesn't believe that I love her. She reads my letters and writes back as though she hasn't understood a thing—she says she's happy we're 'just friends' now."

"Maybe she's worried that someone else will read the letters. You can't exactly be out in the army and professing your love to a girlfriend back home. What if someone intercepts the letter?"

Gina shook her head. "It's fucked up. Who cares if she loves a woman? She's out there fighting and doing just as well as any other soldier." Gina stood up from the barstool and grabbed the jacket hanging on the bar railing. She slipped it over her shoulders and then held out her hand to Kelly. "Can I give you some more advice?"

"From the older and wiser lesbian?" Kelly teased.

"Yeah. Go have fun with Shannon. Get it out of your system and decide if you really want to hang out with her. Maybe you'll be perfect for each other—like Beth and Tasha. But I doubt it."

Kelly nodded. She didn't want Gina to leave but couldn't think of any excuse to keep her longer. "I want you to stay."

"I need to walk off this buzz. Go hang out with the woman who brought you here. Chica, we'd only get into trouble if I stayed."

After Gina left the bar, Kelly pulled Shannon away from her friends and a loud debate over the legality of guns. Kelly convinced her to leave and drove the Jeep back to Shannon's house. The spastic Dalmatian bounded up to greet them as soon as they opened the garage door. Ignoring the dog, Shannon led Kelly to the bedroom. She closed the door as Paco whined for attention, then sank onto the edge of the bed to tug off her shoes. Kelly stared out the window, wondering if she wanted to stay. The streetlight at the corner of Shannon's block cast a yellow glow on the gray sidewalk. The neighbor's sprinklers had flooded the grass and were now watering the cement.

Shannon stood up and joined her by the window. She brushed her fingertips lightly against Kelly's arm. "I didn't know if you were going to come home with me tonight."

Kelly continued to stare out the window. "Why wouldn't I?"

"Gina." Shannon started to massage Kelly's back. "You were talking to her for a long time."

"She was drunk and missing her ex-girlfriend. She didn't really want to talk to me, but I felt a little out of place with your friends." Kelly wished that Gina hadn't left so quickly. She had wanted to talk with her more and almost wished she could have gone home with her instead of Shannon. She sighed and looked over her shoulder at

Shannon. "I just sat down at her table because I didn't want to dance and I can't play pool."

"Why'd you feel out of place with my friends?" Shannon kissed her neck as she slipped her hand under Kelly's shirt and unloosened the clasp of her bra.

"You've all known each other for years . . . I think I just need some time to figure out who's connected to whom so I don't say anything stupid." Kelly murmured as Shannon's hands rubbed her breasts. She guessed Shannon was only being forward because she was drunk. *Do I care?* she wondered. *I've never turned down sex before just because someone was drunk and she's hot tonight.* After seeing her with her friends, it was more obvious how little they had in common and she doubted they'd be together for long. But that wasn't a good reason to go home early. "Or maybe I just need some more time with you before facing your friends again. I wasn't sure if you wanted me to be there tonight."

"I wanted to spend the evening with you and my friends. Right now, I just want you." Shannon pulled off Kelly's shirt and the bra. "Seeing you with Gina made me jealous. I know her too well. She'll flirt with any girl."

As Shannon continued to massage her back, Kelly rested her hands on the windowsill and tried to decide how she should respond. After all, she'd been the one to start flirting, not Gina. "Gina was in a bad mood. I was trying to cheer her up."

"She's always in a bad mood lately," Shannon stated. "But that won't stop her. Trust me, I know Gina well. She's a player." Still standing behind her, Shannon rubbed Kelly's lower back, then moved to her hips and belly. She unbuttoned Kelly's pants and brushed her fingertips along the top of Kelly's underwear.

After pulling off Kelly's pants, Shannon had slipped out of her own clothes and began rubbing her naked body against Kelly's back. Although Kelly could feel herself respond to Shannon's touch and knew she wanted to continue making out with her, she realized it was just her hormones directing her body. Kelly felt detached from the scene. It was as if she were standing on the drenched sidewalk under the streetlight and watching herself through Shannon's window.

Shannon kissed Kelly's neck, just under her ear and Kelly's shoulders flinched reflexively. She quickly apologized. "I'm a little ticklish."

"Uh-oh. That could be tempting." Shannon stepped back and held her out at arm's length. "God, you have a great body. Don't flirt with Gina. Flirt with me instead."

Kelly smiled with embarrassment as Shannon traced her finger over her arms and admired each muscle curve. Finally she pulled Shannon closer and kissed her. Shannon's leg rubbed between her thighs. Through the open window, the smell of watered grass and the sound of crickets pervaded the room. *This is what a summer fling is supposed to be like*, Kelly thought. She massaged Shannon's lower back and kissed her breasts.

Backing away from the window, Shannon moved to turn down the bedsheets. Before she could finish, Kelly pulled her away from the bed and pinned her between the dresser and the bed. As they rubbed their bodies against each other, her hand moved between Shannon's legs and she felt a slip of wetness. She cupped Shannon's breasts with her hands and strummed her fingers lightly over the rings that pierced each nipple. Shannon murmured with pleasure, low and encouraging. She shook her head. "What took us so long to try this?"

Kelly didn't argue as Shannon pushed her onto the bed. She relaxed as Shannon moved on top of her, loving the weight of her body pushing down on her hips. Shannon's knee rubbed between her legs as they kissed and Kelly moaned softly. "I like you naked."

Shannon smiled. "I'll remember that the next time I try to decide what to wear for a date." Kelly's skin prickled at the touch of Shannon's fingertips tracing her body's curve, drawing a line from Kelly's breasts to her hips. Kelly ached to feel Shannon's fingers between her legs. Instead of reaching down, Shannon only continued to rub and massage Kelly's body lightly, teasing her. Unable to handle the constant temptation with no reward, Kelly sighed and relaxed. She lay still for a moment and Shannon looked down at her.

"What's wrong?" she asked.

Kelly smiled. "I can't handle any more teasing."

Shannon opened her mouth as if to apologize. Kelly grabbed her hand and trapped her leg with one foot. She flipped Shannon off of her. In the next moment, Shannon lay on her back on the other side of the bed and Kelly had climbed on top of her.

She smiled at Shannon's expression of surprise. "My turn."

"I almost forgot I was playing around with a karate girl." Shannon laughed. The laugh turned to a soft moan as Kelly rubbed her body. Shannon outweighed Kelly, but not by much and the army training had sculpted Shannon's body with thick muscles. Shannon's eyes closed and her lips parted with an expression of desire as Kelly pressed down on her. Kissing Shannon's open lips, she brushed her tongue inside her mouth, then kissed her neck.

Kelly traced her fingertips lightly along Shannon's skin, tan and smooth in the yellow glow of the streetlight. Her tongue circled each nipple, then moved in a straight line down her belly. She paused to kiss between her thighs as Shannon ran her hands through Kelly's hair. Shannon lifted her hips up from the sheets and pulled Kelly toward her. Kelly pulled back. Although the thought of Shannon's desire filled her with pleasure, she wanted to make the wait worthwhile. Kelly moved up to kiss Shannon's lips again. She pressed her hips down on Shannon rhythmically. She could feel Shannon's muscles dampen with sweat. The sheets tangled around their legs as they moved against each other.

Kelly caressed Shannon's breast and pulled the pierced tip into her mouth, sucking the nipple ring between her tongue and teeth. With the one hand massaging Shannon's warm breast, Kelly moved her other hand between Shannon's legs, parting the folds and letting her finger sink deep inside. Shannon's back arched off the bed as she murmured with pleasure.

Pressing in deeper, Kelly thrust inside, moving faster and faster. In the next second, Shannon's groin muscles tightened around Kelly's hand. Kelly held her fingers inside Shannon, loving the sensation. As she climaxed, Shannon gripped Kelly's wrist and pushed the fingers deeper inside. A soft moan escaped from her lips and her jaw clenched. Finally, her body quivered as the orgasm rushed through her.

Kelly lay down on top of her, letting the weight of her body press on Shannon. Between her legs, Kelly's nerves twitched. Her skin was wet and her body begged for Shannon's touch. She waited patiently for Shannon to make a move but Shannon appeared to be lost in her own feelings of pleasure. Rolling off of Shannon, Kelly leaned on her side and caressed Shannon's face with the back of her hand.

Shannon opened her eyes and looked up at Kelly. A smile parted her lips. "God, that felt good," she murmured. "My head feels so heavy . . . I don't want to be tired, but I don't think I can move right now." She struggled to shift to her side and then rolled back. "Hmm. I feel weak. I've wanted to touch you so much. But I think I drank too much or you just made me feel too damn good."

Kelly touched her lips. "I can wait."

The next morning Shannon apologized for the lack of breakfast food in her kitchen and suggested that they go out to breakfast. Kelly shook her head and pointed to a box of Cocoa Puffs. She had to teach in a few hours but wasn't ready to leave yet. After making out with Shannon last night, she was looking forward to another evening together. It wouldn't hurt to hang around for a while and find out more about Shannon's world, especially with the promise of good sex to come. They sat down on the couch in the family room, each with a bowl of cereal. The conversation strayed from an exchange of embarrassing stories about dates gone awry to coming-out stories. After their first night together, Shannon was more relaxed. Still, something was clearly holding her back. Kelly was aware that Shannon tensed up whenever they touched outside of the bedroom. She'd quickly change topics to avoid any intimacy.

Shannon turned on the TV and flipped through the channels. She settled on the news station. As usual, the broadcast included a segment about the military operations in Iraq. This situation seemed to be getting worse. Shannon switched the station to a cartoon. As they finished their cereal, Kelly quizzed her about her friends and the experience in boot camp. She volunteered to pull out her photo album when Kelly admitted she couldn't remember half of the people she had met at the bar the night before.

The photo album was carefully organized. Pictures were arranged in chronological order and most had neatly written name labels. Shannon pointed out her current friends. Vicky was tall, red-haired and pale. In the one picture of Gina and Vicky, neither was smiling and it appeared as though an argument had just begun. Kelly wondered what their relationship had been like before Vicky left. The album also had a few shots from Shannon's past year of army training. One photo featured five women gathered around a camp stove. Shannon's arm encircled a woman with shoulder-length brown hair and an attractive smile. She was wearing a gray shirt with sleeves cut off to expose the muscles on her arms. Shannon skipped over the camping picture without adding any description to the event. This picture had no name label. Kelly wondered who Shannon was hugging.

Kelly pointed to the woman, stopping Shannon from flipping to the next page. "What about this picture? Same friends from boot camp?"

"No. That was after boot camp. A bunch of the women from the base decided to get together and go down to the river for a weekend camping trip. We all got blasted. You learn how to drink in the army," she said with a laugh.

"Who's this?" Kelly asked pointing to the woman in the gray shirt.

"Hannah. She was one of the officers on the base." She flipped the page without any further clue as to why her arm was wrapped so tightly around Hannah. Kelly guessed that she was Shannon's girlfriend at the time. She didn't really want to hear details about an ex-girlfriend. Yet something about Shannon's tone and her desire to turn the page made Kelly wonder if this was a finished story. No doubt, there was more to Hannah than Shannon would admit. Kelly wondered if Shannon still had contact with Hannah. Shannon continued to describe the rest of the pictures, but Kelly soon lost interest. She wanted to pull Shannon away from her memories and into the present moment.

Shaking off a feeling of repressed desire, Kelly finally left Shannon's house. For some reason, seeing Shannon's affection as she held Hannah in the camping photo made her jealous. Everyone brought baggage to a new relationship, but it was hard to ignore the picture of Hannah that Shannon was so secretive about. She didn't want to get pulled into an unresolved ex-girlfriend issue. Rehashing the events of the last twenty-four hours, her thoughts spun from Shannon to Gina. Kelly knew that she needed to forget her attraction to Gina, who was still in love with Vicky. That would be even more baggage to deal with.

After leaving Shannon, Kelly remembered the surfing trip Alex had scheduled for that morning. She called his cell phone and the answering service picked up the line. He was probably already in the water. She left a message. With Starr as his audience, Kelly knew Alex would be busy showing off on the waves. He wouldn't miss her company today. And the sharks could wait until the next surfing trip.

Chapter 8

049301

Through the bay windows in the library foyer, the sun slipped behind the two red peaks of the Golden Gate Bridge. Kelly waited in the checkout line with her stack of books. Light shimmered over the ripples of water. The university was on the north bank hills at the outskirts of the city and most of downtown San Francisco usually seen from the university library was concealed in a fog that crept steadily closer to the bay windows. Only the red bridge and a stretch of blue water remained visible through the blanket of gray.

Kelly watched the scene at the window with a sudden longing to stay in the city. Unfortunately, the karate summer camp program would begin soon and this was her last Monday off. As of next week, she'd be working six days a week for the rest of summer and didn't know when she'd have time to escape Ashton. She was already starting to miss the city fog. At least she'd have the excuse to come back to the university to return the library books.

The terse voice of the librarian pulled Kelly's attention away from the window. She handed the librarian her ID card and a stack of books. After checking her final exam scores, Kelly had spent the past few hours sifting through a pile of books on her summer reading list. Only a few students wandered the halls and it seemed strange to see the library nearly deserted on a Monday. Judging from the serious, focused expressions of the other library patrons, she guessed that they were probably enrolled in the university's summer school. Kelly was happy she wasn't in their shoes.

Loading the books into her backpack, she headed for the train station. Kelly wasn't eager to leave the city and window-shopped as she made her way through the busy streets. When she neared the station, Kelly paused to watch a group of teenagers loitering by the entrance. Five or six boys were busy harassing the evening commuters. With downcast eyes, Kelly moved through the group quickly. A hand tugged on the strap of her backpack as she passed by one of the boys. His pale face was plagued with pimples, and a smattering of young red whiskers had erupted on his chin. The boys reeked of marijuana smoke. "Spare change?"

"Go home and ask your dad if you're old enough to smoke pot. Maybe he'll give you the money," she snapped at him.

The boy cussed as Kelly freed his hand from her bag. She dodged through the rest of the boys and ran down the staircase. With a quick glance at the station's clock, she slid her ticket through the tollgate. Half past six—the East Bay train to the suburbs was due any moment.

As she ran toward the second flight of stairs leading down to the train platform, Kelly nearly collided with an old couple waiting by the elevator. She skirted around them after a quick apology. A bell rang as the incoming train approached the station. Kelly paused halfway down the steps. An attractive black woman in a stylish gray dress suit was waiting at the bottom of the stairs. The woman appeared to be contemplating which side of the stairwell to move to in order to let Kelly pass. In one hand she held a rolled newspaper and in the other a leather briefcase. Kelly shifted closer to the right side rail to make room for the woman to pass. Someone suddenly shoved Kelly back to the left rail and tugged on her backpack. She gripped her backpack straps tightly, recognizing the boy from the station entrance who had tried to grab her backpack just moments earlier. When he realized he wasn't going to get her pack off her shoulders, he barged past her and tore down the last few steps.

At the base of the stairwell, the boy collided with the woman's briefcase. The briefcase launched into the air and struck the cement several feet down the platform. With a loud crack, the snaps of the case popped open, spilling the contents by the waiting train. The boy cussed and trampled over the briefcase. He disappeared through the open door of the last car. The contents from the briefcase were strewn across the platform. A few other passengers stared at the case with interest, but no one moved toward the mess of papers.

"Are you okay?" Kelly moved down the stairs toward the woman.

"I'm fine. I hate kids," the woman said with irritation. She shook her head as she glanced at the open briefcase.

Papers had flown out of the case in a six-foot radius. After a quick glance at the incoming sign, Kelly confirmed that the waiting train was indeed her ride to Ashton. The train's red light flashed. In a moment the doors would slide closed. The next train to the East Bay was due in thirty minutes. A gust of wind would follow the train as soon as it pulled past the station platform and the woman's documents would be strewn farther down the platform and onto the tracks. With a sigh, Kelly turned away from the open train door and kneeled down to begin gathering some of the loose documents. The station attendant announced the train's departure.

"No, no. I don't need your help. You'll miss your train," the woman called out to stop her.

"As soon as the train leaves, everything will fly onto the tracks."

As she continued gathering the strewn papers, Kelly concentrated on the woman. She glanced at the train, but did not answer Kelly. Instead, she picked up her case and started replacing the contents carefully. She was striking, really, Kelly thought. Dark black hair and brown skin complimented the finely sculpted face, high cheekbones, arched eyebrows and full lips. The woman replaced each sheet of paper in the briefcase with the delicacy of a dancer or a musician. Only years of training would develop fine accurate movements and a body that flexed as beautifully as this stranger's did. Kelly looked away with embarrassment as the woman caught her stare. She glanced down at the documents she'd gathered and noted fragments of legalese. Maybe the woman was a lawyer.

"I really don't need your help," she insisted as Kelly handed her a stack of papers.

"Okay." Kelly nodded. She had collected most of the loose documents anyway. But the train doors were locked and she couldn't board now. The train groaned as the conductor switched on the power.

"Oh damn, I've lost it," the woman swore. She immediately began rifling through the loose papers, as if searching for something specific.

"What'd you lose?" Kelly asked. Hopefully she'd find it and not blame Kelly if something was misplaced.

Slowly, the train began to move past the platform. As it gained momentum and the last car rolled by, the predicted gust of wind roared through the station. Kelly noticed a small rectangular card fly past her. It disappeared in the dark space near the end of the platform. The woman continued to rifle through the papers. Kelly headed past the stairwell toward the end of the platform. This area had no overhead lights and she had to hold her hand out to avoid bumping into anything.

After a short search through the dark recess at the end of the platform, she spotted the white card. Her hand moved through a cobweb and she shivered involuntarily. She grabbed the card. Shaking the cobweb off her hand, Kelly squinted in the faint light.

What she had thought was a white card was actually the backside of a photograph. She stared at the picture. A woman with shoulder-length brown hair and bloodshot blue eyes gazed back at her. She looked as though she had just survived a fight. A large bruise claimed the right cheekbone and her lower lip was cut and swollen. Several notes were scribbled on the back of the photo—phone numbers and addresses. She stared at the woman in the photo again and felt a rush of nausea mix with the recognition. Despite the swollen lip and bruised face, Kelly knew this was the same woman she had seen yesterday in Shannon's photo album, Hannah the army officer. Kelly read the date printed on the picture. The photograph was taken last month. What had happened to her?

Kelly jogged back to the stairwell. "Miss?"

No answer.

"Miss, I think this is yours too," Kelly said louder this time.

Spotting the photo, the woman nodded and took the card from Kelly's outstretched hand. "Yes. Thank you." In a quick motion, she slipped the photo into the front pocket of her suit jacket and snapped the briefcase closed with her other hand.

"I'm sorry about the accident on the stairs," Kelly apologized. She wished she could have grabbed the punk before he'd crashed into the woman's briefcase.

"No harm done. It wasn't your fault."

"Is the woman in your picture a friend of yours?" Kelly asked.

"Hmm?" she asked.

Kelly repeated her question, thinking that the woman was stalling. She was sure that she'd heard her question the first time.

"Oh, the picture. Yes." She smiled. "Yes, she's a good friend. Thank you again for your help." The woman turned toward the stairs.

"Wait . . . I'm sorry to bother you, but can I ask a question? Is she in the army by chance?" Kelly knew there was a story that went with this picture. The muscles in the woman's neck tensed with Kelly's question. Why did this woman have the photo of Shannon's ex-girlfriend? Although Kelly didn't really know if Shannon had dated the woman or not . . . She hated to press this stranger for any information, but she couldn't suppress her curiosity. Kelly had an eerie feeling that the photo had some significance. The woman gave no response and Kelly finally continued, "I think I know her, but I can't remember her name and it's bugging me now. I think she was in the army, right?"

The woman turned to face her. "I doubt that you know the woman in the photo. There are a lot of women who can look similar in pictures. I don't think you know her." Her facial muscles twitched slightly. Was she hiding something? Kelly wondered. She wanted to know more about Hannah the army officer.

"Is her name Hannah?" Kelly asked.

"What?" the woman asked with a hint of irritation.

"Never mind." Kelly shook her head. She was positive that it was Hannah. It was unlikely that she would mistake the face only a day after she had seen her picture. But it didn't really matter. She was just a stranger in a photograph. Kelly turned away. Regardless of the picture, she didn't mind missing her train for a beautiful woman. Kelly wondered if she was a lesbian.

Most of the seats at the station were empty now. Kelly sat down and waited for the next train. She scanned a newspaper that had been left on the bench. There was an article about the war on the front page. Kelly thought about the descriptions Shannon had given of her experiences in the army and the group of lesbians she had met during her training.

After a few minutes, the woman with the briefcase appeared next to her. She was holding the photo out toward Kelly. "Are you sure you know her?"

Kelly nodded. "Why do you have her picture?" She decided that if this woman was now interested in her, she could get a little more information.

"I'm a lawyer. I was just wondering if you had any information that could help us."

"I just know the woman's name is Hannah. She's an officer in the army." Kelly wasn't sure if she was an officer or not but had guessed that she wasn't a new recruit. And Beth had mentioned that Shannon's last girlfriend was an officer.

"Well, she was an officer."

"What? Is she okay?" Kelly asked. The tone of the woman's voice suggested that Hannah had met with a terrible fate.

"She's okay, for now. She was discharged from the army two months ago. What else do you know about her?"

"Nothing," Kelly answered. She had no need to be completely honest to this woman. "I just recognized her face."

"Hannah is attractive."

"From your picture it looks like she's seen some rough times." Compared to Hannah's smiling face in Shannon's camping picture, this second photo was a frightening image.

"She was in an accident. She's fine now. Are you sure you don't know anything more about her?"

Kelly nodded.

The woman replaced the picture in her suit pocket and then handed Kelly a business card. *McMahon, Kinley and Associates* was printed on the top of the card. The woman pointed to her name, Nora Kinley. The card also listed the address of her law firm and contact phone numbers. "I'm Hannah's lawyer. If you think of anything you want to tell me later, give me a call."

"Why were you staring at me on the stairwell before that kid knocked your briefcase?" Kelly asked, taking her business card. She had no intention of calling the number. She really did not have any information she wanted to give to the lawyer.

"You looked familiar, but I'm sure we haven't met before. Anyway, thanks for finding the photo. I hate losing things." Nora laughed. "I go crazy when I forget where I put my car keys."

Kelly wondered why Nora acted so secretive. It wasn't her business anyway. Hannah was Shannon's ex-girlfriend and Kelly didn't even know her. Nora acted as though she were hiding something.

But why? Kelly glanced at the lawyer's business card again. Maybe she would ask Shannon more about the army officer in her photo album. She couldn't deny that she wanted an excuse to contact Nora again. Nora Kinley left the train platform without saying good-bye. She cleared the top of the stairwell and didn't turn back for a second glance. Kelly sighed. She suddenly had a new crush.

Chapter 9

049351

Kelly knew that the only way to find out more information about Hannah and the army was to spend time with Shannon. She left a message on Shannon's answering machine on Monday night, right after meeting the lawyer in the train station. In her message, she invited Shannon out for dinner. On Thursday, Shannon finally called to return her message. Although Shannon had said that she'd been busy and apologized for not calling sooner, Kelly was convinced that waiting three days to return her call was a sign that Shannon wasn't that interested in her.

Shannon invited Kelly to a party that Friday. Her first impulse was to decline. She didn't want to be a token girlfriend again. Then Shannon mentioned that the occasion for the party was Gina's birthday. The friends from the bar were all meeting at Gina's house to celebrate. Kelly agreed to go. She wanted to see Gina anyway, and now there was the puzzle to solve about Hannah.

Tap, tap thud. Tap, tap thud. "Left, left right," Kelly repeated as she focused her attention on the punching bag. She'd had a few bad sparring matches that night and the day's classes hadn't gone well. She knew her attention was focused outside the dojo—she wanted to see Gina again and couldn't wait until tomorrow night.

Each time her thoughts strayed from the bag, Kelly hit harder. Spotting blood on the bag, Kelly paused to check her hands. Blood oozed from the chafed surface on two fingers. She paused to tape the raw knuckles, then stuffed her hands into a pair of gloves and continued her assault. The bag swung from its silver chain directly at Kelly, as though it had developed its own offensive plan.

She could taste the salty sweat on her lips from the sparring class earlier that evening. Her cheek was swollen and tender after Kevin's back fist had smacked her face in her first match. She had stepped in to throw a punch to the ribs just as he extended his fist straight at her helmet. Unfortunately, she turned at the wrong moment and Kevin's fist glanced off the foam and landed on Kelly's right cheekbone.

Kevin didn't apologize after the strike but paused for a moment as she regained her equilibrium. He looked concerned but wouldn't say anything. It would be disrespectful to apologize. Kelly had missed the block. It was her mistake. If he apologized, it would only call attention to the mistake. Blinking to stop the tears from seeping down from her eyes, Kelly had nodded to signal that she was ready to spar again. She couldn't stop the tears. They formed regardless of emotions. She bowed to Sam, and the match continued. After Sam called the last point, Kevin grabbed her in a bear hug. He leaned close to whisper, "Damn, you're tough for a girl."

The dojo emptied quickly after the sparring class ended that evening. After losing the match with Kevin, Kelly had proceeded to lose the next four matches. It was difficult to fight with one side of her face pulsing with blood. She pounded the bag to forget about the sparring mistakes as well as Shannon and her friends.

"Another rough day?" Sam asked from his office doorway. His black hair was trimmed short from a haircut that morning and his face was smooth from a fresh shave. His large build seemed to claim the entire doorway. He had changed out of his black uniform and into a pair of jeans. His belt dangled in his right hand.

Catching the blue punching bag as it swung toward her, Kelly nodded. She was upset that Shannon had not returned her message until that morning, but she didn't want to complain to Sam. Her fist tapped the bag as she tried to hide her frustration. "I just needed to work some things out."

"Yeah, I noticed. Lock up when you finish cleaning. And put some ice on your cheek—you're not going to catch any girls with a shiner." He turned and left the dojo.

Kelly rested her head against the bag. Sweat had dried on her forehead and her hair was soaked. She sank down to her knees and snapped the knot on her black belt, then closed her eyes. Her breathing steadied as she concentrated on the thump of her heart. Its rhythm slowed as she meditated. After a few minutes, Kelly got up and started her cleaning tasks for the night. She moved slowly, stiff from the evening fights, and carefully wiped off each little hand print on the front mirrors. The toddlers in the first class loved to touch the mirror as they stared at their own reflections.

"Is Sam in the office?"

Looking up from the glass and the swirls of window cleaner, Kelly tried to locate the voice. At first glance the waiting room appeared empty. She had turned off the lights in the front of the studio to let any passerby know that the school was closed. The last student had left a half-hour ago. A paper towel was scrunched up in her hand, half wet from the cleaning. Had she imagined the voice? Suddenly, a gray-haired man dressed in a dark suit stepped into view. He was standing in the waiting room, watching Kelly intently. Tossing the paper into the trash bin, she wiped her hand against her uniform.

"No, sir." Her nerves, spent from the long day, made her voice shake. She faced the waiting room, squinting in the darkness to discern the features that belonged to the mysterious voice. Slowly, Kelly recognized Rick, the investor. He moved from the waiting room to lean against the doorway of the studio and his large frame blocked the exit. Kelly realized that Rick and Sam were nearly equal in size. She wondered why she hadn't heard him enter. Apparently he had keys to the dojo.

"Sam left you here to close up shop alone, huh. How do you like that?"

"Fine, sir."

"Fine. Did he leave any message for me? I need to reach him."

"No, sir. He's already gone home for the night. We close at eight. Is there anything I can do to help you?" If Rick knew anything about his investment, he would know the hours of the school.

"No. I don't think you could help me. Does he work tomorrow?"

"Yes, sir. His first lesson is at nine a.m. It's my day off."

"Well . . . He needs to call me. It's an urgent matter."

"Yes, sir. I can leave a message for him." Kelly was sure Rick had Sam's home phone number. If it really was urgent he could call Sam at home. She guessed there was some other reason that he was here tonight.

"I don't think that we've ever been properly introduced. I'm Rick. And by the way, you can skip the *yes, sir* bullshit. You are?"

"Kelly. Nice to meet you, sir." She picked up the roll of paper to begin cleaning the last mirror in the row. Kelly had been teaching for the past few years, but it was true that they had never been formally introduced. Kelly had taught only the children's classes in the dojo. She was not someone Rick would need to notice.

"I don't come by often, but I happened to catch you here twice last week. I saw you teaching the children's class and then I caught one of your sparring matches."

Kelly nodded. She wouldn't forget the ring of his cell phone and Kevin's bloody nose. Her swollen right eye was proof of karate sparring karma. Nearly every mistake made in the dojo was paid off in due time. "Yeah, I seem to remember that you saw me screw up and hit my partner in the nose."

"Actually, it wasn't the first time I've watched your sparring matches. You like to fight with the big boys. Do you ever get scared?" His voice was patronizing.

"It's not that I prefer fighting men—women just don't show up to the adult sparring class."

"Maybe they're scared."

"I think they're smarter than me. They probably want to keep their brain cells and most women are too smart to fist-fight with men."

"It's not often that women win when they fight men," Rick countered. His dogmatic tone made Kelly aware that this was a test. Suddenly, the story she had heard about Rick was a little more interesting. She guessed he was in his early sixties and knew that he had worked for the FBI for several years before retiring. She wondered if the rumors about his private investigation service were true.

"That depends on the rules of the fight." Kelly wasn't in the mood for an exam tonight and the blood pulsing on the right side of her face distracted her. She was waiting for him to tell her that she should let the boys fight their own matches. He was probably concerned that she would get hurt and then try and sue.

"Well, most women can't take a real punch."

"Yeah, I've heard that line before." Kelly was in no shape to defend her position tonight. When she had first started sparring in the adult class, she was paired up with a hotheaded young brown belt in his early twenties. He'd considered it an insult that he should have to fight a teenage girl. After winning the match, Kelly collapsed in the corner as a sharp pain seized her belly. She hadn't noticed the pain until the rush of adrenaline dissipated. Her opponent walked over to offer his hand to help her stand, but she shook her head. She didn't want to appear weak and it was too painful to stand. When she finally struggled to her feet and joined the other students on the edge of the mat, the hothead muttered, "Women don't belong fighting with men—they can't take a real punch." It hadn't mattered that she had scored three points against him in a clean match. She realized then that she should never show pain.

Rick sat down in one of the seats in the dark waiting room. He obviously planned on continuing the conversation even if she was ready to leave. "So, you don't mind the injuries?"

Kelly flipped on the light. If he was staying, she wanted to see him. There was a briefcase by the door that she hadn't noticed before. She glanced at Rick. The light added years to Rick's face. Lines were carved at the corners of his eyes. At first she considered a sarcastic response to Rick's question and then remembered that she was really his employee. Because of him she got a paycheck every week. "It's part of the deal. If you step on the mat, bow to another black belt and agree to spar, you are asking to get hit. No one wants to break any bones. But you can't think about that when you fight." She studied Rick's expression. His jaw line was hard and set. He didn't seem like the kind of man who would particularly care what bones broke in her body. "I lose a lot, but I don't get scared. The 'big boys' go easy on me because I'm a girl."

His head shook. "I don't think so. I've watched the fights. Sam thinks that you're worth my time. And he doesn't usually brag about students."

She knew now that this was an evaluation, not a mincing of words. He was looking for a specific response. She was not the type of fighter who boasted about sparring matches, especially after a bad night and a good bruise. Rick continued to measure her up. She sighed, trying to ease the tension from the day. She was tired of wasting time. "I don't really know what you're suggesting. What do you want to know about me?"

"Do you get scared when you fight?" Rick repeated.

"Honestly, no. I don't get scared. I fight because I love the excitement. Sometimes I win, but mostly I get my ass kicked. But I've been lucky. I don't like beating on people and I'm really not that good anyway."

She picked up a box of carpet freshener and sprinkled the white powder across the floor. It was almost nine o'clock. She wanted to go home, collapse against the wall of the shower stall and let hot water pour over her head.

Rick cleared his throat, apparently frustrated that she was not giving him her full attention. "What do you do when you aren't teaching here? You're on summer break now, right?"

"Yep. I just hang out here and get into trouble." The room fell silent. She could feel his eyes on her back. The white dust flew out of the cardboard box in slow arcs.

"You don't like my questions, do you?"

"No, sir, I don't mind the questions. I just don't have anything exciting to tell you. And I'm wondering why you're wasting your time with me now. I've been at this karate school for years and you usually just walk by without even acknowledging that I work here. You don't know me."

"I'm just the curious businessman. But you're right—I don't know anything about you and I've been paying your checks for years."

"So, why you are wasting your time asking me now?"

"I don't waste my time. I want to know what you do when you aren't working here."

"Fine. This is my job for the summer." She was feeling punchy. "I'm a good teacher and the students like me. I'm worth more than minimum wage. My tuition at the university is due in a month and I don't want to take out another loan. So I'm looking at getting another job. Now you know something about me, sir."

"Have you ever considered putting your martial arts training to use in ways beyond teaching?" he asked.

"No. Martial arts training doesn't offer a lot of job opportunities beyond teaching. I like karate, but I need a real career." She continued, mostly to herself, "And my parents want me to go to grad school. I've been filling out applications, but I haven't really figured out what I'm going to do."

"What about right now? There may be some opportunities this summer . . ."

"Such as?"

"I have other business interests besides this karate studio. Did Sam tell you that I run a private investigation service?"

Kelly nodded. "There are a few rumors about you."

Rick smiled. Wrinkles formed along the edge of his lips and his blue eyes flashed as though he was happy to have rumors circulate. "Well, after I retired from the FBI, I got bored and started working with a few friends—lawyers who needed help investigating their clients and the cases that they're working on. I think you may be able to help me with some easy investigative work. I'd like someone who will blend in and not look like a street thug. You have some martial arts training but no one would suspect that. And I know Sam trusts you. I need someone I can trust as well."

"I don't think I'm qualified for investigative work." Kelly shook her head. "I fight for fun and I lose all the time. I'm not qualified for dodging bullets or knife fights in dark alleys."

"I'm not looking for a prizefighter. I want someone who can tail people, deliver some messages, and who won't look out of place in a crowd. I don't want some big tough guy."

Kelly considered his job description. The thought of investigative work was appealing, and she could use extra money. "I still don't think I'd be good at it . . ."

"I pay well. My one hesitation is that you're used to sport fighting. I need someone who won't pull punches if it does come down to a fight." He held out his fist, an inch from the wall, and then continued, "I've watched you a few times now and seen you come this close to a hit." He paused, his fist frozen in midair. "And then you pulled back. I caught the look in your eye when you were fighting. You looked like you wanted to snap the guy's neck but you pulled your punch. I don't need someone who pulls punches or is afraid of getting hit."

"I'm not afraid of getting hit. I just don't like it. As you can see, I

103

get smacked around here all the time." Kelly shook her head. "And I thought you saw the punch I threw that nearly broke my partner's nose last week. My control sucks. It's not that I pull punches—my aim sucks."

He cut her explanation short. "Your opponent stepped into that strike. But you pulled the other punches. I'm wondering if you pull the strikes because you don't want to go further, or because you can't. I can tell you one thing. You think you're in control when you lose. The opponent only hits what you expose, right? You play a good game and keep your face from getting smashed. Most of the time . . ."

Kelly smiled and gingerly touched the swollen skin under her eye. "Yeah, I hate getting my face hit, but you take that chance when you fight here. I lose because I'm not as good as my opponent. But you're right. I lose on my own terms." She folded her arms and stared at Rick. "Maybe you could just tell me what you think I should consider beyond teaching karate and fighting with the same boys in here. They don't really like to lose to a girl. What are you offering exactly?"

"Part-time work. We'll start with just a package delivery. I'll give you the address and you drop it off at the right place without being seen. Don't ask questions and don't talk about it. You get a hundred bucks for making the delivery. Want to try it once?"

Kelly considered the offer. "Maybe."

"Good." Rick picked up the briefcase by the door and pulled out a manila envelope. He set the envelope on the glass display case. The envelope was blank—no name and no address. "We'll start tonight." He smiled. "If you're ready."

"Tonight?"

He nodded. He scribbled an address on a yellow notepad and handed the sheet of paper to Kelly. "Deliver it at midnight."

Kelly stared at the address. It was in a rich neighborhood in San Francisco not far from her university. She didn't want to make the drive tonight and was a little uneasy at the thought of who might be waiting for the envelope. Rick reached into his jacket and handed Kelly a one-hundred-dollar bill. "Gas money."

"I just drop it in the mailbox at this address?"

"No, leave it on the front doormat. Remember, no one can see you make the delivery." He glanced at his watch. "I won't keep you from your work. You'll see me again soon."

Kelly nodded and went into the back storage room. She pulled out the vacuum and fished the cord free from a stack of boxes. She didn't feel like organizing her thoughts tonight. Why had Rick taken a sudden interest in her? What was in the envelope and why would he pay a hundred dollars for the delivery? Straining against the vacuum, Kelly pulled it out of the closet as the weight of the day sank into her ankles. Rick had disappeared from the waiting room. She walked through the dojo and locked the front door. The manila envelope waited on the display case.

The next day Rick appeared in the dojo again. Kelly's attention was focused on the sparring match between Isaac and Colin. Both boys had been unusually attentive for the past two weeks. Colin was trying hard to earn back his belt. Rick watched the boys for a few minutes and then cleared his throat. When Kelly finally acknowledged him, he held up three fingers and quickly left the dojo.

After calling the end of the sparring match, she ordered the boys to do push-ups and scanned the waiting room. He had left more manila envelopes on top of the glass display case. Kelly hoped that the next deliveries would go as smoothly as the last one. The job seemed too easy. She had found the address without getting lost and delivered the envelope to the front doormat of an expensive house on a hill overlooking the San Francisco Bay. Now, three more manila envelopes were waiting for her. Rick had printed the delivery addresses and times on yellow Post-it notes attached to each envelope. The delivery locations were scattered throughout San Francisco, but each envelope was headed for an expensive neighborhood. Kelly had no idea what connection, if any, there was between the deliveries. The envelopes lacked the names of the addressees, but if she cared, Kelly could probably track down the information. She decided not to investigate her delivery recipients. This was a well-paid delivery job and she needed the money. It was probably better not to know too much information.

Distracted from guessing the contents of the envelopes, Kelly turned back to the boys' karate lesson as Isaac announced he had finished his push-ups. She handed Colin a purple testing certificate at the end of the class. "Don't lose this. It's your ticket to the belt test next week. Ask your father if he thinks that your behavior at home has improved over the past two weeks. If he agrees and signs the form, you can test." She doubted his parents had noticed any change. They ignored Colin. But she knew that Colin's father would sign anything. He thought his signature implied that he was an involved parent.

Colin paled as soon as Kelly handed him the purple form. He gripped the paper tightly. "I won't lose it, ma'am. But what if my dad . . . well, what if my dad hasn't noticed me for the past two weeks?"

"Yeah, Dad never noticed that he lost his purple belt," Isaac added. "But Colin stopped swearing so much. And we haven't been fighting at home."

Kelly stared at Colin. She didn't know how to answer. "Well, I've noticed that you've improved. Have your dad sign the form. We'll consider it a promise that you will continue to show respect—not just for the purple-belt test, but your black-belt test also."

The boys bowed to her and then ran out to the minivan. Colin waved the purple form, but his father ignored him. Colin climbed into the car. He handed the form to his father again. The man glanced at it briefly, then stuffed it into his pocket before closing the minivan door. Kelly shook her head. It was painfully obvious that the boys' father had given up on Colin. Before her next student arrived,

Kelly tucked Rick's manila envelopes in her backpack in the locker room.

After work, Kelly drove to the city. She stopped for a milkshake at her favorite place on Castro Street before delivering Rick's envelopes. The waiter recognized her and smiled. He always wore something pink. Tonight it was a scarf tied around his neck. He started up a conversation about the Giants' winning streak. Kelly was convinced that he only watched the game because he had a crush on the lead pitcher. She confessed she was running late and he cut his story short. He whipped up her milkshake and complimented her on her skin color. A few weeks in Ashton and she already had a good tan. Kelly smiled and paid for the shake.

In a little less than an hour she had finished all three deliveries. She crumpled the yellow Post-it notes into a trash can at a gas station and walked inside to break one of her new hundred-dollar bills. Rick had left a separate envelope with her name on it and three crisp bills. She doubted if she would ever find out what the manila envelopes contained. Hopefully it was nothing illegal.

Chapter 10

049401

Shannon was waiting on the steps of her front porch when Kelly pulled up to the driveway. She waved as Shannon approached her car. After finishing Rick's deliveries, she'd rushed home for a quick shower and then sped to Shannon's house. But she was late. They hadn't seen each other since the past weekend and now Shannon didn't look too happy to see her. Kelly glanced at the clock next to her car's odometer. Gina's party started at eight o'clock and it was already a quarter to nine.

"Hey, Shannon."

"You're late," Shannon replied with irritation in her voice.

"I know. Work ran overtime," Kelly lied. "Did you get my message?" As soon as Rick dropped off the manila envelopes to be delivered, she'd phoned Shannon to warn her that she'd probably be late.

Shannon nodded. "Yeah, I got your message. But you didn't say *how* late you'd be." She shrugged. "Anyway, I doubt Gina will really mind what time we show up to her party. I just can't stay long because of the six a.m. drill tomorrow. I don't really like going out the night before my weekend training."

"Gina will be happy to see you there, I'm sure," Kelly replied.

Gina's townhouse was on the opposite side of town from Alex's place. By the time they arrived, most of the other guests were already drunk. Gina was passing Coronas out to everyone and handed Shannon a bottle as soon as they walked in the door. Gina winked at Kelly. "I'd offer you a beer, but I hate to corrupt people."

Kelly smiled. "Where can I find a soda?"

Gina pointed Kelly down the hallway to the kitchen and pushed Shannon toward a group of five or six people engaged in a loud game of liars' dice in the family room.

In the kitchen, Beth and Tasha were arguing over the number of birthday candles to place on Gina's cake. They both greeted Kelly enthusiastically and asked her to make the tie-breaking decision for the candles, just two to be symbolic, or all twenty-two. The cake was covered in bright blue frosting. She voted in favor of all twenty-two candles and Tasha quickly flashed an I-told-you-so look at Beth.

"So who made the cake?" Kelly asked. There was an empty container of Cool Whip on the kitchen counter and a half-empty vial of blue food coloring dye.

"I did," Beth said proudly. "But don't be put off by the color. Blue is Gina's favorite color. And of course, it's also our softball team's color. But the cake under the frosting isn't blue."

"Thank God," Tasha muttered.

Kelly left the kitchen and wandered out to the patio. The area was small and crowded with potted plants, a patio table and a barbecue. Gina was chatting with three people whom Kelly didn't recognize. She overheard a few comments about giving speeding tickets and guessed that this was a group of cops—Gina's work friends. Gina vowed that she wouldn't be handing out speeding tickets forever.

Kelly made brief eye contact with Gina and was surprised when Gina excused herself from her work friends to greet her. The other three in the group decided to head back inside, leaving Gina and Kelly alone in the patio.

"I didn't expect to see you tonight. Does this mean that Shannon and you are still dating?" Gina asked.

"No, I just came here to see you," Kelly joked. *Damn, she's hot. Why am I attracted to two women who are best friends?*

Gina laughed. "Well, I'm glad to hear that." She replied in the same joking tone, "You guys didn't make a good match."

Kelly didn't know how to respond. *Is Gina really joking?*

Gina motioned to the back door. "Just so you know, you better be careful. Someone at our softball practice told Shannon that she thought I had a crush on you."

Kelly felt her cheeks warm and hoped Gina wouldn't notice her blush. "Who would say that?"

"Beth." Gina picked up a beer from the patio table and took a sip. She continued, "The question is, why would she say that?"

"I don't know. But I'd love to find out if it's true." Kelly wondered why Gina was telling her this. She decided to change the subject. "So, you don't like giving speeding tickets? I thought that was why people became cops."

"Hell, no." She smiled. "I want to be an investigator. But I guess you could say I'm a few promotions away from that. And I'm still young."

"By the way, happy birthday," Kelly said.

"Thanks." Gina suddenly leaned over the patio table and kissed her. She pulled back and smiled. "That was my birthday present." Gina turned away quickly and opened the screen door to enter the house. She looked over her shoulder at Kelly. "By the way, not bad."

Kelly leaned against the patio table. Her heart was racing. The melody of "Happy Birthday" drifted through the back door and out to the patio. She guessed that Beth and Tasha had finally lit the candles. Would Shannon notice that she was missing? When she heard the last note of the birthday song, Kelly reluctantly headed back to join the party.

Despite the bright blue frosting, Beth's cake disappeared quickly. Most of the guests had decided to continue the party at the bar and left after they'd eaten the cake. Gina's house was only a few blocks from the bar and several wagers had been made for a pool tournament later that night. Gina encouraged Beth, Tasha, Shannon and Kelly to stay at her house. For some reason she didn't want to go to the bar with the others.

After clearing up some empty bottles and cake plates left by the other guests, the women settled in the family room. Gina placed a few CDs in her stereo and sank into the couch. Kelly sat down on the floor, consciously avoiding any prolonged stares at Gina. Tasha and Shannon were seated in the couch next to her, avidly discussing something about a problem at their military base. Beth sat on the arm of the couch and argued with Gina about the softball game that they had played earlier that night. Their league alternated the game times for each team and this week they'd started at six p.m. Unfortunately, a few players couldn't make it to the earlier time and they had to forfeit the game. Beth had dropped several hints to Kelly about joining their team, but she ignored the hints and Beth finally left her alone.

The quiet warmth and closeness of five women in Gina's living room was a welcome change from the bustling noise of the party. Kelly was surprised that Gina seemed to be getting along so well with Beth and Tasha and wondered what had changed. Shannon had mentioned that Beth and Gina were trying to form a truce. Maybe it had worked. She started to arrange the CDs in Gina's music cabinet. Shannon placed her bottle on the coffee table and her hands found Kelly's shoulders to begin kneading the muscles. Kelly looked up and smiled at her. Although their evening had gotten off to a rocky start, Shannon had eased quickly into the party mode and Kelly had enjoyed her company. Shannon didn't seem to notice anything between Kelly and Gina. She didn't know what to make of her encounter with Gina on the patio and could still imagine her kiss.

Gina stood up and headed for the kitchen calling over her shoulder, "Who needs another drink?"

"Not me." Tasha swirled pink liquid in her glass and swayed in time to the music from her position on the other end of the couch. An Indigo Girls song was playing and Tasha sang along, slightly off tune. "La la la, shame on you . . ."

Beth watched her, grinning. "You know, Tasha, we can go dancing if you want."

"No. Shannon and I have to be at the base early tomorrow," Tasha replied. After a moment of thought, she added, "I'm waiting for Kelly and Shannon to show us how to wrestle. Shannon mentioned something about a demo tonight."

Shannon grabbed Kelly's shoulders and hugged her body in a tight lock. "Okay, I win. There's your demo."

"Hold on a minute. I have to see this wrestling match." Gina poked her head out of the kitchen with a bottle opener and Corona in hand.

Shannon looked over her shoulder at Gina. "No way. We're not wrestling. You'll start placing bets against me."

"Good idea. Ten to one, Kelly wins. Anyone want to take me up on the offer?" Gina asked.

Gina's interest in the wrestling match made Kelly smile. She wanted to be alone with her so she could ask if there really was something to their kiss on the patio. *Or was Gina playing her?* She longed to kiss her again but reminded herself that she was here with Shannon. Kelly was sure that Gina was flirting with her.

"Come on, let's see a real fight," Beth taunted. "Shannon, I thought you were the tough army chick. You're not afraid of your girlfriend, are you?"

Shannon held up her middle finger without moving from the

sofa. "I just finished my fourth beer. The thought of wrestling makes me nauseous. Besides, she has a damn black belt."

"No way. Really?" Gina asked with disbelief.

Shannon nodded. "Yeah. I'd like to see you wrestle her. She's strong as hell."

Gina's eyes flashed at Kelly. She smiled but didn't say anything.

Kelly looked away quickly. "No, I'm not any good." Kelly added, "But I might have a chance with women who are drunk and easy."

Beth and Tasha laughed as Shannon shook her finger at Kelly. "I knew I was going to be in trouble the first time you flirted with me at the softball field."

"Well, I think it's about time Shannon has some girl who can keep her in line." Gina added, "Too bad the army didn't make you tougher."

Shannon shook her head. She moved off the couch and stretched out on her belly on the floor next to Kelly.

"I'll take a rain check," Kelly said, leaning down to kiss Shannon's cheek. Shannon smiled and rolled over. She reached up and pulled Kelly close to kiss her lips.

A whistle burned through the air and Kelly looked over at the couch where Gina, Beth and Tasha all sat staring.

"Did you gals want some privacy? Because, we can leave anytime . . ." Gina shook her head with mock disapproval. Kelly looked at Gina, unable to resist appreciating the woman's appeal as she relaxed in her home. Her long brown hair was pulled back in the usual ponytail and her loose shirt and baggy jeans didn't hide her perfect figure.

"You know, when I first met you guys I would never have thought you'd be making out on someone else's family room floor," Tasha teased.

"Yeah, you never know what to expect with women," Shannon responded.

Gina caught Kelly staring at her and shook her head. She didn't look away until Kelly finally glanced at Shannon. Fortunately, Shannon did not notice the exchange. Kelly slid off of Shannon, her head filled with images of Gina slipping off her shirt. Kelly shook her head to stop the thoughts.

Glancing down at her watch, she stood up and held out her hand to help Shannon get off of the floor. "It's after one."

"Really?" Shannon asked. "How'd it get so late? Tasha, we have drill in less than five hours. We have to go."

Shannon grabbed Kelly's hands and stood up slowly. Kelly wondered if she could keep dating Shannon and also sleep with Gina. Even as she thought this, she told herself it was a crazy idea. Nothing could happen between her and Gina while Shannon was still in the picture. But maybe Shannon shouldn't be in the picture. She'd waited three days to return Kelly's phone call that week and her hot-and-cold emotions were annoying. They'd only dated for a few weeks and she wasn't committed. Yet something held her back from breaking up with Shannon. She was still attracted to her. But the more she flirted with Gina, the harder it was to ignore that attraction as well.

After saying good-bye to the rest of the party, Kelly drove to Shannon's house. She parked the car and waited for Shannon to climb out of the passenger seat.

"Aren't you coming in?" Shannon asked.

"No, I think I better go home." Kelly faked a yawn.

"Why?"

"I want to sleep in and you have to go play army early tomorrow. I don't want to wake up at five a.m." Was that the real reason she didn't want to spend the night? She still couldn't decide if she liked Shannon enough to continue dating her.

"Okay, whatever." Shannon shrugged. She didn't seem to believe this excuse. "Can you come visit me at the barracks tomorrow night? I'm stuck there all weekend."

"Maybe." Kelly felt uncomfortable meeting her at the army base. It didn't seem like a good idea for Shannon to be seen with another woman in her barracks. She didn't want to jeopardize Shannon's position on the base.

"Just for a little while—stop by to visit me in my prison cell."

"I don't want to get you in trouble." Kelly shook her head.

"Don't worry. I'm used to being careful about the lesbian thing." She kissed Kelly lightly. "I'll call you tomorrow."

On the drive home, Kelly's thoughts drifted from Shannon to Gina. Shannon had seemed cool and detached even while kissing Kelly good night. There was no desire in her eyes. Yet every look from Gina made Kelly's body burn. She pictured Gina relaxing in her family room, and remembered the look they'd shared. It was hard to believe that Gina was a police officer when she relaxed at home with her friends. She didn't fit the tough image.

Kelly glanced at the clock. She had left Gina's house twenty minutes ago with Shannon. Shannon was probably already climbing into bed and would be in her army uniform in less than five hours . . . What about Gina—would she be awake? Kelly knew she should go home to sleep, but she wasn't tired. She turned into the left lane and made a U-turn at the next intersection. Would Gina want to see her? Would she tell Shannon?

After knocking on the front door, she waited on the dark porch and stared at the glowing second hand on her watch while fighting the urge to run back to her car. *What the hell am I doing?* The second hand circled the face of her watch once. She knew that coming back to Gina's house tonight might destroy any hope for a relationship with Shannon. *Do I care?* She realized the answer was probably no. Probably. Another minute passed. Kelly stepped off the front step and headed back toward her Volkswagen. The porch light flickered on and the corner of the front window drape raised up an inch. Gina was checking to see who had knocked.

Finally, the door opened. Gina's arms were crossed and she stared at Kelly. The thin blue fabric of her pajamas outlined the full curves

115

of her body. Gina was in perfect shape. Her dark hair was finally loose from the ponytail and fell just below her shoulders to frame the flawless lines of her face. "Why are you here?"

"Can I come in to talk?" Kelly asked.

"I don't think that would be a good idea. No."

Kelly stepped up to the front door, closing the distance between them. "What if we don't talk?"

"You're crazy, chica."

"I know, but I can't stop thinking about you. Have you ever had sex with no strings attached?"

"No. Sex without strings doesn't exist," Gina replied, shaking her head.

"Okay, would you agree to a one-night stand—then we won't touch again after this one time?"

Gina's eyebrows arched. "You just want to get it out of your system?"

"No, but I'm willing to take what I can get." She was worried that her feelings were stronger than an attraction that dissipates after one night. But she wanted at least one night with Gina. She wanted to feel Gina move under her hands. They stared at each other silently. Kelly's body begged to reach out to caress Gina's smooth skin.

Gina sighed. "Come in, I'm freezing in these pajamas." She pushed the screen door open and waited for Kelly to enter. They eyed each other silently as the door lock slid into place. Finally Gina shook her head. "Kelly, I'm Shannon's best friend. What are you thinking?"

"I don't know." She reached forward and tentatively traced her fingertips over Gina's hips. Gina glanced down at Kelly's hands but didn't move. Kelly stepped closer and Gina backed away.

She shook her head. "Shannon was right, you are trouble."

"No I'm not. I'm not usually like this. I mean, I don't just show up on women's doorsteps in the middle of the night." Kelly laughed nervously. "But there's something about you that I can't get out of my head. Every time you look at me, I want you to touch me." Kelly

116

knew she was crossing the line and wasn't sure how Gina would respond. Maybe she was crazy for even coming back to her house tonight, but she didn't want to go home now.

"I can't do that. You're dating Shannon."

"We can do whatever we want." Kelly pulled on the string that held up Gina's pajama pants. "What would you like to do if no one had any rules? We can talk for a while and then make out . . . Or just skip the talking and spend more time taking off our clothes."

Gina leaned toward Kelly. Their lips brushed lightly and then parted. Her hand slipped behind Kelly's head. Gina pulled her forward into another kiss. She pressed her lips against Kelly's and slipped her tongue inside. After a moment she released her hold and stepped back.

"You're persuasive." Gina smiled. "Do you always cause this much trouble with women?"

"Well, I'm still learning."

Gina reached out to grasp Kelly's hand. She traced her fingertip over the lines on Kelly's palm. "I haven't been able to think straight since I left you at the bar last weekend."

"Why were you trying to think straight?" Kelly teased.

"I don't know." Gina dropped Kelly's hand and shook her head. "I can't believe you're here. You've got have a lot of nerve to come back. Is that a black-belt thing? Do you really have a black belt?"

"I left it at home." Kelly grinned.

"Too bad. I bet it looks sexy on you." Gina caressed her cheek.

The two women stared at each other. Kelly's arms slipped around Gina's waist and she pulled her into a kiss. She pulled back and eyed Gina sheepishly. "I didn't think it would be this easy to break the rules with a cop."

"Well, I'm going to tell your girlfriend."

"We haven't been dating for that long. She's not my girlfriend yet."

"She definitely won't be after . . ." Gina's voice trailed off as she slipped her hand under Kelly's shirt to caress her breasts. They

117

kissed again and Kelly flicked her tongue inside Gina's mouth. Gina pushed away from her and continued, "After I tell her how you seduced me."

"Is that a challenge?" Kelly asked.

Gina didn't answer. She pulled Kelly down the hallway, heading toward the staircase that led up to the bedroom. After passing through the family room, Kelly pushed her against the wall. She ran her fingers through Gina's hair as she kissed her, whispering, "I want you now."

Gina responded with obvious desire. She slipped out of Kelly's hold on the wall and started to climb the stairs leading up to the bedroom. Kelly grabbed Gina's hand, stopping her on the first step. They kissed again.

Gina squinted at Kelly. "I still don't know why you came back tonight. Just for sex?"

"I just wasn't ready to go to sleep," Kelly replied simply. They both knew the real answer was too complicated. Their bodies moved together again. Gina held the railing as she waited on the first step. After pulling off Gina's soft cotton shirt, she gently pushed her against the wall of the stairway. The railing was against Gina's lower back and her hands clutched it as Kelly kissed her. Kelly moved down Gina's body, kissing her breasts and below her belly button, and then pressing her head between Gina's legs as she pulled off the blue cotton pants. She kneeled on the first step, caressing Gina's smooth skin. Gina murmured softly and Kelly glanced up at her face. Was she moving too fast?

With her back pushed against the wall, Gina spread her legs and pulled Kelly's head toward her. Kelly licked the wetness between her thighs and thrust her tongue inside, searching until she found the swollen clit.

Gina gently pushed Kelly away. "Damn, chica." Gina moaned softly as Kelly kissed between her legs. Gina cupped Kelly's chin and looked down at her. "You know, I thought you were just teasing me tonight. We're seriously getting into trouble now."

"Are you telling me to stop?" Kelly asked. She hoped Gina's answer would be no. All she could think of was Gina's body. She wanted Gina to come with her touch.

"No. But you are not going to do this just once. This is not a one-night-stand offer. Come up here for a minute."

Kelly stood up and kissed Gina's lips. She massaged Gina's back and then moved lower to stroke her thighs. "Will you really tell Shannon that I came here tonight?"

"That depends . . . I want to feel your hand inside me when you lick. We'll see how good this goes."

"If you promise to keep both of your hands on that railing."

"Hmm . . . Too bad I don't have my handcuffs."

Kelly kissed Gina's nipples, sucking on the tips and massaging her breasts with both hands.

Gina interrupted her, easing Kelly's chin away from her chest. "So, babe, what's your sign? Can I get your phone number?"

Kelly shook her head and smiled. "Careful, my girlfriend is a tough army chick."

"Don't worry. I could take her on anytime."

"Okay, no more talking," Kelly said. "I'm getting distracted." She grabbed Gina's nipple with her lips. This time she bit lightly and Gina grabbed her shoulders, moaning softly. Letting the nipple slip out of her mouth, Kelly glanced up. Gina's eyes were closed and she gripped the railing. Kelly stood up and pressed her hips against Gina's. She loved the feel of their breasts pressed together. Then she pressed Gina back on the wall and stroked her hand between Gina's legs. She moved faster, feeling her own body burn with desire as they met each other. Kelly slipped first one finger, then two, then three in and out of Gina as they rhythmically pulsed against each other. Gina's hands pressed down on Kelly's shoulders. She knew Gina wanted her to move lower and lick her again, but she ignored the suggestion.

"Get down on your knees." Gina's voice was quiet but commanding as she kissed Kelly's neck. "And don't pull out those fingers."

Kelly dropped to her knees and kissed the soft skin between her legs. With one hand still between Gina's legs, she parted the folds and licked the wet clit. Gina gripped Kelly's shoulders, and pushed her hips forward.

Kelly grabbed Gina's hand and pushed it back toward the railing. "You don't play by the rules."

Gina laughed. "Neither do you. Keep going, chica." She let go of the railing and clutched Kelly's head as she pushed forward with more force. Kelly pressed her tongue inside as her fingers slipped in and out, harder and harder. Gina moaned as Kelly sucked the wet folds into her mouth. Her tongue found the swollen clit again and she continued sucking. Her hand moved faster, pressing her fingers inside rhythmically.

Pushing her hips forward once more, Gina opened her legs wider and grabbed Kelly's hair. Gina moaned with building anticipation as Kelly moved inside her. Her nails dug into Kelly's shoulders as she started to climax. Then, just as she came, her muscles quivering, she pushed Kelly away and sank down on the steps, hugging her knees to her chest.

Kelly sat down next to her and wrapped her arms around Gina's trembling body. Gina's eyes watered. Gradually, she stopped shaking. She brushed the tears off her face with the back of her hand. Kelly released her hold and Gina stood up quickly. She climbed the stairs up to her bedroom without saying a word. Kelly sat on the stairs, still not quite sure if she could believe what had just occurred.

A moment later, she heard the sound of water in the shower. She climbed the stairs and pushed open the bathroom door. Water pelted down on Gina's body, filling the tub. Kelly stepped through the shower curtain. She carefully avoided any contact now. Gina wouldn't meet her gaze. The water ran down their bodies, streaming off skin and dancing over the surface in rivulets.

Finally Gina looked at her. Gina's hair was drenched and her skin glistened. "Will you sleep with me tonight?"

"I don't want to be anywhere else," Kelly replied.

"We need to talk about this later."

"Maybe." She leaned forward and kissed her.

"You can't fuck with me too much. I'll fall for you." Gina's words were clipped, as though she were holding back another flood of emotion.

Kelly wondered where the tears had come from. She knew she wanted more than sex with Gina but was afraid Gina might not be ready for anything more. Gina had mentioned she was still in love with Vicky. Was this true or did she just miss having a lover?

Gina reached out to caress Kelly's cheek. Kelly breathed out slowly. She could think tomorrow. She held Gina's hand and kissed her fingertips. She wanted to hold Gina all night. Later she would decide if this was a mistake. "We'll talk later," Kelly agreed.

"I just look at you and want you again, right now. But this time, I get to have my hands on you." Gina lightly traced her fingertips against Kelly's body. She moved forward and gripped Kelly between the legs. Kelly gasped as a spasm raced from her clit throughout her body. Gina let go instantly and smiled. "Yeah, I know what you want . . . But you have to wait until we get out of the shower and I have you pinned on my bed." She rubbed her hand across Kelly's breasts and down to her legs. "I like having someone like you for competition. Let's see if I can improve on your act."

121

Chapter 11

049451

The next evening Kelly drove to San Francisco to meet Shannon at her base. She hadn't brought a map and got lost following Shannon's directions. After several wrong turns and two detours, she nearly decided to drive back to Ashton. She had only planned to spend a few hours on the base with Shannon and wasn't sure she really wanted to spend time with her tonight at all. Just as she decided to turn around, she spotted the soldiers' housing barracks and one of the base entry gates. There was no guard at the checkpoint and the gate was open, but a sign warning against unauthorized entry was posted with a picture of a red gun target. She'd never been on a military base and had expected at least a guard at all of the gates, especially after 9/11. Maybe they didn't guard the housing barracks as strictly as the other areas of the base, she decided. No one appeared to stop her and no alarm sounded as she drove past the checkpoint.

Kelly approached the barracks and squinted to read the numbers under the flickering porch lights. Buildings that faced the coast were in a continuous need of fresh paint. The white paint identifying the number of each barrack had flaked off several buildings, suggesting that the war was keeping the army too busy to paint, and apparently too busy to guard the gates on the base. She found the building mark that looked most like a "3a" and parked near the entrance.

Kelly was about to knock when the door swung out at her. Bright red hair and a dark green uniform burst out of the building. Kelly quickly jumped off the front step as the girl in uniform rushed by her.

"Oh, gee, I'm so sorry. I've almost knocked us both over!" The redhead grinned. Her accent was thick from what sounded like a home in Minnesota. She seemed completely unsuited for the harsh fabric of a masculine uniform. "Bet you're here to see Shannon, right?" Without waiting for a response she continued, "I'm her roommate. She's been waiting for you. Room sixteen. Go on up the stairs and we're on your right. Have a good visit."

"Thanks."

"No bother at all. Have a good time with the boys tonight. Wish I could go along, but I'm underage. Oh, remind Shannon about the midnight curfew. She doesn't pay much mind to the rules. But I heard they're patrolling tonight. Well, gotta go! There's a movie playing at the Recreation Hall—entertainment for all of us in the underage crowd. It was so nice to meet you." She waved and then turned down the pathway. Her red curls bounced behind her as she crossed the parking lot and skipped down the street.

Kelly climbed the stairs, hoping that she wouldn't bump into anyone else. Shannon had insisted that it was perfectly normal for visitors to stop at the barracks and that no one would notice but Kelly was still cautious. She found the door to room sixteen ajar and spotted Shannon sitting on one of the two metal beds in the room. Her eyes were focused on a paperback that rested on her knees.

During the drive to the base, she debated admitting to Shannon that she had slept with Gina. Kelly had left Gina's bed sometime after ten a.m. and she could still feel those smooth hands caressing her body. Now, as she stared at Shannon, she felt overwhelmed by a desire to apologize for everything that had happened last night.

Sex with Gina was unbelievable. Kelly had come almost as soon as Gina's tongue touched her. They spent the hours tangling the sheets around their legs and trading massages. The sun rose before Kelly or Gina was ready to slow down long enough to sleep.

As she watched Shannon read, Kelly tried to make up her mind on who she wanted to date. She'd been with Shannon for a few weeks but there was still a distance between them. Would her relationship with Shannon develop into something serious if she gave it more time?

On the other hand, she'd felt comfortable with Gina the first night she met her. Unfortunately, Gina had admitted last week that she was in love with Vicky and said she couldn't handle anything beyond a "casual sex" relationship. Ironically, for the first time in her life Kelly wanted more than casual sex. Maybe she could juggle both women temporarily. The entertainment of sleeping with two women would keep her out of other trouble.

Shannon smiled and closed the book as Kelly entered the room. "You found me! Wait, who let you inside?"

"I don't know. Some redhead who claimed to be your roommate."

"Leanne. Perfect—I was worried that you'd knock and one of the guys from the first floor would harass you. They might start asking questions, you know . . . Leanne is great."

"She looks a little out of place in army greens."

"Yeah, she's from the Midwest and doesn't quite feel at home in the military, let alone California. But I think she's the best roommate I could have on this base. She's young, innocent, keeps me laughing, and she's completely trustworthy. Tasha and I were going to be roommates, but for some reason they placed us in different barracks after our first weekend drill." Shannon grinned and then added in a whisper, "I think the sergeant realized it'd be a bad idea to put two lesbians in the same bunk space." Shannon tossed the book onto her nightstand and stood up. "I'm glad you came. Let's get out of here. The guys at Sweet Stream will already be on their second round by the time we get there."

Kelly was reluctant to take Shannon off the base after Leanne's warning. "Are you sure you want to leave? Your roommate mentioned something about an early curfew."

"I'm not worried about the curfew. They don't really enforce it. Beth already came to pick up Tasha, and some other guys from the base were heading to Ashton as well. I gotta get off base for a little while anyway. No one will notice what time we get back. And my Jeep will still be parked here."

Kelly shook her head. She knew that Shannon had asked her to meet her at the base so that she could leave her Jeep here. That way, no one would suspect she'd left. "But if you get caught—"

"Relax, I'll be fine. Don't worry about it. It's my ass on the line and I know what I'm doing. Come on, let's go."

Shannon recounted her day on the base while Kelly drove to Ashton in silence.

"You know, I really wouldn't mind doing this army thing if we were actually doing something useful. I spent this morning setting up a big military communication outpost up in the hills behind our base. Then I spent the afternoon disassembling the site. What a waste of time."

Kelly nodded and Shannon continued. She described details of organizing the communication outpost and the desert survival training. Kelly tried to concentrate on Shannon's story. Her thoughts kept returning to Gina. She was feeling torn between hoping that Gina would stay home tonight and desperately wanting to see her at the bar. If Gina was not at the bar, Kelly would try and convince Shannon to leave early. She had no desire to stand around in a straight bar watching Shannon's friends get plastered.

Shannon touched Kelly's elbow as soon as they parked behind the bar. "Are you okay tonight?"

"I'm fine."

"Look, I know you haven't really gotten to know my friends, but I think you really will like them, eventually. Tasha and Beth think you're great. And I can tell Gina likes you."

Kelly looked out the window. She didn't want Shannon to read any emotion on her face. Gina had promised not to tell anyone about their night together—as long as Kelly promised to drop by her house again.

"Don't worry," she said. "I like your friends. I'm just a little shy in big crowds."

Shannon smiled. "You don't seem like the shy type." She pushed the car door open and stared at Kelly. Kelly had not pulled the key out of the ignition yet and was not ready to face the scene at the bar. Shannon tapped her fingers on the window. "Well, are you coming?"

The group of friends had gathered around the two pool tables in the back of the bar. Kelly recognized the same faces from the last bar scene. She found a stool and sat down next to one of the guys playing pool. Kelly had forgotten his name, although they had been introduced twice. She carefully avoided eye contact with Gina, who stood by the bartender, waiting for her drink. Tasha and Beth were also waiting at the bar. On Gina's other side was an older woman who had been at the party last night. Kelly had been introduced to the woman but she wasn't sure about her name. Maybe it was Carol, she thought. Carol had left the party early, complaining about a headache. She was several inches shorter than Gina and had pale skin and a voluptuous figure. Carol swayed to the chords of a country song that played on the old jukebox behind the pool tables.

Kelly felt a ping of jealousy as Gina reached out to caress Carol's cheek. Gina paid the bartender, then handed Carol a shot glass and a beer. They toasted and downed the shots. Carol grimaced when the alcohol coated her throat and Gina laughed at her expression.

Kelly turned her attention to the pool table. She didn't want to watch Gina flirt. The men playing pool were happy to have an audience for their game. They tried to entertain her with flashy pool moves and bad jokes. As a new pool game began, Shannon sat down next to Kelly.

A few of the guys playing pool were from Shannon's base. They were arguing about whether their reserve unit would be called to active duty. The local news reported on the military's progress in Iraq and there was no end in sight to the U.S. presence there. Reinforcements were still being shipped out every day. Shannon joined in the debate, confident that their reserve unit would stay in California.

"I'm going to the restroom," Kelly said quietly. "I'll be back in a minute." Shannon nodded, too interested in the debate to pay attention to Kelly.

As Kelly walked past the other pool table, Tasha stuck out her hand and smiled. "Hey, stranger! You didn't say hello when you came in tonight. What's wrong?"

Kelly shook Tasha's hand and returned the smile. "I'm sorry. Guess I wasn't paying attention. It's good to see you here." Tasha was an easy person to like. Her smile was infectious and she seemed to genuinely care that Kelly felt included in the group. Kelly didn't understand why Tasha had joined the military. She seemed better suited to playing a game of soccer than cleaning a gun.

"Do you want to play the next round? Beth, Gina and I have dibs on the next open table. But Gina doesn't have a partner. I don't think Shannon will mind if you abandon her to play with us. She's too engrossed in army talk. And you'd think they'd get tired of the same topic, but they never do . . ." Tasha laughed.

"Sure, I'll play. But I'm not very good," Kelly replied. She wondered if Gina would still want to play when Tasha told her who her partner would be.

"Don't worry—Gina is a pool shark. She can beat Beth and me single-handedly. But I'd love to have your company at the table. Beth and Gina get a little competitive if there aren't buffers between them."

"Gina is a pool shark? She won't want me on her team then. I'm really bad—I sink the cue ball all the time. And I think she may already have someone in mind for her partner." Kelly pointed to the corner of the bar by the jukebox where Gina sat with Carol.

"I just asked Gina to play and she said she wouldn't play unless I asked you to join the game. I think Carol is leaving soon."

"Hmm, maybe . . ."

"Well, your other option is to go listen to the war debate for the rest of the night."

"Okay. You convinced me."

Tasha nodded. "Good. I'm guessing we'll have a table soon." She turned to face the pool table and the current four players. In a louder voice she added, "But it might be a while before these pool sharks finish. The boys are more interested in bragging about their cars than sinking the balls."

The pool players ignored her hint. The next player chalked his stick and prepared to shoot, exaggerating each movement. He had a pockmarked face from recent pimples and Kelly guessed that he had stolen someone's license to get in the bar tonight. There was no way he was twenty-one.

"We're just taking our time so you gals can watch and learn, seeing as how you all don't get much experience holding a stick . . ." He had a Southern accent. After this remark, the young man winked at Tasha and aimed his next shot. "It's all about aim—"

"Buck, you're not one to talk about aiming. I saw you out at the shooting range this morning. Your drill leader kept shaking his head after your gun fired. Were you aware that bullets are supposed to hit that target?" Tasha shook her head. "And I know a thing or two about sticks that would make you blush."

One of the other guys at the table whistled and smacked his hand against Buck's shoulder. "Watch your step with the ladies around here, Buck. You're not in Texas no more."

The other players laughed at the exchange. Cowed into silence, Buck hit the cue ball without looking over at Tasha. The ball ricocheted off the corner rail and struck the striped thirteen ball with a resounding crack. The ball dropped into the hole and Buck smiled. "All about aim and luck."

As Buck positioned for his next shot, Kelly tapped Tasha's shoulder. "I'll be back in a few minutes."

"Take your time. Buck will get nervous with all of our attention. He's not used to girls eyeing his stick."

"Go to hell, Tasha," Buck said as his stick hit the cue ball.

"I'll see you there, Buck," Tasha returned evenly.

Buck would get used to the culture in San Francisco soon, Kelly thought with a smile. She nodded to Tasha and headed toward the bathroom. Someone had switched off the light in the back and the long hallway to the restroom was dark. As she searched the wall for the light switch, her fingers caught a cobweb. A metallic click caught her attention and her heart stalled while she tried to localize the sound. She shook the web off her hands and shivered as a chill raced down her spine. Kelly closed her eyes and breathed out slowly. She opened her eyes and scanned the hallway. A fluorescent green exit sign shone at the far end of the hall and she could make out two glowing stickers on the restroom doors.

Shaking her head, Kelly abandoned the search for the light switch and headed toward the glowing sticker on the nearest door. Just as she pushed on the door, a hand brushed over her shoulder and clamped over her mouth. Kelly spun to the side and trapped the man's arm in an elbow lock. She pressed on the back of his hand, separating the knuckle joints as she squeezed between the bones. Within seconds, the spasm of pain from the joint manipulation forced him down to his knees. She pushed down harder, silently threatening to dislocate his elbow, and he gasped in pain. She dropped his hand and lunged away from him, waiting for his next move. He squatted on the ground and rubbed his elbow, then started to chuckle. Her eyes focused and Kelly suddenly recognized Rick. She couldn't understand why Rick had tried to grab her or why he was at the bar at all. He stood up slowly, pointed once at her and then at the exit sign. Kelly followed obediently down the hallway.

"What the hell were you thinking?" Rick asked as they stepped out of the bar. He jammed the door with a matchbox to keep it from locking.

"I'm sorry. I just reacted to your hand. It was dark and I didn't see who had grabbed me. Why didn't you say something?"

"I wanted to see what you would do."

"Then why are you mad? I took you down to the ground and had control. You were crying out in pain from a little elbow twist. I did exactly what I've been trained to do."

"Who trained you to let go? After your attacker fell to the ground, you had the elbow locked and the wrist pushed back to the forearm. God, excruciating pain, beautiful really . . . Then you just dropped the hand without even asking me why I grabbed you." Rick slid his hand inside his jacket and in the next moment had the barrel of a handgun pointed at Kelly's chest. "Were you waiting for me to pull out a gun?"

Kelly swallowed hard and looked directly into Rick's eyes. She could feel the cold metal press through her thin shirt. She opened her mouth to explain and in the same moment shoved Rick's hand to the left as she lunged to the right. Her finger slipped between the trigger and his finger so quickly that he didn't have time to pull away. Suddenly she was holding the gun in her hand and pointing the barrel at Rick.

"Damn, woman. Not bad."

"I hate guns." She checked the safety before palming the weapon back to Rick. "I shot my dad with a BB gun when I was ten. He still has a scar on his shin. After that experience, I forgot how to shoot."

"You'll remember."

Kelly shook her head. "I don't want to."

Rick shrugged and returned the gun to his holster. "If you work for me, knowing how to handle a gun will be essential."

"What does a gun have to do with the mail delivery service?"

"Pretty soon there will be more to your job than delivering packages. So, what do you know about Private Wallace?"

"Private Wallace? Doesn't sound familiar . . ." The name didn't ring any bells. "But I don't know the first name of half the people in here tonight, let alone last names."

"You were sitting by her at the pool table. You picked her up at the base tonight."

"Oh, Shannon?" Kelly realized that she had never thought to ask Shannon her last name.

Rick nodded. "Yes, Shannon Wallace. How do you know her?"

"She's just a friend. I don't really know much about her."

"She's your date and that's all you know?" Rick asked.

Kelly wondered how he knew that Shannon was her date. Had he been watching them before tonight? "She's in the army—the reserves. But I guess you know that." There wasn't any reason to give Rick too much information, she thought. "I met her at a softball game two weeks ago here in Ashton. That's about all I know."

Rick nodded. "And she works in the shoe department at Ashton Sports. I want you to find out more details about her past. Start asking about her work in the army and her experiences during her training. You know her friends. Ask them who Shannon knows, or knew, at the last base where she was stationed. Try and get as much information out of her without letting her suspect that you are prying."

"So, why am I prying?"

"We don't have time to talk about everything now. You'll know more soon." He smiled with tight lips. "By the way, did you notice any cars following you when you left the base tonight?"

Kelly shook her head. "I wasn't paying attention."

"You need to start paying attention."

Kelly remembered giving the same advice to Colin before taking away his purple belt. Rick's criticism stung. He explained that he had followed her for the past three hours and detailed everything that she had done since leaving the karate dojo. After he finished his speech, he suggested she go back to the bar. He opened the back door of the bar, snatching his matchbox before it hit the ground and handed her a business card. "Good luck in there. And don't be late to this."

Reluctantly, Kelly took the business card. The door slammed behind her as she stepped past the threshold of the dark hallway. Dance music coupled with the clash of pool balls and loud voices formed a sharp contrast to the quiet air outside the bar. Kelly entered the restroom and squinted in the bright fluorescent lights. Goose bumps crawled up her skin as she read the first line on the business card Rick had given her. "McMahon, Kinley and Associates." She recognized the card immediately. Nora Kinley, the lawyer at the train station, had shown her the same card. She confirmed the address of the law firm and then flipped over the card. Rick had scribbled on the back, "Lawyer wants meeting Monday at 20:00. Pictures at train stations are important. Ask around for details."

Now she had to find out if Shannon or her friends would talk. As soon as she'd seen the photo from Nora Kinley's briefcase, she knew the army officer was somehow important. But why did Nora Kinley want a meeting with her? She wondered what information she could glean about Hannah from the crowd at the bar tonight. Kelly contemplated Rick's connection to the lawyer. Did this have anything to do with the envelopes that she had delivered?

Kelly glanced at the mirror above the sink. Her blue eyes were unflinching, despite the unsettling meeting with Rick. The image of his gun was frozen in her mind. She shivered at the memory of the metal pressing against her chest. The bullet had waited in the barrel only inches away from her lungs. Rick had said that he followed her car to the army base and waited outside the gates at a nearby gas station. Then she led him to the bar. It was unnerving to think that someone could be watching her every move. Had anyone else seen her car on the base?

Under no circumstances, Rick ordered, could Kelly drive back to the base tonight. He didn't offer any suggestions as to how to get Shannon back. He only claimed it was imperative that she was not seen with Shannon. Someone may have already noted her car, checked her license plates and identified who she had taken off the base. Rick confirmed that there were cameras on all of the barracks as well as the gates. Why was Shannon Wallace important to Rick? Unfortunately, he had not shared any details.

Kelly glanced at her wristwatch. Twenty minutes had passed, but she doubted if any of Shannon's friends would notice how long she had been missing from the pool table. Shannon was probably still engrossed in the discussion about the war. Beth and Tasha had each other to concentrate on, and Gina was entertained with Carol. As Kelly washed her hands, Beth came in. She nodded a greeting to Kelly.

"Hey, Kelly. Fancy meeting you here." Beth's tone was friendly. "I hear my girlfriend convinced you to play a game of pool. We're about to start. By the way, how the hell did you convince Shannon to come out and party with us tonight?"

Beth entered a stall. Kelly cupped her hands under the faucet as warm water filled her palms. She splashed the water on her face. Water dripped off the tip of her nose as she stared at the reflection in the mirror.

"She didn't need any convincing," Kelly replied.

"You know, I probably shouldn't say anything, but she's had some problems with the army."

"What do you mean?"

"Well, for the past few months she's been ultra-paranoid about the lesbian issue and all of the military rules." Beth paused. "It's good to see her relaxing a little."

"Why was she paranoid?" Kelly asked.

"Maybe *paranoid* isn't the right word. She had some reason to be cautious. Her ex-girlfriend was an army officer who got kicked out because she's a lesbian. I guess someone knew that they were dating and had pictures of them together. Ever since Hannah was dishonorably discharged, Shannon's anticipated getting kicked out as well. But they've ignored her, so far. I think she's finally starting to relax a little."

Kelly wondered if the distance Shannon placed between them

was because of Hannah. "Wow, I wonder why they didn't go after Shannon . . ."

"Tasha thinks that the army is more concerned with finding queers who are in the higher positions—you know, the officers get the dishonorable discharge rather than some peons in the reserves. It's not like a couple lesbians in the reserves are worth the effort to even investigate homosexual charges—think about the headline, 'Lesbians subvert our nation's Army one weekend each month.' Maybe we wouldn't have to wage any more wars." Beth laughed as she came over to the sink where Kelly still stood.

"If my girlfriend was dishonorably discharged because of our relationship, I'd be walking on eggshells for the next few years." Kelly shook her head. "I'm surprised Shannon isn't more worried. When did it happen?"

"I don't know exactly. Hannah was discharged about a month after she was caught with Shannon. The military did this investigation on Hannah and asked everyone who knew her if she was a 'mentally stable person.' According to Shannon, nobody said she was a lesbian at first. Then they got some testimony saying that Hannah had been seen with a female recruit. A picture of Hannah hugging a recruit surfaced. They kicked Hannah out immediately. Shannon was the one in the picture, but I guess that they couldn't identify her because the face in the photo was mostly hidden in shadows."

"They didn't investigate Shannon?" Kelly thought it was strange that Shannon had escaped unscathed even if she was a lower priority for those instigating Hannah's discharge.

"Well, they asked her if she had any contact with Hannah that was against conduct rules. From what I understand, officers aren't supposed to hang out with new recruits. They told Shannon that they weren't asking if she was a lesbian, but they did ask if she knew of anyone who was queer. Shannon told them that she didn't know anyone who was queer and didn't have any contact with Hannah that was against conduct rules. She claimed she wasn't the woman in the picture." Beth tugged on the paper towel dispenser, fighting to free the edge of the paper lodged in the reel. After a few seconds of frustration, she dried her hands on her jeans. "Anyway, they let her go. Just like that. You know, sometimes they just want to make an example."

"Shannon was lucky."

Beth nodded. "I don't think she should press her luck either. She doesn't act like Hannah's investigation was a big deal at all. I'm sure the army's got a long record on Shannon that they're waiting to pull if she steps on anyone's toes. Personally, I think the military only goes after queers if they piss somebody off." She opened the door and smiled at Kelly. "I'm just glad I'm not in the military—not that I'd last through boot camp! But I couldn't handle pretending to be straight again. I played that game for too many years. Anyway, ready to hit some pool balls?"

"I guess so. But I'm not very good at pool," Kelly admitted.

"Well, then, I'm glad you're not on my team. You can slow Gina's winning streak down a little."

Kelly smiled. "Gee, thanks. And I'm sure Gina will love having me as her partner," she finished sarcastically.

"Just watch how much love you feel. Shannon's got her eye on you and Gina."

Kelly swallowed hard. She wondered just how much Beth knew. "Shannon's caught up in the war debate. I think she'll ignore our pool game."

Beth and Kelly joined Tasha and Gina at the pool table. Gina kept strangely quiet throughout the game. Carol had left the bar and Kelly wondered if Gina was quiet because of this. Kelly tried to pull Gina into a conversation several times and then gave up the effort. She had other things on her mind. After the meeting with Rick, she realized she needed to find out more about Hannah. Shannon was caught up in a drinking game at the other end of the bar and ignored the pool players.

As Tasha chalked her stick, Kelly brought up the subject of Hannah's discharge. Tasha was happy to add details.

"Shannon and Hannah dated for six months. After the discharge,

Hannah moved to San Francisco to work for some queer political committee." Tasha paused and looked over at Shannon. She was too far away to hear their conversation. "I don't think she's talked to Shannon since. Maybe she's worried that Shannon would face a dishonorable discharge as well. Two months ago, Hannah had called to break off their relationship. Broke Shannon's heart. I think she'd still be with her if all this hadn't happened."

Beth interrupted, "Kelly, you're up." She whispered something in Tasha's ear.

Kelly considered Tasha's last comment. Ignored by Gina and knowing now that Shannon was still pining for Hannah, she felt acutely out of place in the bar. When the pool game ended, Kelly complained of a headache and hinted that she wanted to leave. Beth volunteered to drop Shannon off at the base along with Tasha. Following Rick's advice, she agreed to this plan and left the bar after a quick explanation to Shannon. She watched the rearview mirror as she drove out of the bar's parking lot. No cars trailed her Volkswagen.

A white Ford Escort was parked in Alex's driveway. There was a Grateful Dead sticker and a peace sticker on the bumper of the car. Kelly entered the house cautiously, hoping not to disturb Alex or his guest. A small purse was lying on the kitchen counter by the phone. She eyed the purse and considered investigating it. Alex would be pissed if he knew that she snooped but she wanted to watch out for her brother. Starr's ID, three credit cards and ten bucks were inside. She smiled. Starr was exactly what Alex needed to distract him from the breakup with Laura. Kelly sifted through the rest of the purse's contents. She found a plastic baggie half filled with pot, a lighter, lipstick, a pack of gum, a cell phone and a crumpled receipt. Kelly smoothed the receipt. Starr had bought pancake mix and eggs yesterday at six a.m. from a grocery store in San Francisco. She knew Starr lived in Ashton and wondered who she'd been with in the city at that time.

After reassembling Starr's purse Kelly glanced at the phone. She resisted the urge to call Gina and headed for the shower. Right now she needed to rehash the conversations she'd had at the bar to understand Hannah's role in her world. There were a few issues that still didn't make sense. She knew Hannah was the link between Shannon, Rick and Nora. But why was Rick involved at all? If Nora was Hannah's lawyer and this was a simple army discharge case, why was there a private investigator involved? And why did Rick want Kelly to investigate Shannon? She didn't mind delivering Rick's envelopes, but she wasn't comfortable spying on Shannon.

If there were as many lesbians in the military as Shannon claimed, why bother kicking out Hannah? She was just a drop in the bucket. And both Tasha and Shannon admitted that most queer people weren't discharged, even if they did little to hide their identity. Kelly figured that there had to be some other reason that Hannah was discharged. Maybe she had been too outspoken or the lesbian issue could be a cover for some other reason to get rid of her. Was she just an example for the rest of the soldiers? Maybe Monday night's meeting with the lawyer would answer some questions.

The phone rang once and Kelly ran to pick up the receiver. "Hello?" She had just stepped out of the shower and hoped the ringing would not wake Alex or Starr.

"Hey, chica."

Kelly smiled as she recognized Gina's low voice. "Hey, yourself. Do you know what time it is?"

"Yeah, I know what time it is. How's that headache?"

"Magically disappeared as soon as I left the bar," Kelly replied. "Why'd you ignore me tonight?"

"You're coming to my house, right?"

"Maybe. But you didn't answer my question. Why'd you ignore me?" Kelly tied her towel around her waist.

"I wasn't ignoring you. I was watching you all night. But I didn't want to get you in trouble."

"Yeah, I'm not buying that excuse." Kelly was annoyed that Gina could be completely detached at the bar and only want sex now. Yet maybe that was what she wanted also. "So how was Carol tonight?"

"She's nobody," Gina replied. "And don't even try to give me crap for hanging out with her. You're the one cheating on a girlfriend."

"Shannon's not my girlfriend. We've only been dating for a couple weeks," Kelly said defensively.

"Whatever. Lesbians are considered girlfriends after the second date. But I don't care what you call her. Anyway, Carol's married. Her husband would lay me out flat if anything happened between us." Gina added, "And I'm not interested in Carol."

"Why not? You don't seem to mind if the women you take to bed are single or not. As long as we're hot for you . . ."

Gina laughed. "Get over here. I want my hands on you if you're talking like that." Her authoritative tone was enticing.

A pager on the bedside table buzzed at five a.m. Gina crawled over Kelly to silence the noise.

"Oh, crap," Gina said after a quick glance at the pager screen.

"What's wrong?" Kelly rubbed her eyes and looked over at Gina. The sheets smelled of sex and she could still feel the pressure of Gina's hands between her legs.

"I know the number. If you recognize the page number, the message can't be good. Nobody accidentally dials a pager at five a.m." Gina picked up her phone and dialed.

Kelly closed her eyes and drifted back to sleep.

Gina nudged her shoulder. "Hey, there, sleeping beauty. Bad news."

"What's wrong?"

"That was Beth." Gina sat down on the bed and draped her arm around Kelly. Her naked body had perfect curves. Kelly reached out to trace the line from under her arm, past her breasts, along her ribs and down to her hips. Gina looked down and smiled at her. "You can't get me started now . . ."

"Why did Beth call?"

"She dropped Tasha and Shannon off at the base about an hour ago. They got out of the car and started walking to the barracks and Beth drove away, but I guess she didn't get very far. She said a military patrol car pulled her over before she passed the gates."

"Oh shit."

"Yeah. I didn't get many details. It sounds like she doesn't know if they even saw Tasha and Shannon get out of her car. Apparently the guy said he pulled her over because he suspected she was drunk. She said he grilled her about why she was on the base. Then I guess he let her go . . ."

"I wonder if Tasha and Shannon are okay."

"Beth's worried that they could get kicked out because of this—they were both drunk and out after the curfew. Ordinarily, they'd probably just get a slap on the back of the hand for those offenses. But they're lesbians. Beth's on her way here now."

"What?" Kelly pulled the covers up to her chin. "Why is she coming here?"

"She said she didn't want to stay alone at her house. She's really freaked out about the whole thing and wants to talk."

Kelly rolled onto her side and stared at the clock. It was a quarter after five. The doorbell rang and Kelly rolled onto her back again. "That's not really Beth already, is it? How close does she live?"

"She paged me from her cell phone. She was parked outside the house. She didn't want to just barge in unannounced."

"She knows you well. So, how often do you have late-night visitors?"

"I'm not answering that . . ." Gina smiled. "Better get dressed and figure out a good lie or an escape route now. Beth might not be able to keep this from your girlfriend."

Kelly shook her head. "She wouldn't tell Shannon, would she?"

"Of course she would—they've been friends since high school."

"I thought she was her ex." Kelly groaned softly as she realized she'd become part of their lesbians-stuck-in-suburbia sex ring.

"Yeah, that too. But we're all somebody's ex in this group. So,

139

what's the story we're telling Beth to explain why Shannon's girl-friend is at my house at five in the morning?"

"I'm a terrible liar."

"Well, it's a short drop if you climb out the window," Gina replied, pushing off the bed. She opened her closet door and pulled out a robe. "Just watch out for the rose bush."

Kelly shook her head. "Oh, hell no. It's too damn early to be crawling out of windows. Just don't bring her upstairs. I'm going back to sleep."

Gina laughed and pulled the covers over Kelly's head. "All right, I'll try and stop Beth from ripping off my clothes and seducing me on the staircase."

Kelly grabbed a pillow and threw it at Gina. She ducked to miss the pillow and smiled. Kelly immediately hurled another one at her. It hit her in the belly and she laughed and jumped on the bed to wrestle Kelly under the covers.

"Why are you throwing pillows at me? I can't help it if the women can't resist me . . ."

"You're such a player."

Gina smiled. "You're the one who knocked on my door." She stood up and headed to the bedroom door. "Hey, just in case, if I cough twice, she's on her way up here and you better be looking for a good hiding place."

Kelly sighed as Gina left. After a moment, the sound of Beth's voice drifted up the staircase. She lay in bed, fighting sleep and trying to discern the voices. The walls muffled the sounds. She finally wrapped the comforter around her shoulders and crept over to the bedroom door. Gina had left the door ajar and through the crack, Kelly could peer down into the family room. Beth and Gina were sitting on the sofa. Two cups of coffee were on the table in front of them. Their voices were perfectly clear.

Beth held her knees against her chest. She shivered once and then relaxed. "Gina, I'm scared as hell. What do you think will happen to them?"

.

"I don't know." After a moment of uneasy silence, Gina continued, "Do you think the guy pulled you over because he saw them get out of your car?"

Beth shook her head. "I don't know. He just said that he was pulling me over because he thought I was drunk."

"And you weren't speeding?"

"No."

"So, what did he say?" Gina took a sip of her coffee.

"He asked if I would agree to a Breathalyzer and the sobriety tests. You know, walk on the line, say the alphabet backwards and follow the light—he did all those damn things and I passed. I'd been drinking water for over two hours and I only had two beers."

"And after the tests?"

"After I passed the tests, he asked why I was on the base. I told him I was coming home from a party and got lost."

"And did it seem like he believed you?"

Beth shrugged. "No. I think the whole sobriety test was just an excuse to detain me on the base—maybe while they searched for Tasha and Shannon."

"But he let you go without any ticket?"

"Yeah. He asked me if I knew anyone on the base. I didn't really answer the question—I just started crying and repeating that I was lost. After I cried my eyes out, he finally just told me to go home. I asked him for directions back to the freeway, but I don't think he believed the story that I was lost." Beth shivered and reached for her coffee. She took one sip and shook her head as she replaced the cup on the table. "I'm just worried about what could happen if Tasha and Shannon got caught."

"I don't think that the MP would have let you go if he saw Tasha and Shannon get out of your car. I bet he didn't see them at all." Gina pulled a blanket off the chair by the couch and handed it to Beth. Beth placed the green wool over her lap and settled back against the sofa cushions.

"The guy had to have seen them. He pulled me over about a

block away from where I dropped them off—just outside the barracks. Someone must have seen them get out of the car. They were both drunk. Do you think they could be kicked out of the army if they were caught out after curfew and drunk?"

"No. Not if they were two straight girls. But it might look bad if two dykes come back to the base drunk and after curfew . . ."

"Shit, I don't even want to think about what would happen if they asked Tasha if she was a lesbian. I know she won't lie about it." Pulling the blanket up her neck, Beth squeezed her fists on the wool.

"Well, I don't think now is the time to kick out any soldiers. We're going to be in Iraq for a while. A minor curfew infraction will probably be ignored and they may not have even been seen. Maybe you distracted the MP."

"Maybe. But that's not the whole story." Beth sighed. She still shivered occasionally, despite the blanket. "Some car started following me after the patrol let me go. A black sedan stayed on my tail until I hit the freeway. After a few miles I thought I had lost it so I drove home. As soon as I parked, I spotted the same sedan turn down my street. I ran inside the lobby and just waited by the elevator. I didn't want anyone to follow me up to my apartment. The car was parked outside my building for a few minutes and then finally drove away. I didn't want to hang around and see if they were going to come back and bust into my apartment. Can someone get your address from your license plate number?"

Gina nodded. "And you probably gave the MP your driver's license. So, they already know who you are and where you live. When did the other car start following you?"

"I noticed it just after he let me go. There were no headlights behind me at first. But when I reached the first intersection on the main road, someone was tailing me. It's not like I'm going to pick up a stalker at four in the morning. I'm sure it was someone from the military. Damn it." Beth reached out from the blanket and grasped Gina's hand.

"It could be just some crazy guy with nothing better to do but stalk young women at four in the morning. Maybe the car wasn't from the military." Gina brushed a few stray hairs back into place behind Beth's ear. "I'm glad you didn't stay home alone though."

"Gina, don't put any more ideas in my head, okay? The last thing I need to think about right now is some crazy stalker." She shook her head and let go of Gina's hand. "I hope they won't do anything to Tasha or Shannon. Do you think they will? I feel responsible for asking Tasha to come out tonight. She doesn't like leaving the base on the weekends when she has drill . . ."

"You're not responsible for their choices. You didn't drag them off the base. And just because the MP saw your car doesn't mean they caught Tasha or Shannon."

"Yeah, I guess so. I just feel terrible. And the thing with the car following me home was just creepy."

Kelly shifted her position by the door and the floorboards creaked. Beth glanced up the staircase toward the bedroom. Kelly held her breath.

Beth shook her head. "God, now I'm hearing things. Carol didn't come over last night, did she?"

"Hell, no. She went home to her hubby after getting a good buzz."

She stood up and walked over to the front door to peer out the peephole. After a moment, she returned to the couch. "Gina, I'm starving. Do you have anything to eat?"

Gina nodded and got up to head toward the kitchen. "You're sure no one followed you here?"

Beth was silent for a moment, as if trying to recall her drive to Gina's house. Gina returned with a bag of chocolate chip cookies. Kelly heard her belly growl and realized she was suddenly starving. She enviously watched as Beth bit into her cookie.

"No, I don't think anyone followed me here. I'm pretty sure I would've noticed," Beth answered finally.

Right, Kelly thought. She stood up and went to the window. Lifting the corner of the drape, she surveyed the street below. Her

143

Volkswagen was parked one block away. Now she realized that she should have parked on a different street entirely. Fortunately Beth seemed too preoccupied to have noticed her car. Beth's silver Toyota was parked in Gina's driveway. A black sedan was parked at the corner of Gina's block. As she watched, the car pulled away from the curb and came down the street. She recognized Rick's face in the driver's window. He was alone.

Gina and Kelly made breakfast after Beth finally left. Gina relayed her conversation with Beth while layering salsa over scrambled eggs and fried potatoes. She was convinced that the military had been watching Shannon for the past few months. Shannon had told Gina that she had noticed suspicious cars parked outside her house and on a few occasions had been tailed around Ashton. Although Gina had warned Shannon to be careful and advised her not to hang out with anyone from her base, Shannon had ignored her. She was sure that they already had a case on Shannon and were just waiting for an excuse to discharge her.

Kelly wondered who else had been watching Shannon. Why was the military tracking her? Was she still in danger because of her connections with Hannah? She remembered seeing a black sedan parked outside of Shannon's house before and also at the movie rental store in town. She didn't think this had been Rick's car, but knew she hadn't been paying enough attention to details then. After breakfast, Kelly left Gina's place and went home to take a nap.

She woke that afternoon to the ringing of the phone. Someone left a message on her answering machine. As soon as she heard Beth's voice on the recording, she turned off the machine and called Shannon's house. Shannon wasn't home yet. She wondered how Beth had gotten her number and then remembered that Gina had given it to her that morning. She considered calling Gina but decided she needed a break from the lesbian drama.

Armed with a spackle spreader and sandpaper, she headed outside to scrape the peeling paint off Alex's picket fence. Alex had left a few cans of Alabaster white latex in the garage. She wanted to tackle the fence before facing the Daisy Yellow paint for the house. The painting project was something she could handle. Everything else was becoming too complicated.

By eleven that night, Kelly still hadn't heard from Shannon. She'd left three messages on Shannon's machine and finally decided to return Beth's call. Shannon could be in serious trouble if they had not released her from the base yet.

"Hi, Beth. I just got your message. I'm sorry to call so late." Beth's message had described her experience on the base with the MP and mentioned her concern that someone may have seen Shannon and Tasha get out of her car.

"Don't worry about the time. I'm glad you called. Have you heard from Shannon?"

"No," Kelly replied. "I was hoping you had heard from Tasha."

"Damn it. No, I haven't heard anything yet."

"When are they usually released from their weekend duties? Five, right?"

"Yeah, five p.m. God, it's almost eleven, isn't it?" Beth's voice was shaking.

Kelly confirmed the time. "Listen, I'll call as soon as I hear anything."

"Thanks." Beth sighed. "Gina thinks I'm crazy, but I have this awful feeling that they're going to get kicked out because of this. The whole thing really scared me."

"Hey, I'm getting another call," Kelly interrupted. "If it's Shannon, I'll let you know." Kelly disconnected Beth's call and answered the other line. "Hello?"

"Hi." Shannon sounded weak with exhaustion.

"Shannon—wow, you sound beat. Are you okay?"

"Yeah." She sighed.

"I'm glad you called," Kelly said. "Beth got pulled over by the military police after she dropped you guys off last night."

"I know. We saw the whole thing," Shannon replied. "Is she okay?"

"She's fine. She's just been worried about you guys. What happened to you?"

Shannon sighed again. "Long story."

"Are you home?" Kelly asked.

"Yeah, I'm home, finally. This was the longest weekend . . . Can you come over? I don't want to sleep alone."

"I'm on my way." Kelly grabbed her keys and wallet. "Can you call Beth and let her know that you got home okay? Tasha was released too, right?"

"Yep. They let us both go home, finally."

Kelly drove directly to Shannon's house. The past two days weighed heavily on her conscience. She'd enjoyed sex with Gina, maybe too much, and she knew they had a connection that was missing from her relationship with Shannon. How could she give this up? Maybe she wouldn't have to. Beth hadn't caught her with Gina. Maybe no one would ever find out. Unfortunately, she was more attracted to Gina than to Shannon. But even if she broke up with Shannon, she couldn't turn around and start dating Gina. They were best friends and there were strict rules in the tight-knit lesbian circuit.

Shannon opened the door and stared at her with half-closed eyes. She was still wearing her camouflage green pants and the standard white undershirt. "Thanks for coming over tonight."

Kelly nodded. "You look exhausted."

"And I'm not going to be good company. Do you mind if we just go to bed?"

Kelly reached out to hug her. "I should have given you a ride back to the base."

"It wouldn't have mattered." Shannon grabbed Kelly's hand and headed toward the bedroom. They undressed silently and climbed under the covers. Shannon hugged Kelly tightly for a few minutes and then relaxed her hold. "I want to forget everything that happened today."

"What happened? Did you get caught when Beth dropped you off?"

"No. The MP drove by our barracks as soon as we got out of the car. Just outside the gates, he flashed his lights and made Beth pull over." Shannon stifled a yawn. "Tasha and I ran inside the closest barrack and watched Beth through the window of some guy's room. The MP did a sobriety check on her and then let her go after what seemed like an eternity. We went to our rooms thinking that was the end of it—hoping anyway."

"The MP didn't see you?"

"No. But someone else on the base reported us. We went to the six a.m. drill and they called Tasha and me out of line. God, it was a long day. They tested our blood alcohol level and we were both in the legal range. Thank God." Shannon sighed. "Then they asked us why we missed curfew and if we were out together because we were girlfriends. A bunch of the other guys missed curfew, but they only called Tasha and me out of line. They said that they knew we were girlfriends and that we'd face a full investigation unless we admitted why we missed curfew and explained ourselves."

"Is that their revised *Don't ask, Don't tell* policy? Girlfriends?"

"Their policy is bullshit. They ask whatever they want to know. And behind closed doors they can make you tell. If someone calls you a lesbian you don't have to defend yourself, but if they have what they consider to be *proof*, then you're stuck. Tasha refused to answer a couple questions. I just denied everything."

"Denied being a lesbian?"

"Yep. I told them I liked men. I even said I had a crush on one of the guys in my squad—Matt. When they questioned him, he admitted that we had kissed last night. It was a stupid drinking game, but I did kiss the bastard and he saved my ass today. Did you meet Matt?"

"I don't remember, maybe." Kelly hadn't paid attention to the

147

men at the bar. She couldn't remember meeting Matt and was glad she hadn't seen Shannon kiss him. "So, you can miss curfew as long as they think you're straight?"

"Hell, they know I'm not straight, but they didn't have any evidence against me. All they got me for was missing curfew. So, that'll be on my record. They didn't have any problem with my kissing Matt."

She wondered what else Shannon's military record included. This wasn't the first time that there was speculation about her sexual preference. Would they take this into account? "So, what about Tasha?" she asked.

"She wouldn't lie when they asked her if she was a lesbian. She just said she didn't have to answer the question. You have to play by their rules or not at all, you know? She should've lied. Now, she's facing a full background investigation."

"That sucks. And if they investigate her, they could find out information about you. I mean, they'll ask people from the base. A lot of the guys know she's dating Beth, right? Guys like Buck might talk about what they've seen at Sweet Stream." Kelly thought of the pockmarked pool player Tasha had teased last night. At his tender age, his ego was easily bruised. Kelly knew that if questioned, he wouldn't be on Tasha's side.

"He's just a punk-ass kid and underage. I think he just turned nineteen. He won't say anything about bars if he knows what's good for him. And most people aren't out to point fingers. I don't have any enemies. And everyone likes Tasha. But I don't know how clean her record is . . ."

"It won't be clean after this for either of you."

"As long as I keep to the story about being hot for Matt, I'll be fine. I already called Matt and told him what was up. He's a good guy. If they ask him, he's going to say that we've wanted to date for the past month but can't because we're in the same squad. I've requested a transfer to a different squad. Matt's been looking for a transfer anyway. He wants to go to the sandbox." Shannon paused.

"His brother joined the air force at the same time that Matt joined the army reserves. I guess his brother's been flying bombers in Iraq and Matt can't stand that he's not out there too."

Kelly shook her head. "I can't understand why anyone would want to fight in that war . . . But I'm glad you think everything will blow over with the charges against you and Tasha."

"Well, I don't know that the charges will blow over against Tasha necessarily. I have a bad feeling that she may get kicked out because of this. And she needs the money. We both need the money. She could have lied, but she's too stubborn."

"Some people aren't good at lying."

Shannon smiled. "It's a skill that has saved my butt many times. I don't even want to think about what would have happened today if I had told the truth . . ."

Chapter 12

049551

On Monday night, Kelly called Shannon to find out any news regarding Tasha and the proposed background investigation. Unfortunately, Shannon's information was as expected. Tasha had received a letter that morning from the U.S. Army. It was a brief notice to inform her that a full investigation was being made because of the questionable circumstances that surrounded her recent breach of military policy. The letter did not suggest anything about the homosexual charge.

After hanging up the phone with Shannon, Kelly headed to the bathroom to get ready for her meeting with Nora Kinley. She grimaced at the mirror's reflection and tugged on the strands of hair that fell on her forehead. Her hair was too short to conceal the marks where Kevin's fingernail had scratched her face. In the first match that night, his thumb had gouged a perfect diagonal line from her temple to the middle of her forehead. Kelly's thrust punch to Kevin's floating ribs won the tied match but sweat stung the cut on her head and the win didn't mean much when she had more injuries than her opponent.

With a sigh, Kelly turned away from the mirror. The meeting at the lawyer's office was in an hour and she didn't have time to worry about her appearance. Kelly grabbed her wallet and keys and hollered good-bye to Alex as the front door slammed. He would guess she was spending the night at Shannon's and was too distracted with his own relationship now to worry about hers. She hadn't pushed him for details about his night with Starr. He'd been in a good mood all weekend and she'd heard him humming a Grateful Dead song that morning.

After a quick knock, Kelly waited outside the door to suite 402. *McMahon, Kinley and Associates* was printed on a plaque hanging on the door. The lock turned and Kelly instantly recognized the lawyer from the train station. The woman stretched out her hand and smiled warmly. "Nora Kinley."

Kelly grasped her hand and smiled. "Since we're being formal, Kelly Haldon. It's good to see you again."

"Please come in," she said, stepping back from the doorway to let Kelly enter. "I'm glad you could make this appointment. Hope you didn't bump into any problems at the train station this time."

"Actually, I drove today." Kelly followed Nora down the hallway to her office. She counted four offices in the suite and wondered who else Nora worked with.

"Excellent, then I won't worry about keeping you late."

"Do you usually set appointments after eight?" Kelly asked, taking the seat that Nora pointed to as they entered her office. The blinds were pulled up and the office window had a perfect view of the Bay Bridge stretching across the water.

"No, I'm usually home by now. You were an exception."

"So, why did you want to see me tonight?" Kelly crossed her legs and then uncrossed them. Her chair, black leather seat with carved mahogany arm rails, appeared identical to the one behind Nora's desk. She felt out of place in the deluxe office.

"Why? Well, let's start with the woman in the picture that you recognized."

"Hannah."

"Yes. Hannah Esslinger. How do you know her?"

Kelly shrugged. "I don't know her. Not really anyway."

"What's that supposed to mean?" Nora spun her chair to the side and flipped the power switch on the radio by her desk. "Do you like country music?"

"No." Kelly shifted in her chair uncomfortably and straightened her back. Why did she have a crush on every attractive woman she met?

"Neither do I. For some reason, the only station that has good reception in this office is New Country. I don't know why they call it new, still sounds like country music." She adjusted the volume dial. "Do you want something to drink? A Coke or something?"

"No, thank you." She felt out of place in Nora's office. Or maybe she was just nervous about being alone with Nora. Every time Nora looked at her she could feel herself start to blush. "Is Rick coming tonight?"

"No, not tonight." Nora had pulled a Diet Coke out of the half-size refrigerator behind her desk. She popped the lid and took a sip, eyeing Kelly closely. Kelly glanced around the room, avoiding Nora's gaze. The refrigerator was paneled in mahogany to match the desk and the bookshelves. Dozens of leather-bound books were lined up on the shelves. Nora set the can on a coaster by a stack of papers and cleared her throat. "Actually, I've never met Rick. He was hired to do some investigative work for Hannah's case by my firm. We've done a lot of work together for this case but we've never seen each other. We both have busy schedules."

"Oh, I see." Kelly thought that it was odd that they'd never met.

Who was avoiding whom? Maybe Nora didn't want to be seen with a private investigator. Or maybe Rick didn't want to be connected to this lawsuit.

"Okay, I need to give you some information about Hannah's case and to discuss the opportunity we have for you." Nora smiled. "But first I need to know how you recognized Hannah's picture."

"Actually, I'm kind of surprised that you don't already know." Kelly didn't want to tell her about Shannon. She had guessed that Rick would've already explained Shannon's connection to Hannah Esslinger, but if he hadn't mentioned it . . . "I saw a picture of her. I've never met Hannah in person. She's just a friend of a friend."

"A friend of Shannon's—that's all you know?"

Kelly wondered how much Nora knew about her relationship with Shannon and the circle of friends in Ashton. She didn't like Nora's condescending look after the last statement. "Hmm. I have a feeling you know quite a bit about me. Why are we wasting time asking questions when you already know the answers?"

Nora took another sip of her Coke. Only the arch of her eyebrows acknowledged that she'd heard Kelly's question. "So, what else do you know about Hannah?"

"I don't know her," Kelly repeated. "Look, I saw a picture of Hannah in Shannon's photo album—the day before we bumped into each other at the train station. In Shannon's photo it's obvious they were more than just friends. I was curious about her because Shannon wouldn't tell me any details. Then I recognized Hannah in the photo from your briefcase."

"She was Shannon's girlfriend for six months. They met at the army base in North Carolina. You didn't ask Shannon about her after you saw her picture again?"

"Well, Shannon didn't seem to want to talk about it. I asked her friends and they told me the story of Hannah's discharge and that she was working on some lawsuit against the military. Then some other things happened and I didn't really get a chance to talk to Shannon. That's all." Kelly stopped to wait for Nora's reply.

Nora's cell phone rang and she held up her hand to pause their conversation. Pushing her chair away from the desk, she answered the line. Kelly stood up from her chair. She went over to the bookshelf and skimmed the titles. Nora's collection covered everything from tax law to the First Amendment. Kelly eavesdropped on her phone conversation. She was telling someone to expect her home within an hour. Kelly didn't want to waste Nora's time. She was ready to leave now.

As soon as Nora hung up the line, Kelly stretched out her hand. "I almost want to apologize. I think I gave you the wrong impression at the train station by asking about the picture. I really don't know anything about Hannah. I know you're busy and I think I should just go."

"Please sit back down. I'm sorry for the interruption." Nora ignored Kelly's outstretched hand. "Rick thinks you can help us out."

"Honestly, I don't know how I can help you," Kelly said, still standing.

Nora sighed and handed Kelly a manila envelope. Kelly pulled out a color photograph of Hannah Esslinger and studied it. A large black bruise discolored the skin around her right eye and the lid was swollen shut. Hannah's brown hair was caked with blood above her right ear. A thin red line cut vertically down her bottom lip. One word was printed across the front of her gray sweatshirt: ARMY.

Kelly shook her head and replaced the photo in the envelope. The picture she had found in the train station was a smaller copy of this same photo. "When did this happen?"

"Three weeks ago," Nora replied.

"But wasn't that after she was discharged?"

"Yes. The claims for that were filed several months ago. I'll fill you in on that later. We have other business to discuss today. Please sit down," she said firmly. Nora paused and replaced the manila envelope in her desk. She waited for Kelly to sit before continuing. "You've met Rick. I've contracted him to help me with this case. He's the one that did the background check on you."

"Yeah, I know Rick. He's one of the owners at the karate school where I work."

"Well, that's one side of him. What else?"

"He's retired from the FBI and works as a private investigator," Kelly answered. She wished that Nora would just cut to the chase. Why did Nora want her help? It was too time-consuming to fish for answers all night.

Nora nodded. "Rick does contract work now through his own independent investigation service. I think he got bored with retirement. He runs background checks on witnesses for various law firms and does odd jobs for lawyers. After our meeting in the train station, I decided to ask him to track you down. I showed him your picture and he just started laughing—told me that I had stumbled onto the perfect person for the job. I told him it was more of a collision."

"Perfect for what job? How'd you get a picture of me?"

"I took a shot at the train station."

"Why?"

"You recognized Hannah's picture and I had a feeling you might be able to help somehow. Strange intuition, I guess. Hannah Esslinger asked me to represent her on a lawsuit against the U.S. military for their policies toward homosexuals. She's working for a group called the GLB Political Action Coalition and they've filed a suit claiming that the 'Don't Ask, Don't Tell' policy is unconstitutional."

"Hasn't that already been done?"

Nora shook her head. "Not like this. Hannah has gathered evidence on hundreds of discharge cases. But the strongest case that could overturn the policy is Hannah's. She was a perfect officer. Except for her sexual orientation, the military couldn't find a better officer. The dishonorable discharge was unwarranted. We think this is the best chance we have at overturning the military policy. And the military leaders know it. Hannah was attacked three weeks ago as she was jogging on the beach. Two guys attacked her. Rick tracked down the two men—they were both military boys." Nora paused and picked up a mechanical pencil and tapped it against her desk. "And this is where we finally come to your part . . . I'd like your help."

Kelly shrugged. "I don't see how I can help."

"We're going to announce the lawsuit against the military in a press conference this week. We think we'll have good timing. They're talking about increasing the forces in Iraq again. And it'll be a nice tie-in for the case when we mention the lesbians and gays *silently serving our nation* in all branches of the military." Nora emphasized the last line with a click of her pencil.

"And my part?" Since 9/11, she'd attended nearly every peace rally held in San Francisco. And it was only a few months ago she'd marched at a big war protest. Kelly still couldn't understand why anyone would want to be in the military now, especially gays who weren't wanted in the first place.

"On the day of the official announcement about the lawsuit, I want to have someone watching Hannah. But Hannah won't want some obvious bodyguard. She thinks the attack was just a fluke and refused to hire any protection. I swear that woman is more stubborn than I am," Nora stated, snapping the lead that dropped out of the pencil. She glanced at her wristwatch. "Basically all you have to do is hang out behind the scenes. We'll do the press conference and then head to the banquet hall for a cocktail reception with the GLB Political Action Coalition. After a few hours at the hall, Hannah will leave the city and you're off the hook. I'm going to tell Hannah that you're there only as our lookout, nothing more."

"A lookout?" Kelly had no desire to stand around at a press conference watching Shannon's ex-girlfriend. She cringed at the thought of meeting Hannah under the guise of being a hall monitor. Hopefully Nora wouldn't tell Hannah anything about her connection to Shannon. "You're really serious? I'm not sure what Rick told you about me, but all I do is teach karate. I'm no bodyguard and—"

"Exactly," Nora interrupted. "I'm not looking for a bodyguard. Hannah would never agree to that. And, no offense, but you don't look very tough. I'd never guess that you're the fighter that Rick claims. But by that swollen lip and the cut above your eye at least we know you don't mind taking a few hits."

Kelly reflexively covered the cut on her forehead. "Yes, but it's different when you are fighting in a dojo. Even if we don't pull punches there are, for instance, no guns. I'm not a street fighter and I really don't think I would be any help. Why don't you just hire a couple rent-a-cops?"

"Hannah is against that idea. She really doesn't think anything will happen with all of the media buzzing around the scene. Look, you can decide if you want to do this or not—I'm obviously not forcing you." Nora sipped her Coke as she eyed Kelly. She seemed to be expecting Kelly to immediately agree to the job. Her tone hinted at annoyance when Kelly didn't jump at her suggestion to play Hannah's guard. "I'll be notifying the banquet hall to increase their security and the SFPD know about the press conference. You're just an extra precaution. And it's very likely that nothing will happen. But you never know when some crazy person might try to steal the media attention."

"So, what happens after the press conference? Isn't Hannah still in danger?"

"We're keeping her out of the city. She's going straight back to the suburbs. I just want her watched while she's here on display." Nora shook her head and tapped the stack of notes on her desk. "I've been working too hard on this case. I can't risk having anything happen to jeopardize the case now."

"You're worried about losing her just because of the case?" Kelly had heard stories about lawyers who would only take on cases with good odds for a win. They were often more concerned with their batting averages than finding justice. But Nora must have known that this case was no easy win and Kelly wondered if there was more than a client-lawyer relationship between Nora and Hannah.

Nora smiled. "No, not just for the case. We've become close friends over the past few months. She's a wonderful person, but if you are asking that question in that tone of voice, the answer is no. We're not friends like that. I'm dating a man. And I'm happy with him."

"I didn't mean anything, I mean, I wasn't . . ." Kelly paused. She realized anything that she said would just dig a bigger hole. She'd assumed that Nora was a lesbian because of her association with Hannah but this wasn't the only reason. Nora had a strong personality, an independent attitude and a habit of staring at Kelly for just a moment too long. But apparently she was reading too much into the long glances, Kelly decided. She sighed and reconsidered the job. Would this job pay as well as Rick's envelope deliveries? She wouldn't mind making another hundred bucks just for standing guard at a press conference. "Okay. If you aren't expecting much more than a body between Hannah and some crazy attacker, I could probably find time in my schedule for this press conference."

"Good." Nora smiled. "Rick is going to give you the details and set everything up for me. I just wanted to meet you tonight to make sure I felt comfortable with you." Nora stood up and shook Kelly's hand. As she led the way to the door, Nora added, "Hannah's life is definitely in danger. Too many people would like her to disappear. It is hard to decide whom to trust. I'm lucky we bumped into each other."

Kelly wondered why Nora trusted her. She was dating Hannah's ex-girlfriend and had no reason to help this lawsuit succeed. "Where is Hannah now?"

"Hidden in the suburbs. The press conference is this Thursday. Rick will find you before then. Follow your regular schedule so he can track you down."

"Wouldn't an appointment be easier? Or he could call me." Kelly didn't want another surprise visit at the dojo.

Nora shook her head. "As you will learn if you work with Rick, he doesn't make appointments for his meetings. He just schedules them for other people."

Chapter 13

049601

Alex left a note taped to the refrigerator the next morning inviting her out to dinner. Even though they were living in the same house, they rarely seemed to see each other. Over several plates of sushi and soybeans, Kelly hinted at her problems with Shannon, and Alex mentioned his growing attraction to Starr. After dinner they headed to the café to order some biscotti for dessert. Starr was working at the front counter. She pointed to a table near the back of the café and promised to join them shortly. Alex had not stopped talking about her since they left the restaurant. The pair had become inseparable over the past week.

When they reached their assigned table, Alex glanced back at Starr and smiled sheepishly. He admitted quietly, "You know, Kelly, it's so different with her. She spent the night last weekend and we just talked, the whole night. It was great. Maybe there's something wrong with me. I've never flirted this much in my life. She's supposed to be my rebound from Laura but I think I really like her."

"If it were me, you'd say I just need to have sex. That way I'd get her out of my system." Kelly sipped her coffee. The hot liquid burned the tip of her tongue and she immediately set the cup down to cool.

Alex laughed as she stuck her tongue out and waved her hand over the scalded surface. "Yeah, I would tell you that. Thank God I'm not you. I don't jump into things too quickly." He grinned when Kelly finally closed her mouth. "Remember, I like long-term relationships. Speaking of which, I haven't thought about Laura at all since I met Starr. She's inside my head and I can't think of anyone else. We're going surfing again this weekend. Do you want to come?"

"Maybe. Or maybe I'll let you guys go alone. It's great to see you smiling all the time. Your relationship with Laura sucked. I don't know if Starr will last, but she's perfect for you right now."

Alex nodded. "And what about you? Did you say you were having some problems with Shannon?"

"Hell, I don't even know where to start."

"What's wrong? You're not breaking up with her already?" He blew on his cappuccino for a few seconds before sipping.

"No. But I started sleeping with one of her friends—Gina. She's a cop and incredibly hot." Kelly paused to blow the steam off her drink. Alex kept watch on the front counter where Starr was taking drink orders. She smiled, happy to see Alex wrapped up with Starr, and then continued, "The really crazy thing is that I think I like both of them. I don't know exactly how long it will last. I can't decide if I want to go to bed with the Army Reserves or the police department."

"Damn, Kelly. You're a dog. So, what's the plan? Sleep in both beds until you decide which pillow you like the best?"

"Well, I don't really have a plan. Here's the deal. Shannon doesn't know I'm sleeping with Gina. But Gina knows I'm dating Shannon.

Gina just wants to have sex with me and doesn't want a relationship. She says she's still in love with her ex-girlfriend—this woman who's stuck in Iraq. I think I like Gina more than Shannon, but I really can't decide. And Shannon hasn't gotten over *her* ex-girlfriend either. She apparently was crushed a few months ago when this officer from the army dumped her—I'd explain more, but it's a really long story. So, I figure that since neither of them is emotionally ready to be in a monogamous relationship with me, I'll just sleep with both of them and see who gets over which ex-girlfriend first."

"That plan sucks. What if they both are great people, but you never realize that because you're trying to swing two at a time?"

"So, you're a swinger?" Starr asked, winking at Kelly as she set down another plate of biscotti. "Can I get you guys anything else?"

Alex shook his head. "Can you sit down for a minute?"

Starr squeezed past Alex's chair and kissed his cheek before taking a seat at their table. "Well, don't let me stop the conversation about swingers. What were you about to say, Kelly?"

"Oh. I'm not a swinger," Kelly started. "I'm just having trouble with some relationship issues and Alex is giving me a hard time. But I think we can switch topics. I hear you kids are going surfing. Which beach?"

"We're probably going south of Santa Cruz. I like to surf Pleasure Point. There's a great pizza place near the beach and there's nothing better that a hot slice of pizza after freezing your butt riding the waves all day. Speaking of waves, my friend said they had awesome sets yesterday." She looked at Alex. "Did you check the forecast?"

In a few minutes, Kelly realized she was no longer needed in their conversation. She was content to let Alex and Starr continue their discussion about waves and weather forecasts. Starr was pulling Alex out of the slump that he had fallen in since Laura had entered his life. Kelly loved to see him laughing at Starr's jokes and eagerly planning their trip. At least this relationship was going well.

"Hey, kids?" Kelly interrupted after a break in the debate over surfboard lengths. "Do you mind if I leave? I have to meet Shannon."

"Wait, which one is she?"

Kelly grinned at her brother. "Don't worry, I can hardly keep track and I wouldn't expect you to. You have something better to think about."

Starr smiled and kissed Alex. "You know, your sister sounds like a player. How do I know the trait doesn't run in the family?"

Alex shook his head. "We definitely inherited different genes. In fact, I don't think we share the same parents. I remember some postman that used to flirt with Mom a long time ago . . ."

Kelly decided to call Shannon from a pay phone outside the café. They didn't have an official date and she wasn't comfortable showing up at Shannon's house unexpectedly. As she dropped her change in the slot, she vowed that her next investment would be a cell phone. But first she had to pay next term's tuition. Kelly was relieved to hear Shannon's excitement at the unannounced visit. Tasha's comment about Shannon's continued attachment to her ex-girlfriend still weighed in Kelly's mind. It was easier to spend evenings with Gina knowing that Shannon was really still in love with her ex, but she also selfishly wanted Shannon.

Shannon turned on the stereo as Kelly lay down on her bed. Paco was still whining in the hallway. The Dalmatian had pounced on Kelly as soon as Shannon opened the front door. He refused to calm down after several minutes of ball tossing and they finally decided to leave him with his favorite rawhide bone and escape to Shannon's bedroom.

Shannon joined Kelly on the bed and stared up at the ceiling. "How are you?"

"Good," Kelly replied. She wanted to kiss Shannon but something was holding her back. "I was glad you were home tonight. I really wanted to see you." The blinds were pulled up on the window by Shannon's bed. The night sky seemed to stretch out forever. A crescent moon hung low, just above the ridge of the coastal mountains. Tonight, the moon made a perfect smile as though it were looking down at the earth and laughing. Shannon got up to change the music playing on the stereo. She stared at her CDs without making a selection. Kelly wanted to point out the moon but said nothing. She couldn't read the emotion on Shannon's face. Something was wrong. "Shannon, are you okay?"

"Yeah, I'm fine," she responded without looking up from the CD rack. "Just fine."

Kelly sighed. Now she knew something was wrong. She reached out to tug on Shannon's sleeve. "Play your favorite CD."

"Why?"

"Because I want to know what you like. And you're upset about something. Maybe it will make you feel a little more relaxed."

Shannon shook her head. "Thanks, but I don't need to relax." She slipped a CD into the machine, then began to sort a pile of clean laundry. Kelly could tell Shannon was avoiding her but didn't want to press for a reason. Halfway through the pile, she looked at Kelly and said, "I'm not mad or anything. But I missed you last night. I called your house and your brother said you were gone for the evening." Her voice trailed off in a sigh. She sat down beside Kelly and waited for an explanation.

On the stereo, a woman was singing something about angels. The smell of lavender candle wax pervaded the room. "I had to work late."

"I called at ten. I think I woke your brother up. Since when do they have karate classes at ten at night?" Shannon shook her head. "You know what? Forget I asked. It's none of my business who you're sleeping with."

Kelly clenched her jaw and stared out the window. She didn't want to answer. The moon laughed back at her, as if to say that nothing was as important as it seemed. The day was done and she wanted to relax with Shannon.

Kelly had spent the day coaching: "Kick higher, snap your punches, move faster! Okay, nice strike. Now just hit more. Think about what you're doing—don't just react. Plan a second and third strike." She doubted if they heard her words, with their adrenaline pumping and their fists clashing, so as class ended she added the advice she had been given before her own first tournament. "When your body gets too tired to fight, only your mind can win the match. It's not about beating up your opponent. The tournament is about proving to yourself that you have improved. You don't need to win every match to know that you're stronger and faster than you were before training for this." For the students going to the sparring tournament, her advice was simple. The five boys going to the tournament were between eight and thirteen years old. Pain and empathy were foreign concepts at their age. One concept they understood: hit things, don't get hit. Control was the hardest skill to learn.

Kelly touched Shannon's arm. Shannon pulled back reflexively. "We had a tournament meeting at the pizza joint next door to the dojo. A bunch of the students are going to a tournament this weekend. I slept in my own bed, alone, last night." For once, she really had slept in her own bed, but she didn't need to tell Shannon about the meeting with Nora.

Shannon turned to stare out the window. "Look, I'm sorry . . . I shouldn't have said anything. I just had this feeling that . . . You know what? Forget I brought anything up about this. I'm not thinking clearly right now. You're probably right. I need to relax."

Kelly brushed her hand against Shannon's leg. Shannon didn't pull away. For the first time, Kelly felt close to her. "The moon is beautiful tonight," she said quietly.

Shannon smiled. "It's laughing at us. God, I don't know what's wrong with me. I can't believe I just accused you of sleeping with somebody else. I'm just on edge lately. I feel like I can't trust anyone."

"What's wrong?" Kelly asked. "I know something else is bugging you."

"Nothing." Her shoulders rose and fell in a tired shrug.

"I don't believe you," Kelly said.

Shannon stared at the night sky. "A friend called last night to warn me that I should be careful over the next few days," she began, her gaze focused on the moon. "She said someone from the army might be watching me more closely and that I could be in danger. She wouldn't tell me exactly why. I don't know if she had heard what happened to me last weekend or if it was something else . . . I just want to forget about it all for a while."

Kelly guessed the caller was Hannah Esslinger. Resting her head on the pillows, she debated if she should tell Shannon about the upcoming press conference or her meeting with the lawyer. Nora had not told her that their conversation was confidential. But it was implied. "Shannon, I think you should be careful. After what happened at the base last weekend, who knows who's watching you?"

"I don't really care." Shannon dismissed her comment with a wave. "The army won't kick me out. I've had my ass in the fire before. They let me go with only a mark for missing curfew." Shannon continued, "Let's change subjects. Do you want to hear about our plans with Beth and Tasha for this weekend?"

"Sure," Kelly said with a sigh. She doubted Shannon's confidence in her position. The warning call had obviously made Shannon nervous, and someone could be watching her house even now. Any plans they made to go out for the weekend could jeopardize Shannon's future in the army if anyone saw the four of them together. Kelly was also not eager to make plans for the weekend with Shannon because of the situation with Gina. She wanted to admit that she had slept with Gina, but she didn't want to hurt Shannon's feelings.

"Sure? Wow, that sounds convincing. You know, we don't have to do anything together this weekend—if you already have plans . . ."

"No, I don't have plans." Kelly wanted to continue sleeping with both women, but she knew that she'd have to choose eventually. "What are we doing?"

"What's wrong?" Shannon squinted at her, puzzled.

"Nothing," Kelly lied. She could not tell Shannon about Gina. "I was just thinking about the call from your friend and everything that happened on your base—maybe we shouldn't go out this weekend."

Shannon shook her head. "Relax, I can take care of the army boys. Don't worry about me. Beth and I talked about it at lunch today."

"Oh." Kelly was dreading that Beth would find out about her weekend with Gina. She would instantly tell Shannon.

"It's not bad. We had a long conversation . . . I told her I want to go back to school. I joined the army for a few reasons—you know, serve my country, maybe get to travel, but also to get money for college. Anyway, I keep putting off the college applications. And I don't know what will happen with the war. It sounds like they need more troops in Iraq than they expected. They keep saying that our unit is staying here in San Francisco but I don't know if I trust them anymore." Shannon sat down on the bed. Kelly stared at Shannon's hand, resting a few inches from her leg. She wore a silver thumb ring with a snake pattern across the band and a thin leather bracelet on her wrist. Several small scars etched the back of her hand. "Then Beth brought up your name. I admitted that I don't know what to do about you either."

"What do you mean?" Kelly asked cautiously.

"I don't know if I'm ready for something serious."

"Okay, then we won't have a serious relationship." Kelly paused, trying to gauge Shannon's response.

Shannon shook her head. "It's not that easy. I like you. But I don't know if I'm ready to like you."

Kelly shook her head. It was ironic that on the first night that she had finally felt close to Shannon, they were going to stop seeing each other. "So, this is one of those 'I like you, but not right now' conversations?"

"No, not at all. But I just . . ."

"What?" Kelly took Shannon's hand and held it for a moment, staring at her and waiting for an answer. Shannon looked away as

166

Kelly tugged off her thumb ring. She held Shannon's ring up in the air, read the engraving of Shannon's initials on the inner surface of the band and then slipped it on her own thumb. "Your turn to talk, girl."

"I think I may be giving you the wrong signals. I really like you. Maybe I should just tell you this . . ." Shannon paused and looked at her ring now on Kelly's thumb. "I got screwed by my last girlfriend. After she dumped me, I decided I would just have casual relationships for a while, but now I don't know what to do. I feel you pull away because I'm not really acting interested. But that's not what I want to do at all. I just don't know how much you'll like me."

Kelly leaned forward and kissed her. Shannon pulled back. Kelly slipped her hands behind Shannon's head before kissing her again. Shannon's response was immediate and strong. Kelly felt her pressing desire and knew what Shannon wanted. Kelly shifted back after a moment, their lips separating. "Wait, what were you saying about our weekend plans? I think I'm responsible for getting us off track."

"Mmm, I don't remember what we were talking about. I like this track better." Shannon pushed her down, pinning her to the bed. She kissed her again, slipping her tongue inside Kelly's mouth.

"You don't remember?" Kelly moved her hands underneath Shannon's sweatshirt and unclasped her bra. Shannon pulled off the sweatshirt. Reaching up to cup Shannon's breasts, Kelly licked her nipple, then pulled at the nipple rings with her teeth. She let the metal slip out of her mouth and stared up at Shannon. "Or you don't want to think about the weekend plans right now?"

"You're not giving up?"

Kelly shook her head and smiled.

"All right, if you're going to make me . . . Beth and Tasha want to abandon the usual bar on Saturday. Instead of Sweet Stream they want to try one of the all-women dance clubs. What do you think?"

Kelly unzipped Shannon's jeans and lightly traced a line down the center of her silk underwear with the tip of her finger.

Shannon grabbed Kelly's wrist. "Look who's distracted now."

"I'm not distracted. A lesbian club sounds perfect."

"Yeah, I figured you wouldn't mind leaving the boys behind. And Tasha doesn't want to hang out with the military crowd this weekend. I don't blame her. I'm sick of the whole war debate and I don't even want to remember everything that happened last weekend."

"Yeah, I think a change of scenery will be good. And it'll be nice to go somewhere with just another lesbian couple. Less drama."

"Oh, yeah, that reminds me . . . Gina is tagging along with us. Hope you don't mind. She may bring a little drama."

Kelly shook her head and encircled her arms around Shannon's naked back. "Well, what would a girls' night out be without a little drama?"

Chapter 14

049651

Over the next couple of days the conversation with Nora kept replaying in Kelly's mind. She was flattered by the offer, but doubted that she could really help. If they only wanted someone to buffer bullets, why didn't they ask some bar bouncer? Once Rick gave her the plan she knew it would be too late to back out of the deal.

"Knock, knock."

Kelly looked up from her place on the dojo mat and saw Rick watching her. She had lost track of time as she meditated. "Hey, it's my secret agent man," she started. "I've been waiting for you."

"Don't tell me, I'll guess. You had a vision that I'd arrive while you meditated."

"I was just getting bored and was about to lock the door. Wednesday nights are slow around here." Since her conversation with Nora, Kelly kept imagining that someone had followed her every move. She was relieved to see Rick.

"Are you meeting Shannon?"

"Why do you ask?"

"Well, I've noticed that she isn't your only interest. I've seen your car parked around other neighborhoods."

"You're right, she isn't my only interest."

"Who else are you sleeping with?"

"I don't want to answer that question," Kelly answered. She guessed that Rick had seen her car parked in Gina's neighborhood when he tailed Beth to the townhouse. There was no reason to get Gina involved in this.

"Well, if we work together I need to know who your friends are and who you're about to piss off. You can make me a list. You never know when you could get into trouble."

Kelly stood up from the mat and approached him. "I don't see how a list of my dates is important for our work together. I can take care of myself." Kelly shook her head. "And I already have two parents and an overprotective brother."

"Well, then you have experience dealing with people like me. Don't worry, you'll get used to it," Rick replied with a tight smile.

"I don't know if I want to. Maybe I don't trust you."

"Well, now is the time to decide." He stared at her. "Do you want to back out?"

Kelly waited for a moment before answering. He had pulled a gun on her once just to prove a point. What would he do if she made a mistake later? She had no reason to trust him but she did so implicitly. "No, I'm not backing out."

"Then moving on to the business at hand . . . Sam has been notified that you won't be at work tomorrow."

"Tomorrow? What excuse did you give?"

"I didn't give an excuse—you just weren't able to make it. He didn't ask any questions."

"He'll ask me." Kelly knew that Sam would not question Rick.

She also knew that Sam would grill her on Friday morning to find the reason she'd taken Thursday off.

"He doesn't need an answer. Tell him you can't explain and he'll just drop it. He's worked on projects with me before. He understands why some things aren't discussed."

Kelly nodded. "Yeah, but you don't have to spar with him after pissing him off." The wounds from the last sparring session were almost healed but the scab above her eye was a reminder to stay on Sam's good side.

Rick ignored her comment. "As far as our plan, the Civic Center train station is your base. The press conference is at eleven a.m. Plan on arriving at the Civic Center Plaza by nine o'clock. Two black guys, Terrance and Mike, will be setting up a stage near the fountain in front of the old Veteran's Building. Terrance looks like the poster boy for a fitness magazine and wears earrings in both ears. Mike is overweight and has a tattoo on the back of his neck. Make sure you pay attention to details."

Kelly nodded. "I got it, earrings and tattoos."

"Nora hired them to stand by the stage until the press conference. Your job is just to walk around the plaza for a while. Keep your eyes and ears open for anything out of the ordinary. You know the city—look for people that don't belong. Hannah will be dropped off at the plaza at a quarter to the hour. Nora should arrive at the plaza around the same time. Two other representatives from the Gay Veterans Association will be in the car with Hannah—John, a tall white guy with a beard, and Marcus, an overweight white guy with a crewcut and silver ID bracelet on his right hand. The driver of their car is a bald Asian man, Lee." Rick stopped for a moment and glanced at Kelly. "Are you keeping track of all of this? Details are important," he repeated.

"Terrance and Mike are the two guys setting up the stage," Kelly began. She kept her tone even and curbed the urge to give a sarcastic reply. Rick's paternalistic behavior was annoying her but she knew better than to antagonize the situation with sarcasm. "Lee is the guy driving the car. Hannah will be in the car with John and Marcus. Nora will arrive separately. They talk to the press at eleven a.m."

"Right. Lee will park and wait with the car in the closest space he can find to the plaza. We'll have a spot cordoned off for him, but you know the city—people prize a good parking space more than their firstborn kid. I wouldn't be surprised if one of the news vans takes the spot." A shadow suddenly blocked the light passing through the window from the street lamp at the front of the dojo and Rick glanced at the front door. An older couple stood on the sidewalk, staring at the Summer Karate Camp flyer posted in the front window. He waited to resume their talk until the couple finally moved away from the door. "And Lee will stay with the car so we don't want to have to deal with car bombs or anything."

Kelly nodded. "What does the car look like?"

"Black Chevrolet sedan with tinted windows and California plates," he answered.

"Just like your car. Do all bad guys drive the same car?"

Rick smiled. "Chevy threw a big sale on black sedans."

"And then what?"

"For the most part, we play it by ear. This job should be easy. Just hang out in the background and watch everyone in the crowd. I'll be there so if you see anything strange, page me." Rick set a cell phone on the front counter in the dojo waiting room. "Our phones are linked, so just hit the green button and start talking—just like a walkie-talkie, only smaller, and the phones receive text messages also. But stay off the lines if you can. Cellular connections are easy to tap."

"Then we go directly to the cocktail thing?"

"Yes. It's a big banquet hall—and just don't make yourself too obvious. Watch Hannah the entire time. Nora will tell Hannah that you're there and she won't be too happy to have you for a guard. Just don't let her out of your sight. If anything happens, all you have to do is page me. After the cocktail reception, Lee will drive Hannah home alone. I'll give further directions as they're needed. Once

Hannah leaves the banquet hall, make sure you accompany her to Lee's car. Lee will be waiting in the garage of the hotel—the banquet hall is on the first floor of the Grand Marquis Hotel. Once she's in the car with Lee, you're officially off the clock. By the way, Nora pays well for our services."

"That's it? Sounds easy." Kelly grinned. She wanted to show him that she wasn't nervous even if their plan didn't flow well tomorrow.

"Well, as fair warning, Hannah has received two death threats in the mail. She was also attacked—I think you've seen the picture—when the military was first advised of her lawsuit." Rick shook his head. Kelly remembered Hannah's injured face in the photo. "We're hoping everything goes smoothly tomorrow, but there's no guarantees."

"Great." She realized that Rick was not joking but was still trying to keep their conversation light. "You know, I don't think I'm qualified to do this."

He shrugged. Maybe he was agreeing with her. "Relax, you'll be fine. Tomorrow will be a breeze."

"And where are you in all of this?"

"I'll be parked close by the whole time." He picked up the cell phone and tossed it to Kelly. "Just think about how easy it is to beat up guys twice your size. You'll have the element of surprise if anyone tries anything."

"That isn't comforting," she admitted. "Maybe I can just go back to delivering envelopes for you. I can handle that job."

He shook his head. "So, do you want a gun?"

"I hate guns. And I don't know how to shoot."

"You told me you shot BB guns."

"Only at the rats around the barn where I grew up. I can't hit a target." It had been over ten years since she'd last fired a gun. Alex still had his BB gun but Kelly had sold hers in a garage sale just before her thirteenth birthday. She cashed a birthday check from her grandma and combined this with the money from the sale of the gun to buy a purple CD player. She never regretted the purchase.

"You just aim and pull the trigger."

"No." Kelly felt her stomach tighten. She shook her head to clear her thoughts and then remembered her knife. She always left her pocketknife on the top shelf of the display case in the front waiting room. Kelly reached up to the top shelf and flashed the blade. She always had her pocketknife with her but the one-inch blade would be no match for a gun. Kelly sliced through the air with the blade brandished, then stopped and shook her head. The idea of her guarding anyone was laughable.

"You'll be fine. They won't be expecting a Ninja with a pink pocketknife as Hannah's escort."

"Who is the *they*?"

"Nora didn't tell you?"

"No."

"Well, we don't know exactly. There is a rumor about an underground vigilante group in the military. Hannah thinks she has strong evidence that the vigilante group exists. She's gathered a few names of military leaders that all seem connected to homosexual discharge cases. After Hannah was kicked out, she started collecting evidence from other discharged officers. She made an announcement about a fundraising dinner to raise awareness about the military's discrimination. Her theory is that certain influential military leaders intend to rid the military of all prominent homosexuals. I don't know if the vigilante group actually exists or not. I've heard rumors about it before and I've linked a number of the names on Hannah's list to individuals that the FBI had identified as part of a right-wing paramilitary organization. But I still have my doubts . . . Anyway, we're going to worry about that later. Right now, we need to watch Hannah."

"So, Hannah is going to publicly identify people who she thinks are part of that group?"

"No. That would be too risky. We don't have enough evidence yet that there really is a ring of homophobes organizing all of these cases. And even if the vigilante group is behind everything, we wouldn't want to try and fight the whole group. It's better to pick out some of the prominent leaders in a group and attack them individually. Hannah's plan is to go after the military's policy on homosexuals directly. And we're hoping that the vigilante group won't try and stop a lawsuit that has a lot of publicity and local support. That's why she moved to San Francisco. When she first announced her intent to file a lawsuit challenging the *Don't ask, Don't tell* policy, someone sent her a letter threatening to kill her if the suit was filed. A week later, two guys beat her up when she was out on a run."

Kelly nodded. "And the guys were from the military?"

"Yes. Both men were in the military. I still have friends in the agency that I can lean on for info when I need it. They tracked down the bios on the two men that attacked Hannah, and apparently they had been named repeatedly in the FBI investigation of the vigilante group. The guys left Hannah when they spotted another runner coming down the path. It's very likely they would have killed her if the other runner hadn't distracted them."

This job was over her head, Kelly realized. "Rick, I think you need to hire a real bodyguard for Hannah."

"There will be security guards onsite. Don't worry. All you have to do is be another pair of eyes on the scene. Watch Hannah like a hawk and page me if you suspect anything. I'll take it from there."

On Thursday morning at half past nine, Kelly stepped off the East Bay train at the Civic Center station. Cars clogged the intersection on Market Street. The fog had not burned off yet and the city was still cloaked in gray.

Kelly crossed the street, edging close to the tall commercial buildings that bordered the sidewalk. She carefully avoided any glances from other pedestrians or the street bums as she made her way to the plaza, an open courtyard lined by city buildings, trees and park benches. The bums had laid claim to most of the benches in the plaza, dozing with newspapers covering their faces. Kelly sat down on one of the empty benches. A few men and women in business attire hurried down the tree-lined paths, ignoring Kelly and the homeless men. Kelly had come to realize that most people dismissed her without a second glance. She was too plain and quiet to warrant attention.

After a while, Kelly noticed two men arrive with tools and electric equipment. They started to set up a podium by the flagpole in the plaza. Kelly eavesdropped on their conversation while pretending to read a paperback she'd brought. She quickly confirmed that these were the guys Rick had told her to watch for. Terrance was hand-some, tall and sported a perfect physique. He was obviously in charge. Mike was at least five inches shorter than Terrance, over-weight and much more talkative. They chatted about a baseball game as they set up the podium. Before long they had finished their project and sat down with sodas by the flagpole.

Kelly flipped the pages of her book absently and surveyed the plaza while continuing to eavesdrop.

After popping open the soda can, Mike started, "Well, it didn't take as long as I guessed."

"Yeah, the stage is easy to put together."

"No, man, not the stage. I mean your wife. You know, I figured you'd play the field a while. But you're going down like the rest of us. Don't get me wrong, I'd do anything to have some of that on my plate. Just tagged you for the bachelor and now you've been caught like the rest of us. Terrance, man, it goes downhill fast. Say good-bye to freedom."

"I'm moving in with her. We're not getting married," Terrance replied.

"Not yet, but you will. You'll give her a ring."

"Maybe." Terrance grabbed the power drill and pressed the trigger. He stared at the drill bit as it spun in the air. "Or maybe I'll ask her to marry me and she'll tell me to go to hell."

"No, she won't. I know women." Mike took a sip of his soda. "And they can't keep their hands off a ring!"

Terrance laughed. "Well, I'm not looking to get married yet. And neither is Nora. She's focused on her career."

Kelly caught her breath as soon as she heard Nora's name. Terrance was moving in with Nora?

"And you'll give her a ring. We all fall sooner or later." Mike gulped down the rest of his soda and belched. "Look, she got you to leave your job and come set up this damn thing for her today. You're bending over like we all do. Don't fight it."

Terrance shook his head and jumped off the stage. "Nothing's happening at the courthouse anyway—they won't miss me at work. Hell, her client's paying. And she's paying your lazy ass, too. Come on, it's a quarter after ten. Toss your drill and the rest of the tools in the truck before this thing starts."

Mike grumbled about having to clean up the tools but followed the order as Terrance began a sound check. Kelly watched Terrance with renewed interest. Although Nora had admitted that she was dating a man, Kelly was surprised to see him here. Nora and Terrance had the same rich brown skin. He was as handsome as she was beautiful . . . they made a perfect couple on the surface. But she could not believe that Nora was really straight. It was a shame that a woman so empowered and beautiful as Nora would date a man, she thought. Kelly shook her head and stood up from the bench. She really didn't know Nora or Terrance. She had no business passing judgment on someone else's choice.

A few of the media vans had arrived and cameras were being positioned near the stage, where Terrance stood closely supervising the proceedings. Returning her book to her backpack, Kelly walked through the plaza eyeing the new arrivals carefully. After seeing Terrance by the stage, she decided that she was just an extra on the set. This thought made her relax. She headed over to the hotel bordering the plaza and stowed her backpack in the front lobby's coat check. She had the cell phone in her front pocket but doubted she would use it. They didn't really need her today. And she was getting paid to stand around and watch other people work.

Kelly returned to the plaza and found a park bench farther away from the stage and behind the cameras. She picked up the classifieds section of a newspaper that had been left on the bench and pretended to read while watching the reporters prepare for the interview.

A man in his mid forties sat down at the other end of the bench. Like the other street bums, his clothing was layered in the typical street style, darkened with dirt and frayed at the edges. He didn't seem to notice that Kelly was seated at the other end of his bench and stretched his legs out to claim well over half the seat. With his blue eyes shifting from the stage to a pile of newspapers scattered on the bench next to Kelly, he intermittently repeated the items on someone's grocery list that was scribbled on the edge of the *Chronicle*.

After a few minutes, the man stood up from the bench and shuffled past her. She noted that he didn't smell like the usual street transients. There was no obtrusive sweat or alcohol odor emanating from him. He rubbed his hand along the short gray whiskers on his chin and peered inside the trash can by the next bench along the path. Kelly glanced back to the stage as the bum began pulling out aluminum cans and tossing them into a plastic bag. Bums willingly picked through the trash for the few cents they could get in exchange for the empty cans at the local dump.

A black sedan pulled up to the parking place cordoned off by a yellow rope. Kelly noted the bald Asian driver whom Rick had mentioned. This must be Lee. Two men climbed out of the car, fitting Rick's description of Marcus and John. Hannah exited the car last. She had the same shoulder-length brown hair, pale skin and blue eyes that Kelly remembered from her pictures. She was unexpectedly tall, about the same height as Marcus and John. They walked down the tree-lined path toward the stage together. Terrance was watching their approach closely. Kelly scanned the crowd that had gathered. There were five cameras and at least fifteen reporters. Hannah's statements would be broadcast by the local television and radio station and written up in the national newspapers.

Kelly hadn't noticed when Nora arrived and was surprised to see her stride past the reporters. She smiled with acknowledgment to friendly faces in the crowd, and then greeted Hannah warmly. Nora shook the hands of the other two men, Marcus and John. With a brief nod at Terrance and Mike, she stepped up on the stage. A maze of wires led from the podium's microphone out to the reporters. Nora gave a short speech before introducing Hannah. Kelly watched the crowd as Hannah joined Nora on the stage. She knew that Terrance would be ready if anything happened. He was focused on them like a protective hen with new baby chicks.

As Hannah discussed her army career and the pending lawsuit, a flash of reflected light distracted Kelly's concentration on the crowd. The fog was beginning to burn off and sunlight reflected on an aluminum can wedged between the planks of a bench. The bench was ten feet away from the group of reporters. Squinting, Kelly focused on an object dangling from the can. Fighting a rush of certainty, she ran toward the bench. The dangling object was a burning wick. As soon as she reached the bench, Kelly spit on her fingers. She grabbed the wick and watched the flame crackle and die. A trail of smoke curled up from her hand. Shaking the burning sensation from her fingertips, Kelly inspected the can without touching it. The smell of lighter fluid was strong and gunpowder dusted the edge of a rag sticking out of the can. Kelly wondered what else was inside the can. It would have made a good explosion had it ignited.

Kelly scanned the plaza for the bum who'd been sitting next to her. She suspected he was watching from some lookout point and waiting for the explosion. The man had disappeared past the reporters once Nora had stepped on stage. She hadn't watched him closely and couldn't remember how long it had been since she'd last seen him or which direction he'd headed. There could be other cans waiting . . . He had left a long wick on his handmade bomb. This would give him plenty of time to exit before the explosion. Kelly grabbed her cell phone and pressed the green pager button. "Rick, I hope you can hear this." She paused waiting for his return signal.

"Go ahead."

"Someone set up a little pop bomb—gun powder, kerosene and something else that I can't quite see, all stuffed into a soda can. It was left on the park bench about thirty feet back from the stage—just to the side of the cameras. I just killed the flame."

The phone beeped once and Rick's voice came through after a moment of static. "Okay, I see the bench. A cop is on his way now. And are you sure it's not going to explode?"

"Yeah—it's dead." Kelly stared at the can. Fortunately, this was not the first explosive can she had seen. It was very similar in design to the pop bombs Kelly and Alex used to make to kill rodents around the barn. In place of firecrackers, this one was packed with gunpowder and probably something else more dangerous hidden underneath the gas-soaked rag. She didn't want to poke inside to find out what else may be waiting there. "I'm going to check out the rest of the area around the stage."

"Page as soon as you find anything."

Hannah was still in the midst of her speech and the eyes of the crowd were focused on the stage. Several trash cans, a line of park benches and too many trees to count were all within close range of the stage. There were hundreds of places that the bum, or whoever he really was, could have set another pop bomb. Kelly skirted around the reporters, searching any spot a can could be concealed. It was possible that the bum had only left one bomb. *Would he have had time to set up another?* Kelly looked back at the park bench where she had found the can. Two cops were already standing next to the bench. Kelly was surprised that the police weren't interrupting the press conference to disperse the crowd. Nearly fifty people had gathered behind the press. Hannah had finished her statement, and the reporters were eagerly firing questions, confident that this interview would make the war news for that day a little more interesting. The media liked to give a personal face to the military.

Kelly tried to formulate a good description of the homeless man. She knew the police were going to harass her for details. Maybe he was just a random crazy guy who wanted to make a scene. It was possible he had no idea what the press conference was really about. Or, he could be working undercover for whoever was against Hannah. Suddenly a flash of light reflected off a piece of metal on the flagpole near the stage. She pressed the pager button instantly. "Rick, I think there may be another one. How can we get in touch with the guys on the stage—Terrance is standing about ten feet away from it." Without waiting for Rick's response, Kelly ran behind the crowd of cameras and reporters. The pole was only twenty feet from the stage, but the cameras were focused on Hannah. A can had been placed at the base of the flagpole. As Kelly neared the pole, she paused. She didn't see a wick but she couldn't tell if this can was empty.

"Can't get through to Terrance. Go check it out now."

Kelly moved toward the flagpole, her heart racing. The crowd was still watching Hannah with their backs to the flagpole. She reached out to grab the can. Terrance glanced over his shoulder and spotted Kelly. She backed away from the pole and crushed the empty can in her hands. Terrance seemed to size her up briefly and dismiss her quickly. Apparently he didn't see her as any threat and returned his focus on Nora and Hannah.

When Kelly was just past the reporters, she hit the phone's green button. "False alarm. This one's empty."

"Stay in place by the stage until they clear out the area. That first can you found was definitely a homemade bomb. The cops just confirmed it and they're sending in a special team now." Rick's voice turned to static and Kelly quickly switched off the signal.

Just then Nora motioned to Hannah. Rick must have notified her as well, Kelly thought. Hannah saw the signal, made a final statement of thanks to the reporters and stepped off the stage quickly. A police officer stepped on the stage immediately and began to address the crowd. Nora, Marcus and John accompanied Hannah to the waiting car. Lee ran to open Hannah's door. Kelly listened to the police officer's announcement as the black sedan pulled out of the parking spot.

"The Civic Center Plaza is being evacuated at this time. We've found a suspicious device that may contain explosives and have removed it from this site. We're currently searching for any other devices." When the officer had finished his statement, the reporters broke with a frenzy of questions. He calmly repeated that the area must be cleared immediately and refused to offer further details. "A public statement will be made shortly. We have no reason to suspect that other devices are present, but the area must be evacuated for everyone's safety. The buildings surrounding the plaza will also be evacuated."

After the officer's announcement, Kelly turned away from the stage. She stared at the empty can in her hands, unsure if she should toss it or not. This false alarm had put her more on edge than the real pop bomb. The reporters and their equipment began to quickly disperse as the employees in the Civic Center began pouring out of the buildings. Although Rick had told her to stay in place near the stage, Kelly did not want to attract any more attention. It was likely that the man who had set the bomb had watched his plan unravel and would know that she was to blame. The phone buzzed again and Kelly listened for Rick's voice. This time a text message was displayed on the screen. "The cops need to see the second can. Take it to the park bench where they set up shop."

Several police officers were now at the site of the park bench where Kelly had found the first can. Without looking up from the cloud of dark blue uniforms to see individual faces, she reluctantly approached the group. Her hands were shaking still from the adrenaline rush. She had no desire to be interrogated by the cops. The officer who had made the evacuation announcement appeared to be the man in charge. He noted Kelly's approach and held up his hand to stop her. "Is that the other can that you found?"

Kelly nodded.

"And it's empty?"

"Yes."

"Hey, somebody grab me a plastic bag." He hollered the order over his shoulder and then turned back to Kelly. "So, we need to ask you some questions about the first can you found." The radio on his belt buzzed with static and a dispatcher's voice announced a call number. He glanced down at the radio and then held up one finger toward Kelly. "Don't go anywhere."

"Whatever I can do to help," Kelly agreed.

He unclipped his radio and headed to a drinking fountain several feet away from the other police officers. Holding the radio up to his ear, he kept his gaze focused on Kelly. She wished she could overhear his conversation.

A female officer approached Kelly and held out a plastic bag. "Drop your can in the bag."

Kelly obeyed the order and then glanced up at the officer. She had recognized the voice only after the can had slipped into the bag. Her breath caught when she realized she was staring at Gina. Gina's lips were sealed in a tight line. Neither woman said a word. With her hands covered in rubber gloves, Gina carefully sealed the clear plastic bag. Kelly guessed they would dust the can for her fingerprints. She stared at the SFPD patch attached to the chest of Gina's dark blue uniform, wishing she could explain what had happened. Fortunately, they wouldn't find her prints on the pop bomb.

"Hernandez, start taping," an officer hollered.

Gina spun on her heels and caught the bright yellow roll of plastic tape that the officer threw at her. She quickly returned to the park bench to hand off the can and then began cordoning off the trees surrounding the park bench. It was obvious that Gina was definitely the lowest on the totem pole in this group of officers. Other police officers were directing the crowds that spilled out of the Civic Center buildings around the area encircled with yellow plastic. Two investigators in bomb squad uniforms carefully scanned the area for clues.

The first officer had finished listening to the radio message and cleared his throat. He motioned for Kelly to follow him down the path away from the stage. When they were beyond earshot of the other officers, he began, "I understand that you have pressing business at the banquet hall."

"Well, I'm supposed to be watching—"

He waved his hand to interrupt her. "I don't need details. I've been instructed not to hold you for questioning. However, we need to begin searching for possible suspects. Did you see anyone near the bench where you found the first can?"

Kelly nodded. "Yeah, there was a homeless guy collecting cans from the trash can by that bench. I wasn't really paying attention to him, but after he left I saw the flame burning up the wick."

"Can you give me a description of him?"

Kelly quickly described the man and then added the details about the second can that she'd found. She glanced at her watch. The cocktail reception at the banquet hall would start in ten minutes.

"I know you need to get going." He handed her a business card. "I'd advise you to leave the plaza now. Contact me in three hours to finish this conversation—no later. We'll start combing the area for the man you described."

"One other thing. I'm not sure how important this may be or not, but the guy did not smell like a homeless man. He really didn't smell bad at all."

The officer nodded and thanked her for the help. Kelly took the card and slipped it in her pocket without looking at the name or number. "I'll call in three hours. No later." She knew she had to get to the banquet hall immediately. Kelly realized that Rick must still hold quite a bit of clout if he could convince a cop to let a primary witness—or possible suspect—leave the area before completing questioning. Her stomach was churning with acid. She moved out of the cordoned area quickly, passing Gina without any sign of acknowledgment. How could Gina be here now? Kelly wondered what Gina would think about seeing her here. Hopefully she could talk to her before Gina told Shannon or Beth what had happened.

By the time she reached the Grand Marquis Hotel, Kelly was sweating from dodging through crowds of pedestrians. She grabbed her backpack out of the cloakroom and changed clothes in the bathroom of the hotel's restaurant. Instead of the jeans and T-shirt that she had worn at the plaza, she slipped into a pair of black slacks and a silk blouse she'd stashed in her backpack. The blouse was wrinkled at the sleeves but Kelly guessed no one at the cocktail reception would notice a few creases.

The reception was by invitation only and security guards were checking all bags before allowing anyone to enter the hall. After leaving her backpack in the cloakroom, Kelly entered the banquet hall. A large sign had been placed at the front of the room to announce the event as a fundraiser for the Coalition. Kelly was relieved to find that Nora had remembered to add her name to the list. The guards let her pass.

Guests were just beginning to fill the room and a line was forming at the bar. Nora was in the center of the room, near the table of appetizers, addressing a group of women. Hannah was standing at the back of the room entrenched in a heated discussion with several men. Marcus and John were mingling with a crowd near the bar. Kelly ordered a soda and wandered around until she found a mixed group, thick in a debate over the lawsuit that Hannah had just announced. Everyone agreed that the current military policy discriminated against queer soldiers. The dividing point was the potential for Hannah's lawsuit to proceed to the Supreme Court. Kelly listened to the arguments on both sides while keeping close tabs on Hannah.

Before long, Kelly heard her phone beep. Rick's text message was a relief from the current conversation about the war. She quickly read the screen: "Tell Hannah that Lee is ready."

Hannah had just stepped away from a group of friends and was headed toward the bar. Kelly quickly cut through the room and joined her at the bar. The bartender took Hannah's drink order and began to scoop ice into a cup. Kelly set her phone on the bar counter in front of Hannah. With a quick glance at the message on the phone, Hannah stopped the bartender and apologized. "I think I've changed my mind about the drink. Can I just get some water?"

He nodded and handed her a bottle.

Kelly slipped the phone back in her pocket and headed to the front entrance of the hall. She hung by the door, waiting for Hannah to say her good-byes. She left the ballroom and Kelly followed close behind her. They reached the elevator and Hannah pressed the elevator call button. Kelly wondered if she should say something, but Hannah was clearly ignoring her. *What would she say if I mentioned Shannon?*

The Grand Marquis boasted twenty-one floors and a perfect view of the San Francisco Bay from the suites at the top. At least, that was what Kelly read on the placard on the wall by the elevator. When the elevator finally reached their floor, Hannah entered and pressed the button for the basement garage.

They reached the garage quickly, and Kelly was relieved to see Lee's sedan parked near the elevator door. Hannah nodded once at Kelly as she opened the passenger door. She quickly slipped into the back seat. The wheels squealed as the car sped out of the parking garage. Kelly watched the sedan disappear from view.

She stepped back into the elevator and pressed the button for the lobby. She still had to pick up her backpack from the cloakroom and needed to talk to Rick about the police interview.

She pressed the phone's green button to call him. "Hello? Just to let you know, she's leaving the city."

A buzz of static preceded Rick's voice. "Yeah, I know. You're clear to leave."

Lee must have called Rick as soon as he picked up Hannah. "No, I can't leave yet. I have to call the cops. They want to question me about the thing at the plaza."

"Don't worry about it. I took care of everything. They're out looking for your homeless man. I doubt they'll find him."

Kelly remembered suddenly that the homeless man was wearing gloves. It was fairly common to wear gloves, even in June. Mornings in San Francisco were never that warm. But most bums that she'd seen had cut off the tips of their gloves so the fingertips were exposed. She realized now that his gloves were uncut. Kelly slipped the phone back in her pocket. At least her part was done.

Chapter 15

049701

Six hours after leaving the Grand Marquis, Kelly's phone had beeped. It was just after nine but she'd already fallen asleep on the couch. Alex nudged her shoulder and pointed at the cell phone on the kitchen table. He was watching another ball game. She rubbed her eyes and reluctantly picked up the phone. Squinting at the screen, she read Rick's text message: "Lee's car was tailed."

Kelly hit the green button to page his phone but Rick didn't answer. She left a message asking for further directions. In a few minutes she received his reply. The message listed an address in Ashton. Rick gave her twenty minutes to get to the location. She left the house immediately, telling Alex not to wait up for her. He guessed she was heading to one of her girlfriends' houses and offered to be her alibi depending on who called. As long as she told him the story in the morning, he would cover her for anything.

She parked a few blocks away from the address Rick had given her. She passed several cars parked along the sidewalk before spotting Rick's black Chevy. Rick greeted her with a nod. He unlocked the passenger door and waited for her to climb in before pointing to the house at the end of the block. "Hannah's inside," he said.

Rick explained that Hannah's house was being watched by whoever had tailed Lee's car from the hotel that afternoon. He pointed to a black sedan at the end of the block. Rick guessed they were from the military, but he didn't give details. He handed her the binoculars and began to describe the plan that had been formulated over the past hour by Nora.

Kelly focused the lens on the gray two-story tract house with a neatly trimmed front lawn and a tall sycamore by the front mailbox. Two lights shone from the front of the house, a window on the first floor by the front door and a window on the second floor. A hedge separated both sides of the yard from the neighbors' yards. She shifted the focus to the car parked in front of the house. Kelly tried to swallow, but her tongue felt numb in her mouth. Her eardrums vibrated with a pounding heartbeat as she watched the two men in the black sedan. Everyone drove black sedans, she thought grimly.

Rick gave simple instructions. Kelly was to slip inside Hannah's yard through the back gate. Hannah would open the back door and leave as soon as Kelly arrived. Nora was parked on the street behind Hannah's house. She would take Hannah to stay at a friend's house on the coast, somewhere south of San Francisco. Kelly would stay at Hannah's so that whoever was watching the place would think Hannah was still inside. Rick warned her not to answer any calls and to page him immediately if someone knocked at the door. He would be parked nearby until the military boys left.

After listening to Rick's plan, Kelly nodded in agreement. She was willing to help Hannah out but wished she were back at Alex's house. She didn't want Alex to be her alibi tonight. She wanted to be asleep on the couch. Kelly handed the binoculars back to Rick and tried to relax. This was no big deal, she thought. She just had to spend the night in a house that was being watched by a couple of guys from the military. No big deal, she repeated.

Rick's phone buzzed once and he nodded at Kelly. It was the signal from Nora. She was parked behind Hannah's house now and waiting. Carefully avoiding the ring of light from the streetlamp, Kelly crept down the dark sidewalk. After eleven, most porch lights were switched off. Hannah's light was still on as well as a few of her neighbors'. The prime time news broadcast was over now and Kelly wondered what the television reporters had said about Hannah's press conference.

Kelly jumped a fence near a tall spruce tree and landed in the yard next to Hannah's house. She was surprised at how calm she suddenly felt as she picked her way through Hannah's garden. She knocked on the back door and waited. The second hand ticked slowly around the face of her watch. A minute passed. She raised her hand to knock again and hesitated, holding her breath. Feet shuffled up to the doorway. The lock clicked and the door opened.

Hannah looked at Kelly and sighed. "About time. Do you always run late?"

Kelly nodded.

She clicked her tongue. "You're not in the army."

"No, ma'am."

"You don't look like Shannon's type. And you don't look tough at all. I'm not surprised we almost had a fireworks display this afternoon. I'd have guessed it'd been much worse, knowing now who was on guard. Have you ever stood guard for anything before today?"

Kelly opened her mouth and then closed it. She couldn't think of a response and was surprised by Hannah's frank comments. She wondered why she had agreed to help and then remembered the money Rick had promised her. "There's a car waiting on Spruce Street, behind your house."

"Thanks," Hannah said. "Lock the door when you leave."

After Hannah had disappeared from view, Kelly wandered inside the house. It was a small house with only a few windows facing the front street. Kelly pulled back the corner of the drapes and looked out. The black sedan that had followed Lee and Hannah after the cocktail reception was parked directly across from Hannah's garage. The two men in the black sedan had not moved since Rick pointed them out to Kelly ten minutes earlier. If they were trying to remain unnoticed, they were doing a bad job, Kelly decided. Maybe someone was just trying to intimidate Hannah by following her. Kelly could see Rick's car farther down the block. She let go of the drapes and turned on the television.

The living room was uncomfortably austere. There was one couch, a coffee table and an entertainment center. No pictures hung from the plain white walls. After flipping through the channels, Kelly settled on an episode of *MASH*. Up until a few weeks ago, this show and action-packed war movies had been her only exposure to military life. The military doctors on the screen were attempting to save the life of a man who had just lost his arm when a hand grenade detonated too soon. Kelly watched the show with an uneasy feeling—the man on the surgery table looked remarkably like Buck, the kid who had taunted Tasha over the game of pool. She wandered if Shannon and her friends would indeed remain safely posted at the San Francisco base. Anything could happen.

She started to doze off toward the end of the show and decided to raid Hannah's kitchen. Opening the refrigerator, Kelly inspected its contents. The glass shelves were meticulously clean and all food was arranged in rows of Tupperware containers. The phone rang and Kelly closed the door immediately, feeling like she had been caught with an open cookie jar. After the third ring, the answering machine picked up. Kelly waited for the prerecorded message to finish and for the caller to speak.

The machine beeped and a female voice said, "Hey, it's me. Hello?"

Kelly instantly felt queasy. She stared at the machine, willing it to stop recording. She knew this voice too well.

Shannon started again, "Hello? Are you there? Are you screening calls? Well, I was just watching the news and saw you . . . Wow. I didn't think you were going to take it this far. So, does this mean you're pushing the lawsuit up to the Supreme Court? Hey, I have to talk to you about something that's been on my mind for a while . . . Are you listening and just not picking up the line? I know you screen calls. Hmm . . . Okay, so, I guess you're not home. Or, you're listening to this and just not picking up the phone." Shannon paused, as though she expected Hannah to actually pick up the line.

Kelly hated to admit it, but Shannon sounded like a lover calling to make up after a quarrel. She considered picking up the phone just to interrupt the call but knew that was out of the question. It was possible that someone was tapping Hannah's phone line. Kelly struggled to ignore the feeling that she was the last picked softball player stuck in left outfield.

"Well, whatever," Shannon continued, "I want to see you tonight, but I know you told me not to come over. Look, just call me when you can talk. Or maybe I'll just drop by. Hell, I don't know what to do. Why aren't you home?" The line disconnected and the machine beeped loudly.

Kelly sat down on the counter by the phone. She knew that she couldn't call Shannon from Hannah's phone. There was no way to tell her not to come over tonight. The men that were watching Hannah's house might be military and could recognize Shannon if she came to Hannah's house.

Kelly rifled through a pile of papers by the phone, trying not to think about Shannon's call. A signature on one of the papers in the stack caught her attention as she flipped through the Post-it notes, bills and bank statements. It was folded in half with Shannon's signature at the bottom of the page. Kelly paused for a moment, debating over unfolding the sheet to read Shannon's letter.

The sound of shattering glass suddenly made Kelly's blood freeze. She slipped the letter in her pocket and flicked off the overhead kitchen lights. She switched on the stove light and the kitchen was bathed in a weak yellow glow. Where had the sound come from?

Was it the front window or one of the bedroom windows facing the side yard?

Her cell phone beeped once and she heard Rick's voice. "Get out of the house. Now."

Kelly pressed the green button once, signaling that she had received the message, and ran toward the hall leading off from the kitchen. She reached the back door, unlocked the deadbolt, then heard footsteps. A black overcoat hung from the first peg of a coat rack mounted by the door. Crouched behind the coat, Kelly listened as the footsteps came closer. She wondered if the door hinges would creak if she pulled the handle. All she could think of was escaping the house before the footsteps got any closer. A man dressed in dark blue jeans and a blue jacket strode into the kitchen. He held a handgun out in his right hand as he glanced around the room. Kelly guessed he was in his early twenties. His age and the crewcut hairstyle suggested he was military. He picked up the phone to listen for a dial tone, then replaced the receiver and pulled a flashlight from his jacket pocket. Kelly heard her heart thumping loudly in her chest and realized she had been holding her breath. She quietly exhaled. The flashlight rays brushed into the hallway where Kelly hid, concealed by Hannah's overcoat. She felt her heartbeat slow down as she concentrated on her breathing.

The flashlight beam stopped, inches from the corner where she hid. Listening to the retreating footsteps, Kelly guessed the man was headed toward the family room. She heard the creak of stairs as he started to climb the steps to the second floor. Now was her best chance of escape. The hinges screeched loudly as she opened the door. Kelly bolted out of the house, not bothering to close the door behind her. She knew the man would be on her tail within seconds.

Trampling over the rows of flowers in Hannah's garden at full speed, Kelly reached the back fence and scaled the wood panels. She landed in the next-door neighbor's yard and continued running until she reached her car. Panting, Kelly scanned the street as she unlocked the door of her Volkswagen. Her hands shook as she tried to pull open the door. The man was nowhere in sight. She slid into the front seat and turned the key in the ignition. Her eyes focused on the rearview mirror as she drove past the entrance to Hannah's neighborhood. She reached for her phone and pressed the green button. "I'm out of the house."

"Good to hear your voice," Rick said, after a short buzz of static. "I figured you wouldn't have any trouble getting out of a bind. See how easy this job is?"

"I don't want to talk about it." Kelly's grip on the phone tightened as she tried to stop her hand from shaking.

"We'll talk later. The fun is just getting started."

She swore softly. "Yeah, we'll see. Have a good night." She dropped the phone on the seat and tried to tune in a radio station. Her hand was still shaking. The image of the man in the kitchen kept flashing in her mind. She spun the volume dial and music blasted through the speakers. After tonight, she had no intention of helping Hannah again. She needed a good night's sleep before she could think of what to do with her relationship with Shannon.

It was after midnight by the time Kelly knocked on Gina's door. She hoped Gina wouldn't mind company. Kelly considered calling first but changed her mind. She didn't want to talk anymore. Gina was still awake and let Kelly in without hesitation. Kelly knew Gina wanted to hear the story about the soda can and her link to Hannah Esslinger. Somehow she convinced Gina to go to bed without a full explanation. Kelly didn't know how much she could tell her.

Hugging Gina's back, Kelly snuggled under the covers. She kissed Gina's neck and caressed her cool cheeks against Gina's warm skin. "Thanks for letting me in. I know it's late."

"I was worried when I heard the knock. Especially after what happened at the plaza." Gina waited for Kelly to respond. A few minutes later she asked, "Kelly, are you still awake?"

"No." Kelly had closed her eyes. The heaviness of sleep hit as soon as her head sank into Gina's pillow.

"All right, I'll let you off the hook for now. You look exhausted. But I think that since you're here I should at least get a good story tomorrow."

Kelly shook her head slowly. "I don't think I can tell you."

Gina turned to face her. She kissed Kelly's lips softly. "Well, honey, I wish you could tell me. I don't think I can be appeased with just having the mystery woman in my bed. You should have heard the guys talking about you at the station. It created a stir when we were all sent out to search for the prime suspect—the bum you described—when the prime witness left the scene without full questioning. John was pissed that he had to let you go and the other guys jumped all over him when we saw you walk away. But the captain took John's side. They said you were off limits and would be questioned later as needed. So, the guys have tagged you as everything from CIA to FBI to Mafia."

Kelly smiled. "Too bad none of it's true—sounds exciting. No, I was just in the wrong place at the wrong time today."

"I'm not buying that. Even with your eyes closed I can tell you're lying. Remember, I'm a cop. I deal with liars all the time. Just tell me one thing." She paused. "Why were you at the plaza today?"

Kelly sighed. "Gina, I can't tell you that."

Kelly left Gina's house early the next morning. She slipped out of the bed before Gina woke and left a note of apology taped to the refrigerator. She couldn't tell her anything about the plaza. Alex had already left for work by the time she got home. She made toast and flipped through the Friday morning paper, finding an article about Hannah's press conference and the GLB Political Action Coalition's lawsuit. Kelly was surprised that no mention was made about the pop bomb.

Kelly finished her breakfast and went to the laundry room to start a load of wash. She loaded the machine and then glanced at the jeans she was wearing. She'd worn the same clothes last night at Hannah's house and dried mud was splattered on the pant legs from her run through the garden. She pulled off her jeans and absently checked the pockets for spare change. She found the letter that Shannon had written to Hannah folded in her back pocket. Staring at the letter, she considered tossing it in the trash, but her curiosity was too strong. Unfolding the letter, she noted the date, three days ago. She sighed and read the brief note:

Dear Hannah, I miss you. I know you told me not to write or call, but I can't stay away forever. When can I see you again? I'm worried about you. Don't shut me out of your life. Love, Shannon.

At the bottom of the note, someone had added two phone numbers in pencil. Kelly recognized one of the numbers as Shannon's cell phone. The other number she didn't recognize. The pencil marks didn't match Shannon's handwriting. She started the wash and carried Shannon's note into the kitchen. With some hesitation she picked up the phone and called the unknown number on the note.

A woman's voice answered after two rings. "Hello, this is April at the Emergency Lifeline."

Kelly thought of a quick excuse. "I think I may have dialed the wrong number. This is a hotline for what type of emergencies?"

"Suicide prevention," April responded, too cheerfully.

"Oh, I'm sorry. I must have misdialed." Kelly hung up the phone. She had considered telling the woman that she should tone down her cheery voice. Maybe there weren't many people who called the hotline at ten in the morning.

She stared at the letter again. Why would Hannah have a suicide hotline number unless she was contemplating this? she wondered. Kelly picked up the phone again, this time to call Alex. He answered on the first ring.

"Hey, it's me. Can you talk for a minute?" Kelly asked.

"I'm on a job site inspection," Alex said. He sounded stressed. "I've got about two minutes before the contractor gets back to look at my project. What's up?"

Alex was the one person she completely trusted. She wanted to tell him everything. "I just wanted to call and let you know that I got home okay."

"I may be overprotective, but I figure you can keep the girls in line. Should I have stayed up all night worrying?" His cell phone crackled with static as he laughed.

195

"No, you don't need to worry about me." Kelly wanted to tell him about Hannah's house and the man with the gun. She couldn't get his profile out of her mind. "Did anyone call?"

"No calls. But I would have lied for you if you needed the alibi. So, why'd you need to leave in the middle of the night? What happened? Which girl did you piss off this time?"

"It's a long story. I'll tell you later." Kelly slowly realized she had no intention of telling Alex anything about the past twenty-four hours. "I do need your advice about something though."

"Okay, shoot."

"If you found out that the woman you were dating was still in love with her ex, would you stop seeing her?"

"You're in second place because of the ex-girlfriend?"

"Something like that," Kelly agreed.

"Then I'd say that there are other fish in the sea for you. Drop her before you get hurt. Hey, Kelly, I hate to cut off, but the contractor just came back. I'm going to catch hell if this end of the building isn't wired by noon. Call me later?"

"Okay." Kelly hung up and sank into the sofa cushions. Alex was right—there were other fish. Unfortunately, neither Shannon nor Gina seemed over their ex-girlfriends. And Kelly wasn't willing to move on. Also, she wanted to know more about Hannah and the military case and Shannon was the closest connection she had to Hannah. She was the best lead to press for information. Kelly wouldn't cancel their weekend plans. As far as the letter, she decided against telling Rick about it and tucked it into a paperback in Alex's bookcase.

Kelly relaxed back on the couch in the family room and listened to the ticking of the ceiling fan. Otherwise, the house was quiet. Elvis had curled into a ball at the other end of the couch for a mid-morning nap. His whiskers and eyelids twitched as he dreamed. She decided she could use a nap as well. The phone beeped just as she had drifted to sleep. She reached for the phone and Elvis scowled at her. The cat didn't like interruptions. After apologizing to him, Kelly read the text message from Rick. "Return library books before work."

Shaking her head, Kelly looked over at the cat enviously. Elvis had already closed his eyes, bent on finishing his nap. She wondered what Rick had in mind for her now. She was scheduled for a busy afternoon of teaching. Elvis's simple life looked appealing. As if sensing her thoughts, the cat opened his eyes and yawned. He stretched out his front paw and flexed his nails before tucking his head under his other paw. Kelly reluctantly left the couch and went to gather her library books. She felt uneasy that Rick knew so much about her life and guessed that he had followed her to the library on her last trip. How often did Rick follow her?

The sun moved behind a cloud and the street was cast in a sudden shadow. It was nearly two o'clock and hotter than usual in the city. In front of the university library, drummers pounded their palms against canvas stretched taut over wood barrels and sang in a language that blended murmurs of happiness with cries of pain. Two women with bright orange and yellow scarves danced at the center of the drum circle. They leapt and spun over the ground while their arms swept through the air as if gathering all of the shadows on the cement. Kelly paused to watch the scene. She leaned against a phone booth, her new library books stacked in the backpack at her feet, and half-closed her eyes. The dancers melded into one form and the drums pounded like a single heartbeat.

A few pedestrians paused to glance at the drum circle. Most hurried past as though they were late for something important. They watched the ground to avoid the cracks in the cement and ignored the beautiful dancers. Kelly left her backpack by the phone booth and moved to the edge of the circle. Bowing slow and deep, she began a karate form, the drums urging her to kick higher and punch harder. The form's stylized sequence of techniques prepared her body for the next fight and let her mind relax with the repetition of strikes and blocks.

A man paused by the phone booth. Her backpack was at his feet.

Kelly threw a spinning hook kick in the air and suddenly realized the man was Lee, Hannah's driver at the press conference. His fixated stare held onto her body as she continued the karate form. The drummers' rhythm increased in speed and she was struggling to keep pace. Abruptly, the drumming stopped. Kelly paused, motionless, and looked over at the circle. One of the men raised his stick, beckoning her to join them.

She glanced back at the phone booth and watched Lee's retreating back for a moment. Next to her backpack he had left a black bag. Keeping her eye on the phone booth and the two bags, Kelly joined the drummers as they began packing up their things. Their afternoon practice session had ended but a few of the drummers wanted to ask her about the karate forms. They invited her to practice with them next week. She agreed and then admitted she had to leave. If she missed the next train, she'd be late for work. She ran to pick up her backpack and the bag Lee had left without looking inside.

When Kelly found her seat on the train, she pulled Lee's bag into her lap. There were no marks on the outside. It was just a plain black duffel bag. She had called Rick to ask him if she could open the bag. He didn't answer. She stared at the bag for fifteen minutes, waiting for his reply. Finally her phone beeped. His text message listed only an address: 501A Pacific Coast Highway.

Curiosity finally pushed her to unzip the bag. Wrapped in a blue blanket, she found a handgun nestled next to a small box. The box rattled when she nudged it. She guessed it contained bullets and shuddered involuntarily. A slip of paper was folded under the box. Picking out the slip, she zipped the bag closed. Suddenly uneasy with her possessions, she glanced at the other passengers on the train. Why had Lee given her a gun? Penciled on the note was a date and time. Kelly sighed with relief. This was just another delivery. She would drop off the bag after work at the address that Rick had sent. The gun would be out of her hands soon.

Chapter 16

049801

Thick fog nestled over the bay and the streetlights shone irides-cent on the wet asphalt. During the drive to the city, Shannon dis-cussed her plans for applying to college and her future career dreams. She was particularly talkative and Kelly happily let her carry the conversation. For some reason, she had no interest in Shannon's life plan. Instead of listening, she thought about the gun she had delivered. She guessed that the address on the coast highway, south of San Francisco, was Hannah's new hiding place.

The delivery of the gun hadn't gone as smoothly as dropping off the envelopes. Someone had switched on the front lights just as she tossed the duffel bag on the doormat. She immediately turned and ran out of the yard. By the time she reached her car, the front door had opened and a woman appeared in the doorway. Kelly ducked into the driver's seat of her Volkswagen. The woman picked up the bag and then scanned the front yard. Kelly couldn't tell if it was Hannah. From her parking place, she could see only that the woman was tall with shoulder-length brown hair. Then the front door had closed and the porch lights flickered.

After making the delivery the night before and then helping at the karate tournament that morning, she was exhausted and in no shape to talk about future careers. The tournament had gone well. Her students had earned several sparring trophies and she was pleased with most of the judges' scores on their forms. She had tested Colin that afternoon. His attention strayed only once and he endured a full hour of kicking drills and pushups to earn back his purple belt. He had beamed at Kelly when she tied the belt around his waist. Kelly kept him a few minutes longer than really necessary, hoping that his parents would come to see the test and congratulate him. A babysitter appeared instead.

Kelly found a parking place behind a fast-food restaurant after circling the block near the club several times while Shannon complained about the city's lack of sufficient parking. They crossed the street in front of the restaurant and turned down a road lined by dark warehouses. At the doorway to one of the buildings, a line of women stood waiting as the bouncer checked for identification. Music echoed out from the dark club. Shannon smiled and leaned close to kiss Kelly as they joined the line. The other women from their group approached, laughing. Beth, Tasha and Gina had driven to the club in a separate car. Kelly was happy that she hadn't had to face the ride from the suburbs into San Francisco with both Shannon and Gina in the same car.

Hot air and loud music blasted at the entrance to the club. The dance floor was packed with women and Kelly pulled on Shannon's arm to direct her to the floor. Shannon shook her head and pointed to the bar where the rest of their group had already crowded to order drinks. Kelly nodded and followed her, not bothering to speak in the loud club. Even screams were swallowed by the deafening music pouring out of the speakers.

As they waited for their drinks, Beth tapped Shannon's shoulder and pointed to a girl who had just appeared on the dance floor. Shannon nodded and smiled at Beth. Tasha shook her head. The girl was tall and sexy, her muscles carved beautifully on her belly and back. Her smile was perfect, demure and inviting. Everyone in the group seemed to be appreciating the same scenery here.

When they had finished their first round of drinks, Tasha pointed to the dance floor and Beth followed. Shannon quickly drained the last of her bottle and led Kelly to a space near the center of the sea of swaying bodies. Gina had stayed at the bar. She was talking to an Asian woman and flirting vivaciously. With the bass notes banging through the speakers and Shannon's body rubbing against hers, Kelly tried to ignore the pangs of jealousy she felt watching Gina flirt with the other woman. The rhythm of the music started to relax her and the tension from the past week dissipated as she danced.

On the front stage, two women were dancing close, barely clothed, grinding against each other. Their bodies were well toned, their muscles etched in taut lines on their abdomens, breasts squeezed tight under sport bras, their arms sculpted, skin glistening with sweat.

Kelly scanned the crowd as she danced with Shannon. Her gaze stopped on two women kissing off to the side of the dance floor. She instantly recognized Starr, Alex's new girlfriend. Her stomach turned as she saw Starr pull her date out onto the dance floor. Kelly watched as they danced. Their bodies rubbed against each other suggestively and Kelly wondered if Starr was drunk or laced on Ecstasy. She clung to her partner as though her own feet couldn't support her. Kelly didn't want to tell Alex about this and was upset that Starr would be here at all.

Suddenly, an arm struck Shannon's back. Shannon spun around as a woman with long curly black hair stumbled backward toward her. The curly-haired woman knocked into Tasha as she started to fall.

201

Shannon caught the woman around the waist and a camera flashed twice as all three women blinked in the bright light. The curly-haired woman attempted to stand. A wide swatch of the dance floor cleared instantly as a tall woman threw a bottle at the feet of the curly-haired woman. The bottle shattered against the dance floor. The sound of breaking glass was barely audible over the cacophony of music and shouting voices. Seeing the tall woman's sneer, the curly-haired woman cursed loudly and pushed away from Shannon. She hurled herself at the tall woman. An angry shout erupted as two burly women leapt in to break up the fight. Another body lunged into the circle. The camera flashed again as Shannon and Tasha were pulled into the scuffle. Kelly grabbed Shannon's hand to pull her out of the fight, but she shook loose from the grip and lunged at the tall woman. Finally, Kelly locked Shannon's arms and yanked her out of the fight. At least no one had thrown a punch yet.

"What the hell do you think you're doing?" Tasha yelled as she grabbed the woman with the camera. The woman lurched away from Tasha and ran through the crowd toward the exit. Tasha was close on her heels, despite Beth's screaming for her to stay put.

Kelly watched Tasha near the exit and then glanced back at Shannon. She was angrily shouting at the tall woman who had thrown the glass and hadn't noticed the exchange between Tasha and the photographer. Kelly pulled Shannon to the side and yelled in her ear, "Tasha just took off after the woman with the camera."

Shannon glanced around the room, finally understanding the threat of having her picture taken in the midst of a fight at a lesbian club. Kelly pushed through the crowd of women and out the exit door with Beth and Shannon close behind. As the door closed behind them, Kelly scanned the back alleyway for Tasha. She spotted her less than a hundred feet away and sprinted toward her.

A loud shout came from the back entrance of the bar and Kelly glanced over her shoulder. An obese bouncer was shoving the curly-haired woman and her tall girlfriend out the door. They fell directly into Beth and Shannon.

"Hey, bitch," the tall woman yelled, "you wanna finish this or what?"

Staggering, the curly-haired woman started cussing loudly, "Fuck yeah—I'm ready to settle this. And then I'm gonna sue your ass for assault."

Kelly heard the exchange but continued after Tasha. She hoped that Shannon and Beth wouldn't be pulled into round two of the fight. Fortunately, there were plenty of women gathered in small groups outside the bar smoking clove cigarettes and marijuana. Shannon and Beth would have plenty of help if another fight ensued.

She finally caught up to Tasha at the end of the alleyway. "Tasha, forget about the camera. This isn't the part of town where you want to go for a jog."

"I can't forget about it. I'm already in trouble. If those pictures get back to the army I'm out." Tasha was panting, breathless, as she continued to run. The woman with the camera was nowhere in sight. Near the end of the next block, an old man was curled under a blanket in a doorway to a dark warehouse. The whites of his eyes flashed briefly as he watched the two women pass. He hissed loudly like a cat that had had his tail stepped on and shouted some obscenity. Tasha sprinted down the next block, searching for the photographer. Both sides of the alley were lined with chain link fences or impervious stone warehouse walls. The narrow street seemed to stretch forever and no lights defined the end of the path or a cross street.

Finally, a dark passageway between two warehouses appeared. Tasha took off down the alley. With a nervous glance over her shoulders, Kelly followed reluctantly.

Suddenly Tasha screamed and shrank back toward Kelly. Someone snatched hold of Tasha's arm and yanked her forward.

"Looking for this?" he asked with a sneer.

Even though it was dark, Kelly recognized the face of the man with the crewcut instantly. He'd been in Hannah's kitchen carrying a gun. Kelly gritted her teeth, forcing her body not to freeze up with fear. The passageway was otherwise empty; the photographer from the club had disappeared. Kelly wondered if this man had paid the woman with the camera to instigate the fight in the club. With the pictures, it would be easy for the army to order a discharge for Shannon and Tasha.

The man dangled out the camera and leered at Tasha. Instantly, Tasha grabbed for the camera. It slipped from his hand and smashed on the ground.

"You have no idea what you're dealing with," the man yelled angrily. His other hand still held Tasha's arm in a vice grip.

Without thinking, Kelly aimed a downward strike to the center of his forearm. She hit the nerve and his fist reflexively released Tasha's arm. Tasha lunged away from him as he turned toward Kelly. She drove a side kick directly at his knee. A resounding crack followed the knee strike and his leg cocked to the side. He screamed in pain, clutching his knee.

In the next moment, Tasha scooped up the camera. The man saw her and let go of his knee to reach inside his jacket pocket. A switch-blade flashed silver in his hands.

Tasha gasped as soon as the man turned toward Kelly. She gripped the camera strap.

"Get out of here," Kelly yelled at her.

The man glanced back and forth between the two women. Tasha started to argue but stopped when the man turned the knife at her. Eyeing the camera in her hands, he stepped toward Tasha, taunting her with the knife. Instantly, Kelly threw a second side kick to his injured knee. Jumping to his good leg, he cursed and then focused on Kelly. He slashed the knife at her chest. She sank away from the knife and then sprang forward, catching his wrist. With the blade inches from her skin, she slid her fingers up the knife handle and twisted his arm to the side. While he fought to hold the knife, she wrenched his arm over her back and threw him down to the ground. He fell against the cement, cracking the back of his head on the side of the brick building. Kelly pulled the blade out of his hands and stepped back, waiting. He was unconscious, but his chest quivered with each breath. He would be alert momentarily.

Tasha touched Kelly's arm. Her voice shook as she tried to speak. "We should go."

Kelly pocketed the switchblade and followed Tasha back down the same dark alley filled with the odor of urine. As they passed the old man huddled in the doorway under the thin blankets, he nodded with a strange smile of familiarity. Kelly felt her skin prickle uneasily. Would this old man be questioned later? Would there be an investigation? She thought of the switchblade in her jeans and wished she had left it in the alley. Unfortunately, she couldn't risk leaving fingerprints at the scene.

Back at the club, the same two women were engaged in a shouting match. Gina had joined Beth and Shannon outside the club. The three were anxiously awaiting Tasha and Kelly's return and trying to avoid the two angry lovers.

"Well, I think that's enough fun for one night," Tasha said. "Would anyone complain if we leave now?"

"No complaints. Let's get the hell out of this place," Beth agreed quickly. "I was freaked out that you guys weren't coming back. I wish you hadn't run off after that photographer."

Tasha laughed. "You know you don't have to worry about me. I never do anything stupid. And look, we're fine."

Kelly could hear the nervous energy in Tasha's voice and wondered if the others noticed it also. Beth shivered as a gust of cold air blew down the street.

Tasha hugged Beth tightly. "Are you okay? Did anything happen at the club while we were gone?"

"No, I'm fine. It's just the cold air. And my nerves are a little on edge. Those two women were yelling the whole time but no more fights broke out. What happened with the photographer? How'd you get the film?"

Tasha had pulled the film out of the camera and tossed the camera in a dumpster before they reached the club. "The girl just handed it over when we threatened her. I don't think she really knew what was going on . . ."

205

Kelly didn't add anything to Tasha's lie. She wasn't sure why Tasha hadn't told Beth the truth. Maybe she didn't want Beth to worry. Gina was silent throughout the walk back to their cars. She glanced over at Kelly only once. Kelly returned the look of desire but quickly opened the car door for Shannon. They drove out of the club with no cars following them.

When they reached the freeway, Shannon grabbed Kelly's hand and squeezed it. "I don't know what happened when you and Tasha ran after the woman with the camera, but I know Tasha lied about it."

"It was a crazy night," Kelly replied. "We were just lucky we got the film back. I don't want to think about it anymore. Can we talk about something else?"

"You keep a lot of secrets."

Kelly shrugged. When she saw the camera's flash in the club, she'd guessed that it had something to do with Tasha and Shannon. After the incident at the base last weekend, Tasha was due for a full background investigation. If the military had pictures of them in a lesbian bar fight, Tasha's fate would be sealed.

Kelly couldn't, however, explain the man in the alleyway. She was certain that he'd been the same man in Hannah's house. If he had convinced the woman to take the pictures in the club, this might have nothing to do with the investigation of Tasha. The same people who had been after Hannah could be trailing Shannon now as well. Maybe they had traced the call that Shannon left on Hannah's answering machine . . .

Finally Kelly said, "I think we need something to relax us."

"Hmm. I'd suggest a stiff drink, but I know you'd turn me down. Maybe we can come up with something else that would help." Shannon rubbed Kelly's thigh. "Maybe a back massage?"

"No, I don't think that will be enough."

Shannon grinned. "Let me think about it. I'll see what I can do . . ."

⤫

As soon as they got out of the car, Shannon wrapped her arms around Kelly, pulling her close. "Let's go get some blankets and camp outside tonight."

"Where?" Kelly asked, scanning Shannon's tract home neighborhood. "The front yard?"

"Well, I was going to suggest the backyard, but the sprinklers will soak us at five a.m."

Kelly laughed. "I don't think I want to get wet. Let's settle for your family room floor. It's almost as exotic as camping in the middle of suburbia."

"Mmm. Nothing like hot sex in the conservative suburbs. It's almost scandalous . . ." Shannon grabbed her and tried to kiss her.

Stepping back, Kelly pointed at the sky. "Wait. Look at the stars . . . It's so peaceful here." Stars spotted the night sky. The night air was still warm from the heat of the day. "I love nights like this. It's so quiet," Kelly said. Shannon caressed her arm. A light shone through the window of the second-floor bedroom in the house across the street. The other neighbors had all turned off their lights for the night. She did not see any unusual cars on the street, but it was possible someone was lying in wait for them now. There were plenty of hiding places near Shannon's house. After the scene at the club and in the dark alleyway, she wasn't comfortable making out in Shannon's driveway. But she didn't want to admit that she was scared someone could be watching the house or tracking Shannon.

Shannon kissed Kelly's neck and then arched her eyebrow as Kelly pulled away from her again. "Why don't you want to kiss?"

"I do. Just not in front of the neighbors. And I'm still a little tense after that fight in the club. I wonder what happened to the tall woman who started it all."

"The bouncer said he was calling the cops. They're probably both sobering up in jail as we speak. Just relax, it's over now."

Kelly nodded. "Okay, let's go inside."

After unlocking the door, Shannon headed to the linen closet. She found two thick woven wool blankets and tugged them free from a stack of sheets. "Courtesy of the U.S. Army." She handed the blankets to Kelly then grabbed two pillows and closed the closet door.

"Where's the dog?" Kelly noted that the Dalmatian was nowhere to be seen and the usual chew toys were missing from the hallway.

"Paco? My parents came to pick him up yesterday. They finally finished the repairs on their house."

"Oh." Kelly hadn't thought much about the dog before tonight. Now she wanted him in the house as a watchdog.

"You sound like you miss him," Shannon said, laughing. "Obviously you didn't spend enough time here. He was driving me insane. That dog chewed everything in sight."

"But he would bark if someone tried to break into the house." Kelly couldn't shake the uneasiness that she felt after running down the dark alley with Tasha. She shivered as the memory of the fight and the switchblade flashed in her mind.

Shannon shook her head. "Relax. No one is going to break into the house. Don't worry, okay?"

"Okay," Kelly replied. The switchblade was still in her back pocket. With one hand tugging on Shannon's belt, Kelly followed her into the family room. Shannon spread the blankets over the hardwood floor and was lighting a candle on the coffee table. Kelly undid the top button of Shannon's jeans after unclasping her belt buckle. When Shannon had lit the candle, she pulled Kelly's hands away from the jeans and turned to face her.

"You always get to go first. This time, I want a chance." Their lips met and she pressed Kelly against the side of the couch. She kissed Kelly's neck and loosened the first and second buttons on her jeans. Her fingertips traced along the edge of Kelly's underwear and then reached under her shirt to brush against her breasts. "Sometimes I hate foreplay." She unbuttoned Kelly's shirt slowly and caressed her. "I want to put my fingers inside—"

"Oh really?" Kelly pulled Shannon close and pressed her lips against Shannon's, slipping her tongue inside.

Shannon pulled away and shook her head. "You're not going to win." She leaned against Kelly and kissed her lightly. Her tongue pushed inside as she continued to unbutton Kelly's jeans. Only one button remained. Slipping her middle finger into her mouth, she licked the tip then lowered it to stroke between Kelly's legs. She pushed her hips toward Kelly and said, "This time I'm going to make you come first."

Kelly pulled Shannon's hand out of her jeans and grasped her wrist firmly. She guided Shannon's hand up to her lips and kissed the wet fingertip. "Is that a threat or a promise?"

"Both." Shannon smiled.

Kelly slipped the wet finger into her mouth. Shannon's eyes closed while Kelly's tongue encircled her finger. She sucked on the finger for a moment and let it slide out of her mouth slowly as Shannon pulled back her wrist.

Shannon drew a line down Kelly's cheek with the wet fingertip. "I want you naked, now."

Kelly pulled off her shirt. She liked Shannon's dominant act and wondered how long she could keep it up for. Shannon unclasped Kelly's bra and squeezed her nipples. Kelly's jeans were hanging unbuttoned on her hips and Kelly pulled them off as Shannon watched. As Kelly finished undressing, Shannon directed her down to the army blankets and climbed on top of her. Shannon's body rubbed over Kelly, rhythmically pushing her hips into hers. The sensation of Shannon's clothing and the rough wool blanket on her naked skin added to her arousal.

Shannon pushed her tongue inside her mouth as Kelly tried to kiss her, then moved lower to kiss her neck and lower still to lick slow circles around each nipple. Her tongue brushed down her belly. Shifting her weight, Shannon traced her fingertips along the line of Kelly's thighs, detouring past the wet skin between her legs. Kelly moaned with pleasure. Each time Shannon neared Kelly's middle, her fingers and tongue brushed teasingly close to the swollen clit. Yet she refused to touch where Kelly most wanted to feel her. Waiting was painful.

"Mmm. I thought we were skipping the foreplay. I want to feel you. When are you going to take off these clothes?" Kelly murmured.

"Maybe I won't."

"Please?"

Shannon sighed. "So demanding . . ." She smiled and took off her shirt, then stood up to unbutton her jeans. Kelly pulled the edge of the wool blanket up for a cover. Shannon shook her head and pulled it down. "I want to see. Don't move until I tell you."

Kelly ached to be touched again. Shannon undressed slowly keeping her eyes focused on Kelly. Finally, she had folded all of her clothing and placed it in a neat pile on the sofa. Kelly's clothes were scattered around the room and Shannon reached down to pick up her pants. The knife slipped out of the back pocket and struck the wood floor.

Shannon picked up the knife, turned the handle over in her hand once and then glanced at Kelly. "Where did you get this? An army surplus store?"

"No." Kelly struggled to think of a lie. "I found it near a Dumpster in the city."

"I'd bet whoever lost it was in the army. It's standard issue." She straddled Kelly and crossed her arms, staring down at her as though Kelly was in trouble. She leaned down and kissed her, then pulled back. "Tell me if you've been sleeping with someone else."

"What?"

Shannon shook her head. "You know what I said."

Kelly shook her head without answering. Her nerves quivered in anticipation of Shannon's touch.

"How about just telling me the truth?" She combed through Kelly's hair with her fingers. "I know you're sleeping with someone else. Who is she?"

Kelly didn't answer. There was no way she could tell Shannon that she was sleeping with her best friend and, at the moment, it didn't matter. Right now, she wanted to be with Shannon.

"Fine. Don't tell me who she is . . . But I want you to stop sleeping with her." Her fingertips trailed down Kelly's neck to her breasts and massaged lightly. She sucked each breast in turn, and when the cool air hit, her nipples grew firm, begging for another caress. "I want you to stop sleeping with her because you like me better."

Kelly wanted Shannon to stop talking. Her body was burning for more than conversation. "You're unbelievably sexy when you're mad at me."

"Are you just saying that? I think that line has been used before. And I'm still mad at you."

"Yeah, I'm just saying that . . . and hoping you'll forget why you're mad at me."

"Fine. Let's forget about everything. Have a good life. Maybe you should call that other woman, cause you're too wet to just go to sleep." The exchange was light and the tone teasing, yet Shannon slid off Kelly and now lay beside her. Shannon started to put on her shirt, but Kelly caught her arm.

"No. Don't leave." Kelly squelched the whining tone in her voice. She wouldn't beg for anything.

"Why not?" Shannon asked.

"Because you're sexy and I want you to stay and make out with me. Besides, this is your house." Kelly grinned. "You'd have to kick me out first."

"All right. Get out of my house."

"No," Kelly said, knowing that Shannon didn't really want her to leave. If Shannon knew that Kelly had been sleeping with Gina, she might've really tried to kick her out.

"God, you're stubborn." Shannon laughed. "What am I going to do with you?"

"Make out with me?"

Shannon drew a line from Kelly's lips down to the warm space between her legs. She moved on top of her. Kelly lifted her hips up off the blankets. She was begging to feel Shannon's fingers.

"I want you to tell me what you want," Shannon said, her voice soft, the words slow as she gauged Kelly's response.

Kelly nodded, feeling her throat tighten and a throbbing desire burn between her legs. She pressed her hips up again, but Shannon shoved her down, trapping her on the floor.

"I'm going to make you ask," Shannon said, tempting her. Every spot that Shannon brushed seemed to ignite.

"You're driving me crazy," Kelly murmured as Shannon's hands played along the side of her belly and thighs. Still she avoided the center, wet with desire. "I want you . . ."

"Really?" Shannon feigned innocence. "Tell me exactly what you want."

"You know what I want," Kelly answered.

"But I want to hear you ask for it." The muscles on Shannon's arm flexed as she leaned to the side, her hand supporting her weight. She looked down at Kelly, waiting.

Kelly sighed. She knew what Shannon wanted to hear. Her body easily asked for it, but her mind was fighting against having to ask. Kelly turned away, frustrated and unwilling to bend further to comply with Shannon's request.

Shannon sat down on the blanket. The night sky outlined her body. She brushed her fingertips along the inside of Kelly's thighs. "Maybe you want me to stop?" she asked, her eyebrow arching, the tone seductive.

"No."

Seconds ticked by as they stared at each other, unflinching. After a moment, the corners of her lips pulled up in a sly grin. "Say it."

"Come on," Kelly pleaded again, but Shannon only smiled. Her hands were inches away from the spot Kelly needed her to touch. Nerves fired through her body with every touch. The intensity of her desire was only increasing as Shannon refused. "Please . . ."

Shannon lowered herself onto Kelly. She grabbed Kelly's wrists and pulled her hands over her head to rest on the pillow. "Ask for what you want." Shannon sighed after a moment of silence. "Don't move," she said, letting go of Kelly's wrists. Her hips pushed down on Kelly as she kissed her, thrusting her tongue inside Kelly's mouth.

She rubbed her knee between Kelly's legs and brushed her fingers over the short hair.

Kelly was wet and ready to beg for Shannon's hand. Yet she stopped herself from speaking. She had never had to ask for sex.

"I know how much you want it. All you have to do is ask." Shannon pushed her again.

Her clit was pulsing with desire. Ignoring her pride, Kelly started, "I want your fingers inside—"

Stopping Kelly in midsentence, Shannon parted the folds of skin and thrust deep. She continued to move her hand, two fingers slipping in and out, harder and harder as she kissed Kelly's lips and neck. Three fingers pushed inside. Kelly gave in to every thrust, her body having no control now. Each push of Shannon's hand sent a warm rush through her. Shannon's gaze caught Kelly's and she eased her fingers out.

Shannon smeared the wetness on her fingers down Kelly's chest and past her belly button. She dropped her head between Kelly's legs. Her tongue stroked the swollen clit, flicking faster and faster. Kelly spread her legs farther apart as Shannon's tongue continued the rapid strokes. She was just about to climax when Shannon pulled back. Kelly squeezed her legs together as her muscles quivered. Shannon had stood up and was heading down the hallway to her bedroom. Kelly rolled to her side and closed her eyes. Her body was still shaking as nerves screamed in confusion.

After a moment, she felt Shannon's hand on her shoulder. She rolled onto her back and gazed up at her. Shannon kneeled next to her. She held a bottle of lube and was squeezing the liquid into her palm. Kelly watched as Shannon spread the lube over her hand. She climbed on top of Kelly and kissed her.

"I want to try something with you," Shannon said.

Kelly tried to relax as she felt Shannon's hand move between her legs. She spread her legs. Three fingers slipped inside easily. The lube mingled with her wetness. Shannon pushed in a fourth finger, slowly sliding her thumb over her clit. She watched Kelly as her hand rocked back and forth with the rhythmic movement of her hips. The four fingers pulled out and Shannon kissed her again. As their lips separated, Kelly felt Shannon's four fingers and thumb push at her center. In the next moment, the hand slid through the wet space to move inside her. She cried out involuntarily as a spasm of pain raced up her body.

Shannon held her hand still. "Do you want me to pull out?"

Kelly shook her head. She was unable to speak. Every thought was concentrated on Shannon's hand inside her. Shannon rotated her wrist and the slight change in position made Kelly's eyes water. She pushed her hips up, wanting to feel every movement of Shannon's hand as more nerves were aroused.

Shannon looked down at Kelly and smiled. "I can do whatever I want with you now." Her free hand squeezed Kelly's nipple and then massaged each breast gently. The hand between her legs thrust faster now and Kelly's murmurs of pleasure mingled with gasps of pain. Shannon slid her hand out and lowered her head. She flicked her tongue between Kelly's moist folds. Running her fingers through Shannon's hair, Kelly wrapped her hands around Shannon's head and lifted her hips higher. Shannon pushed her fingers back inside while her tongue circled the clit.

Nerves exploded between Kelly's legs and a warm wave washed over her. A low groan escaped her lips as she gave in to her orgasm. Tremors raced through her muscles until something finally made her relax. Every muscle felt weak.

"You like that?" Shannon asked.

"Mmm." Kelly nodded. "Don't pull out yet."

Shannon collapsed on top of Kelly, still inside her. Her skin was hot and wet. The muscles twitched in Kelly's legs and she squeezed Shannon's fingers again.

"You want more?" Shannon asked, beginning to move inside her again.

Kelly gasped. "Not so hard. My whole body is still lit. But I want to keep you inside."

After another minute, Shannon withdrew her hand. She caressed Kelly's cheek. "I'm sorry if—"

"Don't apologize for anything," Kelly interrupted. "Unless you're about to say that you don't want to do that again."

Shannon shook her head. "I've never come just watching someone else. I can't wait to put my fingers inside you again. I can't wait to touch you again."

Kelly's body still throbbed. The brief moment of pain had been well worth the orgasm that followed. She shifted onto her side and propped herself up on her elbow. "I think it's my turn to touch you."

Shannon leaned back against the blankets and waited for Kelly. "But I'm not as tough."

Kelly kissed her. "Don't worry. Unlike you, I'm not feeling insecure." She added, "I don't have anything to prove."

Shannon shook her head and playfully tousled Kelly's hair. "Watch it, you're already in trouble."

"Well, I'm glad we aren't fighting about sex. I don't know if I could handle another fight now."

Shannon laughed. "Yeah, the scuffle with the women in the nightclub was enough excitement for one weekend."

Kelly hoped Tasha would not tell her about the man with the camera. She guessed he'd wake tomorrow morning with a bad headache. Hopefully he would not come looking for his knife.

Knock, knock, knock.

Shannon bolted upright in the bed, pushing the comforter off of her bare shoulders. Kelly rolled over to her side, propping her head up with her hand. Shannon was holding her breath and waiting for another sound.

"What time is it?" she whispered.

Kelly found her watch on the nightstand. "Eight o'clock. Who the hell knocks on someone's door this early on a Sunday morning?"

"Someone from the army," she replied.

"But you don't have drill today." Kelly peeked through the blinds and saw a box wrapped in brown paper on the front step. The package made Kelly remember her last delivery. She'd had a bad feeling about delivering the gun and came too close to being seen. Hopefully Rick wouldn't give her another job like that. "There's something on the porch. Looks like someone made an early delivery. No sign of any live person or an army drill sergeant."

Shannon nodded, then shivered. She slid back under the sheets, lying on her side, and pulled the comforter up to her chin. "Who delivers anything this early in the morning? On a Sunday? God, I don't even want to think about it. If it was someone from the army I would've been in so much trouble. Do you think I'm paranoid?"

"No. Maybe. Why would they just show up at your house?"

"If you get called into active duty they come to your house, hand you a letter with your orders and say, 'Report in twenty-four hours.' And that's it—your life is theirs."

"And if they found you in bed with some naked chick?"

Shannon grinned. "I'd be screwed." She rolled onto her back and stared up at the ceiling. Finally she said, "My ex was discharged because she was gay. Well, they got her out because of our relationship, but I think there was another reason why they wanted her discharged. She had a job updating personnel files and knew a lot of secrets. There was a whole group of lesbians on the base, but they just singled her out. They questioned all of her friends and still couldn't pin anything on her. There was a rumor that we were dating and someone had a picture of us." Shannon paused and leaned over Kelly to peek through the blinds. The package was still waiting on the porch. "But they let me off without even an investigation. Someone wanted to get her out of the army. I still can't believe she was discharged. Do you know how screwed you are if you have a dishonorable discharge on your record? Every job you apply for will want a full explanation of 'dishonorable' and some people would rather hire an ex-con."

"Why didn't you worry about being a lesbian when you signed up?"

"I was nervous at first. I had a friend in the navy and she told me not to worry about it. The thing is, you can be a lesbian in the army only as long as you don't piss someone off. When you do, they find ways to get you out of the system. Anyway, no, they probably wouldn't be too happy to find me in bed with you."

Kelly pulled Shannon close. "I like the army dyke image. You're very sexy in the green camouflage."

Shannon laughed. "Hmm, I like it when you wear your karate uniform—the black pants with that thin little string holding them on, low on your waist looks hot. Maybe we could try making out in costume."

"I think I'd be too embarrassed."

"Sometimes risks are worth taking. We could have some fun pulling off our uniforms," Shannon said mischievously. She stood up and grabbed a robe. Kelly watched through the window as she picked up the package on the front porch and quickly closed the door.

"It's for my roommate, Vicky. Her grandma sent her something Express Mail—probably another batch of cookies. She sends Vicky little presents all the time. I feel bad just tossing them in a pile, so I've been taking them to the base and sending her everything in a big box each month. Vicky didn't want to worry her grandma so she never told her that she was being sent to Iraq."

Chapter 17

049851

The next few days passed in a fast blur as the karate summer camp started. Kelly started working ten-hour days and Sam even agreed to give her a bonus after she signed an entire Little League team up for a week of karate camp. By next week, she'd regret the signup when the entire team of seven-year-olds were creating havoc in the dojo. Until then, she spent the extra fifty bucks on groceries and happily filled Alex's refrigerator with fresh produce and even indulged in a carton of her favorite mint chocolate-chip ice cream.

That week's Thursday sparring class was canceled. Joe had gotten free tickets to the Giants game and invited everyone from the adult sparring class to join him. Kelly had to teach the karate summer camp that day and couldn't make it into the city in time for the ball game. Sam hated baseball. Usually, he lost students to Little League as the busy parents could only meet so many after-school obligations.

After Kelly finished teaching her last student for the day, Sam asked her if she wanted to hang around the dojo for some grappling practice. Grappling was a blend of sparring and ground wrestling. In their dojo, it was the closest they came to an all-out fight.

Kelly was tired from the long day of teaching but she couldn't say no to Sam. She was always nervous about fighting him. It was certain that he would win every match, but if she made a mistake he could injure her in no time. Despite her own fear, she trusted his control absolutely.

Sam tightened the laces of his shoes and glanced at Kelly. "By the way, why'd you take last Thursday off?"

Kelly had hoped that Rick would have given some excuse to Sam. She didn't want to tell him about the press conference or about the evening at Hannah's house. Selecting her words carefully, she replied, "Rick asked me to run an errand. I know he owns part of the dojo, but do you think it's a good idea that I work with him?"

Sam shrugged. "Not if it gets in the way of your teaching schedule. But, he's my investor so I have to keep him happy. And I guess if he asks you to do something for him, do it. But tell me yourself. Don't let Rick give me the message."

She nodded. Fortunately, Sam wasn't going to press her for details.

"Are you ready?" he asked.

Ignoring the strong urge to step off the mat, Kelly bowed to Sam and then shook his hand. She knew Sam was upset that she hadn't talked to him more about working with Rick. And he was already unhappy with her about last weekend's tournament. Kelly had refused to fight in the tournament despite Sam's request. He said he was disappointed when she refused, but she didn't change her mind. She studied martial arts to learn how to fight, not to win a trophy. But she hated it when Sam was upset with her.

He pressed the start button on his stopwatch and tossed it to the corner of the mat. Their grappling matches only lasted three minutes, but every minute seemed to stretch as long as a year.

Springing into fighting position, Sam threw a punch toward her face. As she blocked the strike, he grabbed the sleeve of her uniform. She turned quickly, shrugging off his hands and shuffled around him. He threw a few predictable combinations that she recognized as bait meant to encourage her to take the offensive role. Kelly didn't move in. Any step closer to Sam would give him an opening to take her down. She was stalling, dancing over the mat in a wide circle around him, hoping that the fear that had caught in her chest would dissipate soon. But the longer she waited to strike, the more time it would take to shake the fear.

Kelly glanced at the stopwatch on the corner of the mat, wondering if she could stay on her feet for the full three minutes. He lunged at her suddenly. Twisting to the left, she narrowly escaped his hands. She threw a strike into his ribs with her right fist and followed with a left backhand to his temple. He caught her wrist and pulled her toward him. Wrenching her arm, she tried to break free, but he only cinched a tighter hold. She spun to the side, his fingers burning on her wrist, and aimed a back kick at his kidney. In the next second, his heel struck her calf in a sweep as his palm slammed her chest.

As she hit the ground, Sam jumped on her, pinning her to the mat. Sinking his weight on her hips, he moved down to choke her throat with interlaced fingers. She wrapped his left arm and locked his left leg with her foot, then, gasping for air, pushed over to her left side. He rolled off her and then turned to grab for her throat again. They wrestled on the ground, each battling for a handhold on the other. The only sound in the dojo came from their bodies rolling over each other and grunts of pain. His legs wrapped around her neck and he squeezed his knees tight, occluding her jugular vein.

Struggling against the pressure, Kelly counted the seconds of consciousness, one, two, three, four. Was the ringing sound coming from the stopwatch? Was their match over? Stars flashed as she closed her eyes, then only blackness and a loss of sound. She knew

Sam was still choking her, but she couldn't localize any pain. Finally, she slapped his thigh weakly. Two slaps to signal that she had lost the match.

Instantly, he released the pressure between his legs. Kelly rolled onto her belly, then crouched on her hands and knees, coughing as her lungs greedily gulped for oxygen. She looked up to see him standing by the doorway to the waiting room. The dojo was dimly lit and his profile was silhouetted in the light filtering in from the front window. She had lost consciousness for only a few seconds. But a minute feels like a year when you grapple, Kelly thought again. The stopwatch suddenly started beeping and they both glanced at the corner of the mat. He picked up the watch and silenced the noise. She stood up slowly, waiting to hear her blood pulse in her ears.

His lips moved before she heard the words. "Do you need a minute?"

Kelly shook her head, swallowing the rising pressure that swelled at the back of her throat. Resolutely, she returned his bow and handshake and the match started again.

They tumbled to the ground quickly this time. Kelly fought harder, yet his hands pressed down, shoving her back against the mat. Pinned to the ground, she reached up to find his throat. Interlacing her fingers around the sweaty skin of Sam's neck, she squeezed as if her life depended on this hold.

His fist pounded into her abdomen and the breath raced out of her lungs. Her fingers forgot their position on his neck as a weakness filled her hands, and suddenly his arms crossed over her throat. She groaned and pushed his arms away, bringing her knees up to her chest to block his body. He only fought harder, and once he had her neck squeezed between his forearms, she knew that there was no way to win the match. Still she was not ready to give up. The muscles in his forearms bulged and as his wrists turned, the pressure increased against her neck. His pelvis pressed down on her hips and his knees rested against the mat, trapping her movement to either side. A rush of nausea overcame her as his crotch pushed between her legs. She pulled her knee up toward her chest and kicked his lower spine with a hard blow. He winced with the strike, but kept his chokehold on her. Kelly hated the warmth pushing between her legs. His hands squeezed harder and she forgot the sensation of the mat under her back, turned deaf to the sound of Sam's breathing and lost the scent of their mingled sweat. Her palm shoved into Sam's face, narrowly missing his nose. She fought the urge to scratch her fingernails into his eyes. His grip only tightened. The air in her lungs was growing heavy.

Finally, she relaxed, letting her arms and legs fall to the mat. She could no longer hear any sounds and was close to losing consciousness again. She slowly tapped his leg to signal the end of the match. He collapsed on top of her as he released the chokehold. She stared at his forehead, waiting for him to get off of her. Seconds passed and he continued to press down, still hard between her legs, his pelvis immobilizing her hips. Finally, he rolled off of her and stood up, shaking out the stiffness in his hands. Without a word, he walked off the mat. She listened to the back door open and slam shut as Sam went outside. Silence. Kelly lay still on the mat, her heart pounding. The air passed painfully into her lungs as the muscles between her ribs stubbornly moved with each breath.

On the drive home, Kelly tried not to think about Sam. It was difficult to get the grappling match out of her mind. By the time she had finally recovered enough to stand, Sam had returned to grab his keys. His eyes met hers briefly, but he did not say a word. She sensed his concern and guessed that he felt bad for what had happened on the mat. In his defense, she reasoned, he hadn't done anything entirely wrong. His body's arousal was mostly beyond his control. And nothing had happened. Then again, she had been unconscious for a few seconds. He should have released the chokehold sooner, but it was her responsibility to slap his leg when she could no longer handle the fight. And although he could have hurt her more, she trusted Sam with her life.

Before their grappling match tonight, she had tried to talk to Sam about the work she was doing with Rick. But she didn't know where to begin. Maybe he already knew. Maybe he was trying to toughen her up for whatever she'd have to face in her work with Rick. Her phone buzzed and she glanced at the screen. Someone had called without leaving a message. A phone number that she didn't recognize was listed on the screen. Maybe Rick had paged her from a pay phone, she considered.

Kelly had called Rick earlier that week. After telling him about the man with the camera and the fight at the club, she admitted she still had the knife. He advised her to lose the knife and then asked her if she'd noticed anyone following her. She told him that she now spent more time staring at her rearview mirror than through the front windshield when she drove anywhere. It was amazing she hadn't gotten into an accident. But no one had been following her—she was sure. She also asked Rick about the duffel bag that she had delivered to the house on the coast. Kelly hinted that she was uncomfortable with deliveries that had dangerous contents. He had laughed and told her not to worry about it. The bag and the contents belonged to Hannah. She had requested the delivery. Apparently another death threat had been made and Hannah was worried about her safety. Kelly doubted that one gun and a little box of bullets would protect Hannah in the house isolated on the coast. If there really was someone sending death threats, she hoped Hannah was taking more precautions.

Kelly dialed the number on the screen and waited as the phone rang four times. She was about to hang up when she heard a soft click. She waited but no voice answered. "Hello?" she said.

"Hi. Do you know who this is?" a woman asked.

"Yes," Kelly replied, recognizing Nora's voice.

"Good. Can you meet me at the office in two hours?"

"I'll be there." The line clicked and Kelly hung up. She guessed that Nora meant her office in the city. In two hours it would be midnight. Why was she requesting the late-night meeting? Kelly rolled down her window and felt a shiver race up her spine. The night air was cold on her body, covered in dried sweat from the grappling match. She had no idea what Nora would want now. Two hours would give her enough time to shower and change clothes before driving into the city.

Alex had fallen asleep on the sofa in the family room. The cat was probably out harassing the neighbor's dog or the local mice. Kelly had heard a scuffle and a cat's hiss just as she climbed out of her car.

Alex opened his eyes and smiled when she entered the room. "You're home late." He sat up and then stared at Kelly with an anxious look. "God, Kelly, what happened to you?"

Kelly glanced down at her karate uniform. The gi was still wet with sweat. Blood was smeared across her chest. Sam must have had a cut on his hands. The dragon patch sewn on her shoulder had been ripped off at one edge. Now the dragon appeared to be lunging off her uniform. "Rough night. I lost. Nothing unusual."

Alex laughed. "I don't understand you. What's surfing with a few sharks compared to someone beating the crap out of you in that dojo?"

Kelly remembered Starr as soon as Alex mentioned surfing and her heart sank. She had not yet told him about the night at the club. How could she explain that she had seen Starr at a club kissing a woman? "I'm fine. A little bruised, but the pain goes away in a few days. Shark bites don't get better in a few days."

Pushing Alex's feet off the sofa, she sat down next to him. The television was tuned to the nightly news broadcast. The anchorman was discussing something about maintaining peace in Iraq and Kelly grabbed the remote control to change the channel.

"They take over a country by dropping bombs and push in a new government but leave all the troops there. Whose brilliant idea was it to call this a peace mission?" Alex asked bitterly.

"I don't care," Kelly replied.

"Really?"

"No, not really. I'm just pissed about the whole thing. The news doesn't explain what's really going on." The station changed and a

224

sitcom family filled the screen as canned laughter erupted from the set. Ignoring the show, Kelly turned to face Alex. An article in that morning's newspaper had predicted that the U.S. would actually be expanding military forces in Iraq. This would mean more reservists would be called to active duty. For the first time, she considered the war on a personal level. By the end of summer, Shannon could be in Iraq. "What are they fighting for?"

"Money, politics and oil," Alex said simply.

"It's bullshit." She sighed, flipping through the channels after muting the volume to silence the canned laughter.

"Well, maybe you would feel different if you lived over there."

"Yeah, then I'd probably hate people like me." Kelly tossed the remote control on the coffee table. A pop music video flashed on the television screen. She didn't recognize the young voluptuous singer but decided the woman was too attractive to switch the volume on. "Alex, if you were gay would you join the army?"

"First off, no." Alex stared at the singer on the screen. "Second, where the hell did that question come from?"

"I don't know. Our country is freaked out about having queer people in the military but they're there. And gay soldiers are fighting in Iraq risking their lives for a country that would stab them in the back if they knew who they were. It doesn't make sense. Why would you sign up for that?" Kelly's voice rose as she felt the tension increasing. "Hell, I don't know why I'm so upset about this." She grabbed a pillow from the couch and squeezed the stuffing into a tight ball.

"Are you mad because you think that the military should accept gays and proudly send them to war? Or are you just mad about the whole war?" Alex asked.

"Yeah, war sucks." She was too frustrated to explain and decided to switch topics. "Alex, I need to talk to you about something else." Kelly paused, debating how to tell him about Starr's presence at the club that past weekend. She knew she couldn't keep it from him. "I don't want to tell you this, but I think I have to."

"Wait, don't tell me." He looked at her and scratched his head. "You signed up for the army?" Alex finished sarcastically, "I knew one of your girlfriends was going to wear off on you."

Kelly laughed. "The army? Hell, no."

"What is it then?"

She picked up the remote control again and flipped the channel without looking at Alex. Another news broadcast was discussing the military. Alex leaned over her shoulder and pressed the power button on the remote. The television screen flashed to black. She said, "I saw Starr this weekend at a club."

"With someone else?" Alex asked hesitantly.

"Yeah."

He stared at the black television screen. After a moment, he sighed and crossed his arms. "Girl or guy?"

"Some drunk girl. I think they were both drunk. Or on Ecstasy. As soon as I saw her at the club I knew I had to tell you. But I'm sorry and I wish I was wrong." She knew that Alex wanted a monogamous relationship and would not be happy dating someone he couldn't trust.

He stood up and went into the kitchen. Kelly heard him open the refrigerator. He returned with two beers and handed her one. "And don't tell me you don't drink," Alex said, popping off both bottle caps, "cause I know we've gotten drunk together." He took a sip and then slapped her knee. "By the way, where have you been running off to lately and why'd you need an alibi that other night?"

"I have another meeting tonight." Kelly shrugged. "I'm in over my head."

"A meeting with a pissed-off girlfriend?"

"No. Right now they're both happy." She'd been thinking about Gina all day and wanted to call her. But Shannon and Gina had a softball game that evening. It made her nervous when they did things together. She was worried Gina would eventually admit that she'd slept with her. But the girlfriend issue wasn't on her mind now. She was nervous about the meeting with Nora. She had a bad feeling about meeting her tonight. Alex stared at his beer bottle. Kelly guessed he was thinking about Starr and didn't want to tell him about her own problems. She wasn't ready to explain her work with Rick. Alex worried about things too much. Nora and Hannah's lawsuit was also off-limits. "It's not really about the girlfriend issue. But I don't feel like talking about it."

"You mean you're not going to tell me?" he asked.

"Not yet. I still have a few things to decide."

"Well, when you figure out which girlfriend you like, let me know." Alex grinned. "I need to know if we're supporting the army or the police."

"I think I'm going to break up with Shannon—the one in the army," she admitted.

"Why?"

"I don't know." Kelly stared at the bottle in her hands. "She still likes her ex-girlfriend and I'm not up for all of that drama. Besides, they'll send more troops on that *peace* mission and she'll be gone."

"And what then? Is the cop waiting for you?"

"No. She still likes her ex-girlfriend. I'll just give up on girls for a few weeks, hang out here and get drunk with you." Kelly laughed. She took a sip and cringed as the alcohol hit her tongue. "Alex, at least waste your money on something that tastes decent."

He sipped his beer. "I'm just trying to get buzzed. Then you forget about the taste and everything, *and everyone*, on your mind."

She set her full bottle on the coffee table and stood up. "Give Starr a call. I could be wrong about the whole thing. I want to be wrong."

"I don't think you're wrong. She called to cancel our surfing plans."

"Alex, you may be the last defender of monogamy." Kelly wished she'd never introduced Alex and Starr. "I think I got you involved in this and I hate to see you get hurt."

"Relax, I'm a construction worker. Hell, I'm tough and I drive a big truck." Alex grinned. "Besides, I'm the one that went back to flirt

227

with her. It isn't your fault at all." He tapped his beer bottle against hers. "Hate to admit it, but I'll miss the damn biscotti. Well, you'll probably have me matched up with some new girl in a few weeks, whether I'm ready or not."

"You got it." Kelly knew he was more depressed over the news than he let on. Maybe it had been too soon for him to meet someone after breaking up with his fiancée. Relationships were too complicated. She stood up and stretched her arms. Her body was already starting to stiffen around the fresh injuries from grappling. "Damn, I've got to get ready. I can't be late to this meeting."

"Whatever you're doing, Kelly, watch your step, okay? You better get your ass home tonight in one piece. I don't want to fill out a missing person report. And I sure as hell don't want to tell Mom or Dad if I get a call from some hospital. They'd kill me."

"Thanks for your concern," she replied.

A Mazda was parked outside the front door of the office building on Market Street. Kelly recognized Nora in the driver's seat. She was smoking a cigarette and looked preoccupied. Kelly tapped the passenger side window and waited for Nora to unlock the door. She slid into the seat and Nora immediately started the car engine.

"Where are we going?"

"Just for a drive. I didn't want to have this conversation inside the office. Thanks for being on time, by the way."

Kelly gazed out the window. They drove in silence through the business center of the city, past the plaza on Market Street and toward the bay. Before reaching the piers, Nora turned back the direction they'd come. She wound her way through the city streets, heading, Kelly thought, toward the Golden Gate Bridge. Kelly was trying to ignore her mounting frustration. She knew there were no cars following them. Why was Nora driving in a circle?

"So, am I supposed to start asking questions? I mean, I don't really know why I'm here. Rick didn't say anything. But I guess you have an agenda tonight? I mean, I don't mind driving around with you, but . . ."

Nora shook her head. "I'm not trying to make you feel uncomfortable."

Kelly blushed and turned quickly to look out the window. She wished that she could act like her usual self around Nora. Every time Nora looked at her, Kelly felt like a kid with a crush. But Nora was not that much older—she guessed she was in her early thirties. Although it would be unusual to partner in a law firm that soon, she could tell Nora was the type who would work hard to secure success early. She fit profile of the perfect lawyer—intelligent, well-spoken, attractive and capable of dominating others. She was also good at masking her emotions. Kelly could sense that something was wrong, but Nora was not giving her any hints.

"Yes, we do need to talk. But we're spinning our wheels for a while. I want to make sure no one is following us," Nora said finally. She turned off the highway at the last exit before the bridge. They zigzagged through one-way streets until the Palace of Fine Arts came into view. Nora parked the car. "This is my favorite spot in the city. Want to go for a walk?"

Kelly followed Nora's lead and got out of the car. The fog covered the city and lights shone in a strange orange haze circling the lake by the palace. They wandered down a path toward the water. Several ducks roosted under the willow trees. They quacked as Nora and Kelly neared the trees, then quickly hid their heads under their wing feathers. Nora sat down at a bench by the water's edge. Kelly went to the sand bank and put her hands in the dark water. It was cold on her skin and goose bumps prickled up her arms.

"Hannah was found this afternoon . . ." Nora began. Kelly looked over her shoulder and waited for Nora to finish, but she seemed unable to continue. The hiss of the wind through the trees surrounding the palace was the only audible sound.

Finally, Kelly decided to push her. "Who found Hannah?"

"Her friend, the woman who owned the house on the coast.

Hannah was staying at her place, you know. The friend had gone to the store for a few hours. When she came home, she found Hannah . . ."

Kelly shivered, but not because of the cold water. Suddenly everything that had occurred over the past few weeks came rushing to form one thought. Hannah was dead.

"With one bullet in her head," Nora finished. Her voice quavered for the first time. Maybe Nora didn't fit the perfect profile of a lawyer. Lawyers were supposed to hide their emotions. Kelly sat down on the bench next to her. They stared at the water without speaking. Nora kicked at a rock next to the bench. It rolled down the slope to the water. The splash of water shook the quiet air.

"I'm sorry."

"Yeah, me too," Nora replied. "She left a suicide note. The crime scene investigators said that it looks like she shot herself but they're doing an autopsy tomorrow."

"She shot herself with the gun I delivered," Kelly added, her stomach turned with this news.

"She asked me to send it to the house on the coast where she was staying. Her friend found a death threat taped to their door. Hannah was concerned for their safety. She wanted her gun for protection. I'd never have guessed that she'd commit suicide."

What if she had never made that delivery? Kelly wondered. For the first time she wished she'd gotten lost and given up. She could have delivered the duffel bag to a different address, but Hannah probably would have just found another way to kill herself.

"I guess the lawsuit was just too much for her." Nora continued, "Hannah wasn't the type to give up on anything. Especially not like this."

"Are they sure it's a suicide? Suicide notes could be forged."

"They sound sure. Her gun was found next to her body, only one bullet had been fired, and there was no evidence of a break-in. Everything points to a suicide." Nora shook her head and swore quietly. "Look, I want you to watch out for your friend. I know you're

230

dating Shannon, Hannah's ex. Shannon was very close to Hannah—even after they broke up. I don't know how she'll take this. She's one of the few people who really knows Hannah's story. I don't think she's in any danger but Hannah did receive death threats and I know she was worried about Shannon's safety."

"Were the death threats from someone in the military?"

Nora nodded. "My guess is that it was someone who felt personally threatened by Hannah. She knew things about a lot of people. She had collected information from countless army discharge cases. I don't know who, exactly, was out to get Hannah. But it looks like the military succeeded in getting rid of one of their problems."

"Are you going to continue with the lawsuit against the military?"

"I'd like to. It depends on what the Coalition decides. Other lives could be at risk and we still don't know who was sending the death threats."

"From what I overheard at the cocktail reception, Hannah was the backbone of this lawsuit as well as the Coalition."

"To be exact, the GLB Political Action Coalition is paying my fee. Hannah was only one of their organizers. The Coalition has a good case to push the courts to overturn the military's policy on gays. I'm sure they won't want to retract the lawsuit. Something as volatile as this issue is risky, obviously, now more than ever."

"If someone was trying to stop the lawsuit, wouldn't they go after everyone involved?"

"Possibly. They could threaten someone else in the Coalition. Personally, I think the death threats Hannah received were from someone who had a personal vendetta against her. She knew too many things about the military. She gave me a list of potential enemies when we first filed the lawsuit, mostly individuals who were involved in other discharge cases against officers. A lot of them were pretty influential outside the military too. Politicians, judges, police officers."

"So she killed herself before anyone else could?" Kelly remembered Shannon's letter that she had taken from Hannah's house.

From the note that Hannah had started to write in response to Shannon's letter, Kelly guessed that the woman was in a severe depression. She couldn't handle the loss of her career and breaking up with Shannon had only pushed her farther off the edge.

"I know she was scared. I think the lawsuit was just too much pressure." Nora paused. The ducks had started quacking and she glanced over to their roost. One of the males had ventured down to the water's edge and disrupted the others. The path past the palace was illuminated with spotlights placed near each tree. Only bums ventured out to the park after dark. Tonight they had the palace grounds to themselves. "The police won't look any further than the suicide. They've been given copies of the death threats but don't seem to care. They know that Hannah was previously discharged from the army because of reported 'mental instability.' Mentally unstable people often commit suicide, I guess."

"So I guess you won't be needing me anymore," Kelly said, focusing on the lapping water at the lake's edge. The duck had waded into the water and floated in a circle, keeping his head cocked toward his roost.

"I've asked Rick to commit to the lawsuit. I want a full investigation of everyone that Hannah knew. We're going to be looking into the files that she collected on all of the military personnel that organized the recent discharges. He is going to hire you full-time."

"Why me?"

"I don't know. Rick wants you." She shrugged and then continued, "To tell you the truth, I'd rather have someone with more experience."

"I'm not an investigator," Kelly said. She remembered the feeling of complete nausea as she watched the man with the gun wander through Hannah's house while she hid by the coat rack. Her second meeting with this man had solidified her dislike for investigative work. Dark alleys scared her and the man's knife was still in her pocket as a reminder that she didn't want to get involved in anything else that involved the military. Maybe it was too late.

"Rick is the investigator. We need someone who will work mainly as our liaison. I've never met Rick in person and don't intend to. He has too many ties to the FBI and likes to keep his distance from things that are under too much public scrutiny." Nora stretched out her legs and leaned back against the bench.

A female duck waddled down to the sand bank and stared at the male. She glanced back at the bench, eyeing the women suspiciously, and then sank into the water to join the male duck in his slow circling pattern.

Nora continued, "I'm going to sort through all of the information that Hannah collected for the case and Rick will follow up with the investigation of Hannah's military contacts. We need someone we can trust to pass information. We'll have a lot of work on our hands with this lawsuit. By the way, no one besides Rick, you and me, knows about the envelopes."

"The four envelopes that I delivered?"

"Yes, I think one of those four people was threatening Hannah. We sent information to some people on Hannah's list of possible threats to the lawsuit—anyone she thought would try to harm witnesses or supporters. Hannah had collected incendiary background information on everyone she thought would be a threat to this case."

"Blackmail." Kelly had wondered if the manila envelopes had something to do with Hannah's case. Every address had been in a wealthy neighborhood. She suspected that only influential people opened the envelopes. But she had been told not to ask questions.

"I wouldn't call it that. Hannah wasn't asking for money. You delivered a letter advising them to keep their hands off potential witnesses and a sample of the information we would release if anything happened. Hannah hoped that this approach would make the biggest potential opponents to the lawsuit back away. She wanted the case to get a fair hearing and we were worried that any discharged officers that we named in the case could be in danger."

"If the guys on Hannah's list continue to retaliate because of the threats that were sent . . . Who will be next in line after Hannah's

233

death? Anyone who received a letter might try to attack the other organizers in the Coalition if the lawsuit proceeds."

"Yes."

"And then their blood is on our hands." Kelly regretted her words as soon as she saw Nora's face. Hannah had only died that afternoon. Kelly stared at the dark ripples that formed on the surface of the water as a breeze swept across the lake. The willow trees whined and the ducks quacked quietly to themselves. She reached out to find Nora's hand. Nora squeezed her hand once and then relaxed. Kelly wondered where the lawsuit would lead. Nora was not going to give up on Hannah's lawsuit. It was the Coalition's main battle and they were still ready to fight.

Chapter 18

049901

Kelly welcomed her busy schedule at the dojo. Since the karate summer camp had started that week, Sam had decided to take mornings off, which meant she was alone with the camp kids until noon. By Friday, she was exhausted and ready for the end of the week. The dojo was crawling with twenty boys and eight girls by nine a.m. Colin came early, dressed in a clean uniform and proudly wearing his purple belt. Instead of his usual quick stop in the parking lot, Colin's father actually came into the dojo. He informed Kelly that Colin and Isaac had been scheduled for baseball camp that week, but Colin had begged to spend his entire summer break in the dojo. Kelly elected Colin to be the camp leader for the day. He fell into the role with gusto and had the younger kids corralled onto the mat in orderly rows by five minutes after nine.

Eight hours later, she sent home the last summer camp kid and went to the café for dinner. Starr wasn't working at the café that evening but the other waiter recognized Kelly and smiled. He only worked as a busboy when Starr worked the front counter and tonight he was scrambling between the cash register and the coffee machine. She ordered a sandwich and collapsed on a chair at a table in the back. The camp kids had worn her out and she told herself that she needed a break from karate and time to think about Hannah's death. But she didn't want to think about it. Her sparring class would start in an hour and she wanted to hit something.

The busboy delivered her sandwich and asked her about Alex. He mentioned that Starr and Alex had promised to teach him how to surf and he'd been searching the Internet for information about wetsuits and boards. She wanted to be left alone and told the kid to research shark bites before settling on a wetsuit. Ashton was too small-town, she decided as she quickly ate her sandwich and headed back to the dojo.

The windows were white from the moisture condensing on the glass. Waiting by the entrance, she listened to the shouts drifting out onto the sidewalk. The familiar stench of sweat greeted her nose as she pushed open the door and swung her bag down on a chair in the front room.

Sam looked up as the door closed. "I thought you were going home for the night."

"Can't miss sparring class," she said.

The students were kicking the bags against the back wall. Sam's nod and smile made Kelly relax. She didn't need to discuss the last grappling match with Sam. Nothing would happen again, she told herself. Nothing had happened before—it was just another fight. But now she wasn't sure she trusted Sam completely.

Unzipping her bag, she pulled on a pair of foam-rubber shoes and a helmet, then fished out her mouthpiece and gloves. The junior students had left their bags and stood facing Sam. She waited at the edge of the mat as the junior class bowed and kneeled to meditate in unison.

"Rise up—class dismissed," Sam yelled.

The students stood up quickly and filed out into the waiting room, dripping with the sweat from their endurance training, their voices subdued as they discussed dinner plans.

Kelly started her warmup exercises and concentrated on the image in the mirror, suddenly surprised that it didn't look any different. Her skin had tanned and there were a few red highlights in her brown hair, but otherwise she appeared unchanged from one month ago. Yet in the past four weeks her world had been completely overturned.

"Anything wrong?" Sam asked as he grabbed her foot, correcting the position of her kick and then scrutinizing the next strike that she threw.

She shook her head and moved through the first set of karate forms. What could she say? Hannah was dead. Shannon didn't know about the death yet. Rick had not called her with instructions for their next step. She hated to wait for his orders but had no choice. Kelly was conscious of Sam's close review and wished he would watch one of the other students. Her form was slow, but he withheld his criticism.

"Hey, before you leave tonight, we need to talk. Someone left something for you." He turned and walked off the mat, bowing as he stepped through the doorway to the office.

Five students, all men, had entered the studio. Two of the men stood stretching by the punching bags. Kevin and Tom both smiled warmly at Kelly and joined her in practicing the karate forms. Their stylized strikes and blocks seemed to be only a synchronized dance but every move could preclude a deadly attack. Tom stopped practicing his form and went to stretch his leg muscles against the back wall, muttering something about a stiff joint to one of the men by the bags.

"All right, find a partner," Sam called out from the window of his office. He leaned through the doorway and continued, "Start with some free-sparring. And I want to see good technique tonight."

237

Tom was six feet tall and weighed just over two hundred pounds. He tapped Kelly's shoulder and they bowed. In the past, their matches had been close but Tom hadn't sparred for a few months. He usually overpowered her, but maybe he'd be slow tonight, she reasoned. His left side kick was dangerous. He preferred to land the kick low on the thigh, narrowly missing the knee. It struck the sweet spot, mid femur, sending a shaft of pain through the bone and a quick spasm of muscle. They shook hands after bowing and started to spar. His green belt was tied low on his waist and the knot loosened as he shuffled on the mat.

"Don't look so serious, Kelly. You're scaring me," he said, teasing. He threw a playfully light right punch toward her nose. Leaning to his left, Kelly threw a roundhouse kick at the helmet, narrowly missing his cheek. As her foot landed, his fist pounded against her ribs. She exhaled and absorbed the strike, coiled back, and in the next instant threw a left back fist to his temple. A resounding thud erupted as the thin foam was struck.

"Nice punch," she murmured through the plastic mouth guard, feeling the muscles along the ribs contract painfully as the air rushed through the chest.

He nodded. "You too."

Sam dismissed the students after the sparring class ended. Kelly pulled off her sweaty helmet and gloves and followed him into the office. "You needed to talk to me?"

Sam handed her a plain white envelope. There was no address on the envelope. This was not another delivery. She opened the envelope quickly, not caring that Sam was watching her, and read the one line on the note. "Practice karate until eight." She set the note on Sam's desk.

"So, can you tell me what you're doing with Rick?" He stared directly at her. His dark eyes seemed to be reading her thoughts.

Kelly shook her head.

"I told Rick that I'd never forgive him if anything happened to you."

"Do you trust him?" Kelly asked. She realized her voice sounded weak and cleared her throat. She didn't want Sam to think she was afraid of working with Rick.

"He worked for the FBI for a long time. He's seen some things go down that you and I only deal with in nightmares. And he's killed people." Sam shook his head. He paused and looked at the note on his desk. "Yeah, I trust him."

"Do you mind if I stay late tonight?"

"No. Lock up when you leave." Sam reached into his desk and grabbed his wallet and car keys. He smiled at Kelly as he headed out the back door. "I know you'll be fine, but watch your back. I don't want to have to train another teacher."

Two hours later, Kelly parked in Shannon's driveway. A light shone through the window of the living room. Rick had met her outside the dojo just as she was leaving. He had given her a brown box this time. It was large enough to hold a handgun, but the box was too light. She still remembered the weight of the gun in Hannah's duffel bag. This time, Rick didn't ask if she wanted to make the delivery. She had accepted his job offer for a part-time position in his private investigation service. He would train her over the next few months and she would soon have bigger jobs than the messenger service.

"Well, look who the cat drug in—what happened to you?"

Kelly smiled. "You sound like my brother. I've been sparring and I know I stink. Is it okay if I shower here?"

Shannon laughed. "Of course. We're supposed to meet everyone at Sweet Stream in twenty minutes."

"But it's Friday. I thought your friends only went to the bar on Saturday nights." Kelly had not anticipated a night out with Shannon's friends. Although she wasn't looking forward to the Ashton bar scene, she also didn't want to spend the night home alone

239

with Shannon. Kelly couldn't keep Hannah's death a secret from her for long, but she had no idea how she could bring up the subject either. When they arrived at the bar, Kelly was relieved to see Gina. Shannon was watching Kelly's interactions with everyone at the bar very closely at first. After two beers, Shannon stopped monitoring Kelly and joined a pool game with a group of guys.

Kelly sat down at the table that Beth and Tasha had claimed. They were flipping through a magazine and pointing out their favorite actresses. Gina joined the discussion and slid into the open seat next to Kelly. Her hand brushed over Kelly's leg. The group bantered noisily about the Hollywood stars' sex appeal. Kelly relaxed and began to enjoy the loose mood of the bar. Gina was in an unusually good mood and Beth was happily drunk already. Every time Tasha looked at her, Kelly felt like she was a co-conspirator, they had tacitly promised not to mention the man and the camera they'd left in the dark alley last Saturday.

Shannon glanced over at the table occasionally but seemed more interested in her pool tournament. After listening to Gina's story about arresting her first DUI, Kelly excused herself to get some fresh air. The bar was stuffy and she needed some time away from the loud group at the pool tables. She sat down on the sidewalk and rested her head on her knees. The door opened behind her and Kelly felt a hand rub her head. She looked up and saw Gina smile.

"It's good to see you again," Gina started.

"Yeah, you too."

"I got a letter from Vicky today." Gina sat down on the sidewalk next to Kelly. "She's not coming home anytime soon. I guess they're going to keep her stationed over there for six months. Things aren't looking bright for her."

"You miss her?" Kelly asked, hesitantly.

"No. I thought I did. But after I read her last letter I realized she really doesn't want a relationship with me. And for the first time, I don't want a relationship with her. We would have stopped dating even if she had stayed here in Ashton. To tell you the truth, I've been missing you."

Kelly smiled. "You're trouble."

"Why are you still dating Shannon?" Gina brushed over Kelly's leg as she slipped her arm around her. "Do you like her?"

"I don't really know," Kelly admitted. "But now is not a good time to break up with her."

"Why not?" she asked, tugging on Kelly's belt.

"Hannah died yesterday. Shannon doesn't know yet," Kelly replied. She trusted that Gina wouldn't share this news. She reasoned that if she trusted Gina enough to sleep with her, she could trust her with this information.

Gina gasped and then swore under her breath. After a moment, she asked, "I want to know how you found out first."

Kelly shook her head. "Someday I'll tell you. I promise."

"Someday, huh?" She sighed. "Shannon was still in love with her. She wouldn't admit it. God, she's gonna take this hard."

Kelly only nodded. She didn't want to think about it anymore.

Gina hugged her tightly and then shivered. The temperature tonight was noticeably cooler and the wind raced through Gina's tank top. "Hey, babe, wanna run away with me? Let's get the fuck out of here."

"Where to?"

"I don't know." Gina paused. "Some sandy beach where we can splash around in warm waves and get to know each other better. In bikinis."

"Okay. I think I might like you." Kelly grinned, and then added, "In a bikini."

Gina leaned over and pecked her cheek. After a moment, Kelly turned and kissed Gina's lips. They held each other close, their bodies begging for more intimacy, as two lovers kept apart for too long. Just then the door opened and Shannon stepped out of the bar. She glanced down at the sidewalk where Kelly and Gina sat, too close. The three women waited in silence. Kelly moved away from Gina and stood up. She opened her mouth to explain, but Shannon held up her hand to stop her. She clearly didn't want to hear the lie. Shannon turned back to the bar and disappeared inside.

"Fuck." Kelly kicked the trash can next to the entrance to the bar and glanced at Gina. "Well, that wasn't a good meeting."

"That's an understatement." Gina shook her head and closed her eyes. "Beach blankets, cool drink, bikinis, ocean waves at our feet, the hot sun overhead . . ."

"Yeah, Gina. I want to join you there."

Gina glanced at Kelly. "Really?"

Kelly nodded. She felt closer to Gina then any woman she had dated. "But I need to figure my way out of this first."

"She'll break up with you."

Kelly nodded. "So, do you want to hang out sometime? As fair warning, I come with baggage."

"Me too."

Wandering to the back of the bar, Kelly found Shannon sitting at the table next to Beth and Tasha. Tasha shook her head at Kelly as soon as she approached. Grabbing Beth's hand, Tasha suggested, "Come help me pick out some music on the jukebox."

Shannon stared at the empty bottle of beer in her hands. "You suck. Gina was one of my best friends."

Kelly sat down on a barstool at the table. "I know."

"Did she ask you or did you ask her?"

"I started it."

Shannon cleared her throat. "Why?"

Kelly didn't answer. Shannon's distance their first night at the bar had pushed her to flirt with Gina. But now she wanted Gina for other reasons. Finally Kelly decided to tell her the truth. "I'm attracted to Gina. You and I haven't been dating long. No one said this was a committed relationship."

"Fuck you, Kelly, she's my friend. There are rules. You don't sleep with your girlfriend's best friend."

Gina entered the bar and Shannon refused to look at her. Gina walked over to the jukebox to join Beth and Tasha.

"Yeah, I know . . . Look, just so you understand, I really did start this. Gina could have said no, but I initiated it. So, blame me," Kelly volunteered.

"I am blaming you. Can you leave now?"

Kelly stood to leave. She wanted to tell Shannon to be careful. Hannah had been worried about Shannon's safety before. Kelly wondered if she was still at risk. Since Hannah's death, would the military ignore Shannon now? Shannon was probably waiting to hear from Hannah. She probably knew that Hannah had been hiding out somewhere, but no one had been allowed to contact her while she was staying at the house on the coast. Kelly couldn't think of anything to say. "I'm sorry about everything. Guess you won't flirt with strangers who show up at your softball games again."

Shannon shook her head and laughed. "No, I have no intention of doing that anytime soon. And don't call my friends."

It was a reasonable request. She waved to the group at the jukebox on her way out of the bar but didn't stop to talk to anyone. Gina's gaze followed her all the way to the door, but she stayed at the jukebox. Kelly paged Rick as soon as she got to her car. She waited for twenty minutes in the driver's seat, staring out the front windshield. Why did she want to talk to Rick anyway? There was nothing to do now but go home.

Chapter 19

049951

Alex shook Kelly's shoulder to wake her on Sunday morning. She opened her eyes slowly and glanced at the clock, quarter after six. He smiled and held up his surfboard. "Want to go splash around in the waves? I'd love the company."

"Alex, why do you get up so early to go surfing? There are still waves at noon." She yawned and rolled onto her other side.

"Yeah, but you miss the sharks if you go later. It's better to go early in the morning when they're hungry." He shook her shoulder again and tapped the board on her bed. Sand fell of the board onto the sheets. "Come on, let's go. We'll grab breakfast on the way down and you can tell me why you slept in your own bed on a Saturday night."

The waves crashed against the rocky coast, sending a spray of saltwater out in a white arc. Kelly and Alex picked their way down the cliff until they reached the sandy beach. Five other surfers were already in the water, paddling on their bellies and waiting for the next set of waves. They changed into their wetsuits and splashed into the water. She had played on this beach as a kid. Their parents had taken them to the ocean nearly every weekend during the long summers. The water was a cool treat from the hot California sun and only an hour away from Ashton. Alex had become an avid surfer. She'd never mastered the sport and, after seeing a shark once while paddling to shore, had developed a strong fear of the open waters. But today there was no fear.

Kelly paddled past the other surfers and lay on her surfboard, feeling the ocean swells rise and fall under her belly. She watched Alex ride the first wave in a set that rolled under her board and then closed her eyes to sleep. The rocking ocean gently carried away all thoughts of Hannah's gun or the next package waiting to be delivered. Her relationship with Shannon and Gina had been resolved. Gina was Shannon's best friend. In the same moment, she'd lost both girlfriends. She missed Gina, but maybe she needed the time alone. Dating was too complicated, she decided.

Kelly opened her eyes and stared at the coastline. She had drifted far from shore. Digging her hands into the cool water, she paddled fast toward the safety of land. She felt something lift the tail of the board and looked over her shoulder at a wave rising up behind her. Kelly paddled faster and then jumped to her feet to ride the wave. She gripped the board with her toes and shifted her weight uneasily across the waxed surface as she fought to keep her balance. Then the board glided onto the smooth face of the wave and she relaxed as the ocean carried her back to the shore.

Kelly sat down on the sand to watch the waves crash on the rocks. She kept a close tab on Alex and noted when his board disappeared under a wave. She waited for his head to reappear, each time, holding her breath until she saw his face. She had no desire to surf now. Dragging her fingers through the sand, she made tiny paths leading up to a small sand castle. As the next wave crashed on the beach, Kelly saw a red glimmer in the sand. Curious, she walked down to the water's edge. A red stone sunk into the sand as the water receded. She picked up the gem and cleaned off the sand that clung in a small crevice on the nearly perfect surface.

An hour later Alex surfed into shore. He toweled off his face after setting down his board. Kelly handed him the stone as he sat down next to their ice cooler. "What do you think?"

"It's a ruby. Where'd you find it?"

"Just washed up here."

"Someone must have lost it. Too bad it has a crack on the side. It's almost perfect."

"I like it," Kelly said. "I think I like it more because of the crack. It has a story." She slipped the ruby in her pocket and followed Alex back up the trail to their car.

Alex turned on the radio as they washed down their surfing gear and packed up for the ride home. A news broadcaster was talking about the country's military influence abroad.

"Hey, Alex, can you change the radio station?" She didn't want to think about the military or the war right now.

Alex shook his head. "Wait, did you catch what that guy just said? Did they just mention a draft?"

Kelly stopped washing off the surfboard and listened to the broadcast as Alex turned up the radio's volume.

"Several thousand troops will be sent to locations in the Middle East over the next week. The U.S. force's continued position in Iraq has been challenged by the U.N. However, due to continued Iraqi separatist resistance to peace negotiations, U.S. military leaders will be stepping up security levels. This move will require a substantial increase in troops. More reservists have received orders for active duty."

❧

Kelly left two messages on Shannon's phone and then decided to drive over to her house that evening. Shannon obviously was not ready to talk to her. She didn't know if she'd found out about Hannah's death yet and wanted to tell her she was sorry. After knocking on the door, Kelly waited outside Shannon's house for several minutes. Finally she wandered to the side yard to peek into the garage window. Shannon's truck was parked in the garage. Kelly sighed and started back to her car. She hadn't thought that Shannon would refuse to see her. Maybe she could stop by Beth and Tasha's house to find out if they had talked to her.

"Miss?"

Kelly spun around and spotted Shannon's neighbor. He held a garden hose over a brown spot on his front lawn. "Yes?"

"Are you a friend of Shannon's?" The man was in his late seventies and talked as slow as he moved.

She nodded.

"She wanted me to tell anyone that stopped by here the message. She's gone for a while."

"What do you mean?" Kelly asked.

"Guess she was transferred to a new unit. She told me they sent her a letter saying they needed her expertise or something in a unit that's headed to Iraq . . . I don't know. She left yesterday. Anyway, she's on active duty now and they've probably already sent her across the country. She'll be headed for the sandbox any day now, I guess."

Kelly drove to Gina's house. She wasn't sure if Gina wanted to see her and decided not to knock. She placed the manila envelope on the doormat and turned to walk back to her car, instinctively looking over her shoulder to ensure that no one was watching. This time, she knew the contents of the envelope.

Chapter 20

050001

Spotting the sign for the diner, Kelly hit her turn signal and pulled off the main road. The box was out of her hands, but she couldn't relax yet. The silver sports car had followed her. Kelly found a parking place in the back lot and contemplated what she should tell Rick. She had broken the first rule—someone had seen the delivery. Kelly had known that the silver sports car was parked across from the stucco house when she arrived to deliver the package. But she hadn't realized it was Gina's car until it was too late. She slipped her pager into the front pocket of her jeans and climbed out of the Volkswagen. No stars in the night sky penetrated the thick layer of fog. The city lights cast an orange haze overhead. Gina jumped out of her sports car and joined Kelly at the entrance to the diner.

"So, how'd you know I'd be at that house tonight?" Kelly asked. "Oakland's not your beat."

"You're not going to start off with thanking me for saving your ass?" Gina grinned.

"Thank you." She grabbed Gina's hands and quickly kissed her. "Now answer my question."

Gina laughed. "Okay. I saw the package in your room last night. The address and time were written on a Post-it so I figured I'd stop by after work." Gina paused and glanced at a car that had stopped at the intersection. The driver was focused on the traffic light and didn't notice them standing by the diner. When the signal turned green, she continued, "The note on the box said Monday at ten p.m. Are you always late?"

"Not always," Kelly said defensively.

"Good. I wouldn't want a partner who was chronically late."

"Who said anything about being partners?"

Gina shrugged. "Looks like you could use the help."

"Maybe I deserved that comment, but I don't think I need a partner." She remembered the growl of the Rottweiler that had nearly lunged at her throat. It was lucky that Gina's gunfire had distracted him.

"So what's the food like at this place?" Gina gestured toward the diner.

"I don't know. Hopefully they make good milkshakes. I'm starving for chocolate," Kelly said. She held the door for Gina and they went inside.

The waiter looked up from a television screen as they entered. The small television was positioned between the kitchen and the front counter. "Have a seat wherever you like, girls. Menus are on the tables and you can just holler when you know what you want. I'm your cook and waiter tonight. As always, I recommend the chocolate shakes."

"Perfect," Kelly said. "Looks like it's my lucky night."

Gina slipped off her leather jacket and Kelly caught the glint of the silver chain on her neck. The ruby hung from the silver at the base of Gina's throat. The crevice where the sand had lodged formed a jagged scar down the center of the stone. "Shannon called me this morning. You know they transferred her to another unit. She's in Georgia now. Apparently she'll be there for a few weeks. Then she's heading to Iraq. She doesn't know when exactly."

"I stopped by her house and talked to her neighbor. Is she doing okay?"

"Well, she isn't looking forward to going overseas. And she found out that Hannah committed suicide. I think she's forgotten about everything that happened between us. Or she blocked it out. She has too many other things to think about right now. She's mourning. For some reason, she doesn't think anything was my fault. She didn't mention your name at all."

"You're still her best friend."

"Yes, and she needs friends right now. Tasha wasn't called into active duty. Almost everyone else in the unit received orders. But she didn't."

"Are they going to discharge her?"

Gina shrugged. "Who knows? Beth thinks they will. Tasha is trying not to think about it. Maybe a discharge would be for the best. She doesn't want to go to overseas. So what was in the package we delivered tonight?"

"I don't know," Kelly responded.

"You almost got eaten by a dog and I woke up the whole neighborhood. We could've been arrested. Don't tell me you don't know what was in it."

"Can a cop get arrested just for shooting a gun?"

Gina shrugged. "Probably not. What was in the package?"

"I don't know."

"Tell me," Gina insisted.

"You're stubborn." Kelly looked over at the waiter. An old episode of *MASH* was playing on the screen. "Can we have two chocolate shakes?"

He nodded and grinned. "Good choice."

As he disappeared into the kitchen, Gina said, "You don't have to tell me everything . . . just what was in that package."

"Okay, I'm not lying. I really don't know." She could sense Gina's frustration and added, "It has to do with an army lawsuit. My job, so far, is just to deliver packages. And I'm not supposed to ask questions."

"They're still going to push the lawsuit after Hannah's death?"

"I guess Nora has some other people lined up at the Political Action Coalition."

"Tell me how you got involved in this. Why were you at Hannah's press conference?"

"It's a long story."

With a swish of his apron, their server presented them with two tall glasses. He set down the chocolate shakes and dropped two straws on the table. "Well, I love to see kids out on a date, but isn't it getting past your curfew, girls?"

Gina shot back, "Gee thanks, Mom."

He smiled and returned to his stool by the television. "Enjoy the shakes, and don't look so serious over there."

"You're hiding things from me. I don't like that." Gina sucked the straw to taste the thick chocolate shake. "This isn't bad."

Kelly nodded at the waiter who was waiting for a sign of approval.

Gina had a serious look on her face and seemed to be mulling over something. "I just don't understand why Hannah committed suicide. Did she know too much about the military?"

Kelly thought again about the letter that she had found in Hannah's house and the suicide hotline number. She couldn't tell anyone about it now. Maybe if she had mentioned the letter to Rick, or not delivered the gun, Hannah might still be alive. Nora had mentioned that Hannah had been depressed at losing her career and she guessed that the lawsuit hadn't been enough to bring her out of the slump. Kelly guessed that losing her girlfriend and getting death threats might have pushed her farther over the edge. There were still unanswered questions in Hannah's case. She hadn't figured out who had beat up Hannah the first time, but Nora and Rick seemed to know it was someone from the military. Also, she didn't know the identity of the man whose knife she now had. Hopefully they wouldn't meet again in a dark alley. And she didn't know who had sent Hannah the death threats. Everything seemed to end in more questions.

She addressed Gina in a lowered voice, "I'll tell you later. Eventually, I promise to tell you as much as I know."

Gina shook her head. "I doubt it. Well, whatever." She sighed and turned away from Kelly to glance at the front door of the diner and then over to the waiter.

"I hate to hear you say that. Nora and Rick want me to continue working with them. I don't know what will happen with the lawsuit and how much information I'll learn, but I promise to tell you."

Turning back to her, Gina grabbed Kelly's hand and stared directly at her. "Just tell me what's going on. I could help you. Ask Rick if I can help with any investigative work. Or I could be your partner."

"Maybe. We know you can shoot a gun. And I guess that could be useful, even if your aim is bad." Kelly tasted the milkshake and smiled. This waiter always used extra chocolate syrup.

"Bad aim? I'm a great shot!" Gina said indignantly.

"Do you always aim for plants?"

"I wanted to scare the dog, but I didn't want to hit him. And you were in the way." She laughed and tapped her glass against Kelly's. "Cheers."

"Cheers. So, I guess I should be thanking you for missing my leg."

"And for saving your ass from that Rottweiler." On a serious note, she added, "I want to help you with this investigation. Shannon told me quite a bit about Hannah and some of the information may be pertinent to her death."

"And you're looking for a moonlighting job already?"

"I'd be a good partner." She paused briefly and glanced out the window. The silver sports car was the only car parked near the entrance to the diner. "Are you interested?"

Kelly considered Gina's suggestion of helping on the investigation. She still wasn't sure what her own job would be over the next few months. Rick might agree to train them together. "I don't know if it will work."

"Yeah, I think there's a rule that you have to keep a relationship on a professional level if you're partners in an investigation."

"Who made that rule?" Kelly smiled. She couldn't resist the closeness of Gina's face and the sweet smell of her skin. "Well, if that's the rule, we might as well give up now. Gina, why did you come to my house last night?"

"I got your letter and I had to see you. I know you told me to stay away, but I didn't understand why. Was it because of the investigation?"

"Yes. I don't know who's watching me and I don't want you to get pulled into this."

"Well, I guess it's too late now. Partners?" Gina asked.

"Maybe." Kelly nodded.

"By the way, I never got a chance to thank you for the package." Gina's hand touched the ruby on her neck. "Does this stone have a story?"

About the Author

Jaime Clevenger lives in Northern California. She currently works as a veterinarian. Some of her other job titles have included karate instructor, chemistry tutor, baby-sitter, horse-ride trail guide and closet writer. It's good to be out.

Publications from
BELLA BOOKS, INC.
The best in contemporary lesbian fiction

P.O. Box 10543, Tallahassee, FL 32302
Phone: 800-729-4992
www.bellabooks.com

WILD THINGS by Karin Kallmaker. 228 pp. Dutiful daughter Faith has met the perfect man. There's just one problem: she's in love with his sister.   ISBN 1-931513-64-3 $12.95

SHARED WINDS by Kenna White. 216 pp. Can Emma rebuild more than just Lanny's marina?   ISBN 1-59493-006-6 $12.95

THE UNKNOWN MILE by Jaime Clevenger. 253 pp. Kelly's world is getting more and more complicated every moment.   ISBN 1-931513-57-0 $12.95

TREASURED PAST by Linda Hill. 189 pp. A shared passion for antiques leads to love.
                                                                      ISBN 1-59493-003-1 $12.95

SIERRA CITY by Gerri Hill. 284 pp. Chris and Jesse cannot deny their growing attraction . . .   ISBN 1-931513-98-8 $12.95

ALL THE WRONG PLACES by Karin Kallmaker. 174 pp. Sex and the single girl—Brandy is looking for love and usually she finds it. Karin Kallmaker's first *After Dark* erotic novel.
                                                                      ISBN 1-931513-76-7 $12.95

WHEN THE CORPSE LIES A Motor City Thriller by Therese Szymanski. 328 pp. Butch bad-girl Brett Higgins is used to waking up next to beautiful women she hardly knows. Problem is, this one's dead.   ISBN 1-931513-74-0 $12.95

GUARDED HEARTS by Hannah Rickard. 240 pp. Someone's reminding Alyssa about her secret past, and then she becomes the suspect in a series of burglaries.
                                                                      ISBN 1-931513-99-6 $12.95

ONCE MORE WITH FEELING by Peggy J. Herring. 184 pp. Lighthearted, loving, romantic adventure.   ISBN 1-931513-60-0 $12.95

TANGLED AND DARK A Brenda Strange Mystery by Patty G. Henderson. 240 pp. When investigating a local death, Brenda finds two possible killers—one diagnosed with Multiple Personality Disorder.   ISBN 1-931513-75-9 $12.95

WHITE LACE AND PROMISES by Peggy J. Herring. 240 pp. Maxine and Betina realize sex may not be the most important thing in their lives.   ISBN 1-931513-73-2 $12.95

UNFORGETTABLE by Karin Kallmaker. 288 pp. Can Rett find love with the cheerleader who broke her heart so many years ago?   ISBN 1-931513-63-5 $12.95

HIGHER GROUND by Saxon Bennett. 280 pp. A delightfully complex reflection of the successful, high society lives of a small group of women.   ISBN 1-931513-69-4 $12.95

LAST CALL A Detective Franco Mystery by Baxter Clare. 240 pp. Frank overlooks all else to try to solve a cold case of two murdered children . . .   ISBN 1-931513-70-8 $12.95

ONCE UPON A DYKE: NEW EXPLOITS OF FAIRY-TALE LESBIANS by Karin Kallmaker, Julia Watts, Barbara Johnson & Therese Szymanski. 320 pp. You've never read fairy tales like these before! From Bella After Dark.   ISBN 1-931513-71-6 $14.95

FINEST KIND OF LOVE by Diana Tremain Braund. 224 pp. Can Molly and Carolyn stop clashing long enough to see beyond their differences?   ISBN 1-931513-68-6 $12.95

DREAM LOVER by Lyn Denison. 188 pp. A soft, sensuous, romantic fantasy.
                                                                ISBN 1-931513-96-1 $12.95

NEVER SAY NEVER by Linda Hill. 224 pp. A classic love story . . . where rules aren't the only things broken.   ISBN 1-931513-67-8 $12.95

PAINTED MOON by Karin Kallmaker. 214 pp. Stranded together in a snowbound cabin, Jackie and Leah's lives will never be the same.   ISBN 1-931513-53-8 $12.95

WIZARD OF ISIS by Jean Stewart. 240 pp. Fifth in the exciting Isis series.
                                                                ISBN 1-931513-71-4 $12.95

WOMAN IN THE MIRROR by Jackie Calhoun. 216 pp. Josey learns to love again, while her niece is learning to love women for the first time.   ISBN 1-931513-78-3 $12.95

SUBSTITUTE FOR LOVE by Karin Kallmaker. 200 pp. When Holly and Reyna meet the combination adds up to pure passion. But what about tomorrow?   ISBN 1-931513-62-7 $12.95

GULF BREEZE by Gerri Hill. 288 pp. Could Carly really be the woman Pat has always been searching for?   ISBN 1-931513-97-X $12.95

THE TOMSTOWN INCIDENT by Penny Hayes. 184 pp. Caught between two worlds, Eloise must make a decision that will change her life forever.   ISBN 1-931513-56-2 $12.95

MAKING UP FOR LOST TIME by Karin Kallmaker. 240 pp. Discover delicious recipes for romance by the undisputed mistress.   ISBN 1-931513-61-9 $12.95

THE WAY LIFE SHOULD BE by Diana Tremain Braund. 173 pp. With which woman will Jennifer find the true meaning of love?   ISBN 1-931513-66-X $12.95

BACK TO BASICS: A BUTCH/FEMME ANTHOLOGY edited by Therese Szymanski— from Bella After Dark. 324 pp.   ISBN 1-931513-35-X $14.95

SURVIVAL OF LOVE by Frankie J. Jones. 236 pp. What will Jody do when she falls in love with her best friend's daughter?   ISBN 1-931513-55-4 $12.95

LESSONS IN MURDER by Claire McNab. 184 pp. 1st Detective Inspector Carol Ashton Mystery   ISBN 1-931513-65-1 $12.95

DEATH BY DEATH by Claire McNab. 167 pp. 5th Denise Cleever Thriller.
                                                                ISBN 1-931513-34-1 $12.95

CAUGHT IN THE NET by Jessica Thomas. 188 pp. A wickedly observant story of mystery, danger, and love in Provincetown.   ISBN 1-931513-54-6 $12.95

DREAMS FOUND by Lyn Denison. Australian Riley embarks on a journey to meet her birth mother . . . and gains not just a family, but the love of her life.   ISBN 1-931513-58-9 $12.95

A MOMENT'S INDISCRETION by Peggy J. Herring. 154 pp. Jackie is torn between her better judgment and the overwhelming attraction she feels for Valerie.
ISBN 1-931513-59-7 $12.95

IN EVERY PORT by Karin Kallmaker. 224 pp. Jessica has a woman in every port. Will meeting Cat change all that?
ISBN 1-931513-36-8 $12.95

TOUCHWOOD by Karin Kallmaker. 240 pp. Rayann loves Louisa. Louisa loves Rayann. Can the decades between their ages keep them apart?
ISBN 1-931513-37-6 $12.95

WATERMARK by Karin Kallmaker. 248 pp. Teresa wants a future with a woman whose heart has been frozen by loss. Sequel to *Touchwood*.
ISBN 1-931513-38-4 $12.95

EMBRACE IN MOTION by Karin Kallmaker. 240 pp. Has Sarah found lust or love?
ISBN 1-931513-39-2 $12.95

ONE DEGREE OF SEPARATION by Karin Kallmaker. 232 pp. Sizzling small town romance between Marian, the town librarian, and the new girl from the big city.
ISBN 1-931513-30-9 $12.95

CRY HAVOC A Detective Franco Mystery by Baxter Clare. 240 pp. A dead hustler with a headless rooster in his lap sends Lt. L.A. Franco headfirst against Mother Love.
ISBN 1-931513931-7 $12.95

DISTANT THUNDER by Peggy J. Herring. 294 pp. Bankrobbing drifter Cordy awakens strange new feelings in Leo in this romantic tale set in the Old West.
ISBN 1-931513-28-7 $12.95

COP OUT by Claire McNab. 216 pp. 4th Detective Inspector Carol Ashton Mystery.
ISBN 1-931513-29-5 $12.95

BLOOD LINK by Claire McNab. 159 pp. 15th Detective Inspector Carol Ashton Mystery. Is Carol unwittingly playing into a deadly plan?
ISBN 1-931513-27-9 $12.95

TALK OF THE TOWN by Saxon Bennett. 239 pp. With enough beer, barbecue and B.S., anything is possible!
ISBN 1-931513-18-X $12.95

MAYBE NEXT TIME by Karin Kallmaker. 256 pp. Sabrina has everything she ever wanted—except Jorie.
ISBN 1-931513-26-0 $12.95

WHEN GOOD GIRLS GO BAD: A Motor City Thriller by Therese Szymanski. 230 pp. Brett, Randi, and Allie join forces to stop a serial killer.
ISBN 1-931513-11-2 $12.95

A DAY TOO LONG: A Helen Black Mystery by Pat Welch. 328 pp. This time Helen's fate is in her own hands.
ISBN 1-931513-22-8 $12.95

THE RED LINE OF YARMALD by Diana Rivers. 256 pp. The Hadra's only hope lies in a magical red line . . . climactic sequel to *Clouds of War*.
ISBN 1-931513-23-6 $12.95

OUTSIDE THE FLOCK by Jackie Calhoun. 224 pp. Jo embraces her new love and life.
ISBN 1-931513-13-9 $12.95

LEGACY OF LOVE by Marianne K. Martin. 224 pp. Read the whole Sage Bristo story.
ISBN 1-931513-15-5 $12.95

STREET RULES. A Detective Franco Mystery by Baxter Clare. 304 pp. Gritty, fast-paced mystery with compelling Detective L.A. Franco
ISBN 1-931513-14-7 $12.95

RECOGNITION FACTOR: 4th Denise Cleever Thriller by Claire McNab. 176 pp. Denise Cleever tracks a notorious terrorist to America.
ISBN 1-931513-24-4 $12.95

NORA AND LIZ by Nancy Garden. 296 pp. Lesbian romance by the author of *Annie on My Mind*.　ISBN 1931513-20-1　$12.95

MIDAS TOUCH by Frankie J. Jones. 208 pp. Sandra had everything but love.
ISBN 1-931513-21-X　$12.95

BEYOND ALL REASON by Peggy J. Herring. 240 pp. A romance hotter than Texas.
ISBN 1-9513-25-2　$12.95

ACCIDENTAL MURDER: 14th Detective Inspector Carol Ashton Mystery by Claire McNab. 208 pp. Carol Ashton tracks an elusive killer.　ISBN 1-931513-16-3　$12.95

SEEDS OF FIRE: Tunnel of Light Trilogy, Book 2 by Karin Kallmaker writing as Laura Adams. 274 pp. In Autumn's dreams no one is who they seem.　ISBN 1-931513-19-8　$12.95

DRIFTING AT THE BOTTOM OF THE WORLD by Auden Bailey. 288 pp. Beautifully written first novel set in Antarctica.　ISBN 1-931513-17-1　$12.95

CLOUDS OF WAR by Diana Rivers. 288 pp. Women unite to defend Zelindar!
ISBN 1-931513-12-0　$12.95

DEATHS OF JOCASTA: 2nd Micky Knight Mystery by J.M. Redmann. 408 pp. Sexy and intriguing Lambda Literary Award-nominated mystery.　ISBN 1-931513-10-4　$12.95

LOVE IN THE BALANCE by Marianne K. Martin. 256 pp. The classic lesbian love story, back in print!　ISBN 1-931513-08-2　$12.95

THE COMFORT OF STRANGERS by Peggy J. Herring. 272 pp. Lela's work was her passion . . . until now.　ISBN 1-931513-09-0　$12.95

CHICKEN by Paula Martinac. 208 pp. Lynn finds that the only thing harder than being in a lesbian relationship is ending one.　ISBN 1-931513-07-4　$11.95

TAMARACK CREEK by Jackie Calhoun. 208 pp. An intriguing story of love and danger.
ISBN 1-931513-06-6　$11.95

DEATH BY THE RIVERSIDE: 1st Micky Knight Mystery by J.M. Redmann. 320 pp. Finally back in print, the book that launched the Lambda Literary Award–winning Micky Knight mystery series.　ISBN 1-931513-05-8　$11.95

EIGHTH DAY: A Cassidy James Mystery by Kate Calloway. 272 pp. In the eighth installment of the Cassidy James mystery series, Cassidy goes undercover at a camp for troubled teens.　ISBN 1-931513-04-X　$11.95

MIRRORS by Marianne K. Martin. 208 pp. Jean Carson and Shayna Bradley fight for a future together.　ISBN 1-931513-02-3　$11.95

THE ULTIMATE EXIT STRATEGY: A Virginia Kelly Mystery by Nikki Baker. 240 pp. The long-awaited return of the wickedly observant Virginia Kelly.
ISBN 1-931513-03-1　$11.95

FOREVER AND THE NIGHT by Laura DeHart Young. 224 pp. Desire and passion ignite the frozen Arctic in this exciting sequel to the classic romantic adventure *Love on the Line*.
ISBN 0-931513-00-7　$11.95

WINGED ISIS by Jean Stewart. 240 pp. The long-awaited sequel to *Warriors of Isis* and the fourth in the exciting Isis series.　ISBN 1-931513-01-5　$11.95

ROOM FOR LOVE by Frankie J. Jones. 192 pp. Jo and Beth must overcome the past in order to have a future together.　ISBN 0-9677753-9-6　$11.95